THE WARD WITCH

UNHOLY ISLAND BOOK ONE

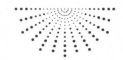

SARAH PAINTER

Published by Siskin Press Limited

Cover Design by Stuart Bache

ALSO BY SARAH PAINTER

The Language of Spells

The Secrets of Ghosts

The Garden of Magic

In The Light of What We See

Beneath The Water

The Lost Girls

The Crow Investigations Series

The Night Raven

The Silver Mark

The Fox's Curse

The Pearl King

The Copper Heart

The Shadow Wing

The Broken Cage

The Magpie Key

For Mum. I wish you were here.

CHAPTER ONE

E sme Gray was up before dawn, as was her custom when she had paying guests. She liked to have everything ready before even the earliest riser was likely to poke their head from one of the two guest rooms. If the island was very busy, something that had happened only a couple of times in Esme's memory, she moved into her painting studio and let out her own bedroom as a third.

Now, she laid out cutlery and condiments on the nicest table in the small dining room. It nestled in the front window and, today, had a view of a choppy grey sea. Esme pulled back the blue curtains and hooked them behind the pewter-toned tiebacks with the sculpted metal shells. The elderly woman she had inherited the house from had had a real thing for seaside decoration. Esme had stripped out the sandcastle wallpaper border and taken several boxes of beach-themed knick-knacks to the charity shop on the mainland, but she hadn't managed to eradicate everything.

She turned on the oil-heater in the corner to take the chill off the air in the room, and made sure that her pictures were all hanging straight and that none had lost their

1

discreet, but very clear, price tags. In Esme's experience, if guests had to wonder how much a painting cost, they assumed they couldn't afford it and didn't even ask.

It was the end of the season and she wasn't likely to sell much more to visitors. She had an online store, which always had a welcome bump in the run-up to Christmas, but she wasn't a skilled digital marketer. She found it easier to chat to the people who stayed in the village and, somehow, they always seemed to leave with a brown-paper wrapped rectangle under one arm. One of the seascapes she couldn't seem to stop painting.

At seven-thirty, the couple staying in the sandpiper room emerged in fleeces and walking trousers. Esme had pegged them as early risers, although it hadn't taken much detective work. Most people who stayed at her establishment were the adventurous, seize-the-day types. Hikers and birdwatchers, kayak-enthusiasts, and obsessive beachcombers. The village was a well-kept secret and would have topped the dictionary definition for 'off the beaten track'. Plus, its location, jutting out into the North Sea just on the border between Scotland and northern England, and nestled on a tidal island that was routinely cut off from the mainland, didn't exactly lend itself to luxury mini-breaks.

Mr and Mrs Allingham, a pleasant couple from York, settled at their table and Esme took their breakfast order. Outside, the day had arrived. The sun pierced the clouds and added a little glitter to the waves. A figure was walking along the beach, too far away for Esme to identify. Which was unusual. It wasn't a large community and she was pretty sure she could pick out the residents blindfolded in the dark.

In the kitchen, she dished out porridge, filled a toast rack, and laid a tray with small dishes of butter and honey.

The husband was vigorously stirring sugar into his tea. 'Are there boat trips from the village?'

Esme shook her head. 'Sorry. No.' Some of the residents had boats, of course, but not even Hammer offered to take tourists onto the sea.

Mr Allingham's face scrunched in disappointment. 'We were hoping to visit that island.'

'Island?'

'The one to the west. Àite Marbh.'

He butchered the pronunciation, which was for the best. It wasn't a phrase that anybody local said out loud. Esme shook her head again. 'Sorry. Nobody goes there. It's not safe.'

'Is that Gaelic?' Mrs Allingham asked. 'Unusual to find on the east coast this low down.'

'Things are a little different here,' Esme said mildly. She tucked a lock of her brown curly hair, an escapee from her ponytail, behind her ear. 'Now, would you like your eggs boiled, poached, scrambled or fried?'

In the kitchen, Esme fried eggs and tattie scones in a skillet, and tried not to trip as her cat wound his way around her legs in a repeated figure of eight. 'Jet, for goodness' sake.' He looked up at her with wide green eyes and let out a piercing wail. The kind that a desperate animal might make before it finally succumbed to starvation. 'Your food is in your bowl,' Esme reminded him and ignored his indignantly arched tail as she took the plates out to the dining room.

Later, after waving off the Allinghams, asking them to please not leave a review for Strand House anywhere online, Esme relented, as Jet had known she would. Sitting on the cold tile of the kitchen floor, Jet on her lap and facing her with a regal tilt to his finely shaped head, she fed him individual pellets of his scientifically engineered, nutritionally balanced, extremely expensive cat food. Every few mouthfuls he would stop accepting the pellets and regard her with an implacable stare until she gave him a small piece of ham.

'That's probably the last lot of the season,' Esme said to the cat conversationally.

Jet blinked at her.

'Let's hope for a long, quiet winter.'

Jet didn't reply, but he accepted his next pellet of food with good grace.

LUKE WOKE BEFORE DAWN. His hike-camping tent was thoroughly waterproof and he had an insulated all-season sleeping bag, but his brain always knew when it was sleeping outdoors and roused him early. There was a sharp coldness in the air and he knew the autumn would be short – winter was already snapping at its heels. He dressed quickly and brushed his teeth standing outside the tent and watching the choppy black waves in the grey pre-dawn light. The horizon was glowing with the promise of the coming day, and Luke ignored the inner voice that told him that nothing would have changed. He would try again. It wasn't unusual for small communities to be a little closed, a little wary. He would persevere.

He looked at his temporary accommodation. He wanted to strike camp, to perform the calming ritual of erasing his presence, but there was the niggling thought that he may well need to spend another night on the beach. Deciding to put his faith in the people of the island – surely somebody would rent him a room today – he took down his tent and rolled everything carefully away into his rucksack. He scuffed over the sand and scanned the area for any stray pieces of litter. His family had camped lots when he was growing up, and the importance of treating the countryside with respect had been instilled at a young age. You stepped lightly, you didn't make too much noise and you always, *always*, left the land as you found it.

The main street of the village on Unholy Island barely qualified for the title. White-washed houses, some with fishing floats outside their brightly painted front doors, were punctuated by the occasional signs of business. One cottage had a red mailbox set into its front wall and a rectangular post-office sticker in the window with a list of opening hours. The door was closed and Luke presumed you had to ring the bell to gain entrance.

About halfway along, there was a small pub called The Rising Moon, and at the far end, just before the village gave way to scrubby land which sloped down to the rocks and the sea, a large, detached house that was a different style to the others. Grander. On one side of the main street were narrow lanes which also led down to the sea, giving views of the watery expanse. Down one of these, he discovered a general store that hadn't been open the day before. With the blinds pulled over the windows and a solid door, it had been easy to mistake as another residential dwelling. Today, the blinds were up. A sheet of yellow-tinted plastic had been put over the glass to protect the goods inside from fading, which gave the displays a weirdly old-fashioned look, like a retro filter had been applied.

A bell sounded as he entered, and he found himself hemmed in by teetering shelves of long-life food. Cans, packets and boxes, along with essentials like candles, torches, matches, firelighters, string, sewing needles, toilet roll, bleach, and painkillers. A giant reel of blue nylon rope barked his shins as he turned a corner in the shelving and he almost toppled a stack of paint tins.

The man behind the counter was watching Luke with interest.

'Morning,' Luke said, shooting for friendly and unthreatening. He knew his size meant that he needed to add extra wattage to his smile, especially when he was in an enclosed space that highlighted his height and breadth.

The man inclined his head, but didn't reply. He must have been at least middle age, there were lines around his eyes and a few streaks of silver at his temples, but he had thick black hair that was swept back from a lightly tanned face.

'Nice day.' This was stretching the truth as the wind was still brisk, but Luke was channelling charm as hard as he could.

The man remained immune, the slightest lift of his chin the only acknowledgement that Luke had spoken.

Luke's next words surprised them both. 'I'm looking for a place to stay, don't suppose you know of anywhere to rent?'

The man's eyes widened in shock. He shook his head emphatically, his eyebrows drawn into a frown that seemed disproportionate to the question. Not one to give up easily, Luke tried again. 'A room would do and I'm not fussy. I can pay cash.' He didn't understand his own actions. The slim hope that he might find his brother on Unholy Island had dwindled, and the place was so small, he would have questioned every resident by the afternoon. There was no reason to change his plans and stay longer. But it was undeniable, the forward momentum that had kept him moving from place to place for the last year and a half seemed to have abruptly disappeared. He wanted to stop here. For a while, at least. At least a week.

The man had retreated from the counter, as if frightened by Luke's questions.

'Right. Well, thanks, anyway.' Luke picked up a bar of chocolate and a packet of flavoured noodles. On one end of the counter, there was a box of paper bags with a hand-written sign. Home-made tablet. He added a bag of the sugary confectionery and asked where he might be able to get lunch later.

The man slid a laminated map of the village across the counter and tapped the main street. His blue eyes bored into Luke as if trying to say all kinds of things and Luke realised something. The man wasn't being deliberately rude, he just wasn't speaking. Maybe he couldn't speak.

Luke turned up the wattage on his smile. 'Thank you,' he said warmly. 'Appreciate it.'

Esme cleared up from breakfast, changed the bedding and put the sheets in the wash, and spent a little time in the back garden harvesting the blackberries and weeding the raised beds. By twelve her stomach was rumbling and her muscles were telling her that she had done enough exercise for the morning. She decided to treat herself to lunch at the pub, even though there was a chance she would bump into the Allinghams.

The Rising Moon wasn't a large pub. The main bar had four stools, which hardly anybody ever used, and six tables of various sizes seating between two and six. The local residents could all eat at the same time, and often did, which meant that tourists were often seated on the small terrace outside. Seren had installed a heater and canopy, which made it a more enjoyable experience, but she some-times moved the locals onto the dreaded stools or told them to 'hurry up and finish' in peak season when there could be as many as three sets of visitors looking for a hot meal on a blustery summer's day.

Seren was wiping down the bar when Esme walked in. Seren was in her forties or possibly older, Esme had never been very good at judging age. She had smooth, olive skin, hooded eyes that always looked languid, and when she wore red lipstick she looked like a screen idol. Today, she was make-up free and was wearing her usual work uniform of jeans and a checked cotton shirt, the sleeves rolled back to expose the tanned skin of her arms. Matteo, who ran the village shop, was already at one of the small tables, reading a paperback book and shovelling casserole into his mouth at an impressive rate.

'Have your lot gone?' Seren said.

'Don't know,' Esme replied. 'They were talking about birdwatching today, walking down to Seal Point. They'll be away by three, though.' The tides meant that the island linked to the mainland via the causeway at specific times. For the Allinghams to make it safely back, they had to cross between two thirty and four and they had received the stern safety talk both before travelling to Unholy Island and from Esme herself. They had stayed two nights, though, so she knew they wouldn't miss the window. They didn't have many visitors to the island and those who did stay, never stayed more than two nights. It was the rule. An immutable law that was rarely stated out loud, because it was implicitly understood and obeyed without exception. The wards that shielded the island from general knowledge on the mainland and discouraged visitors, also ensured that even the keenest holidaymaker found themself desperate to leave after two nights on the island.

Fiona and her son Euan walked in. She dispatched Euan with a stack of old ten pence pieces to the small back room with its ancient Space Invaders machine.

Euan was almost sixteen, but he looked much younger.

He always seemed serious, but that might have been because he was so quiet. He certainly seemed more child-like than his age suggested, but Esme had never asked Fiona about it. One of the best ways to maintain civility in a community as small and closed as the island was to always respect people's privacy. Boundaries were even more important than usual when a winter storm could keep the islanders locked together in the same one and a half square miles for weeks at a time.

Fiona ordered food and then sat at Esme's table. She had taken one of the larger tables, an unspoken invitation for any locals to join her. Unlike Matteo's decision to take a small table, reinforced by the presence of his book. It didn't mean he wasn't going to listen in to everything they said, however, and relay it all to his drinking pals later. For a mute, the man was an incorrigible gossip.

Seren put cutlery wrapped in paper napkins onto their table, along with a condiment set. The scarred wooden table was immaculately clean and Esme rested her elbows on it as she listened to Fiona talk about her morning.

'Did you have a visitor earlier?' Seren asked.

Esme shook her head as Fiona nodded.

'Aye,' Fiona volunteered. 'A man looking for a place to stay a while. Very easy on the eye, but in need of a good wash.'

Seren frowned. 'He's already been here two nights. Camping down on the beach.'

'Does that count? Camping, I mean?'

'Yes,' Esme said. 'Of course.'

'He told me he wasn't looking for a night,' Fiona said. 'He wants a place to stay for a week. Maybe more. He didn't seem to have any pressing plans.'

'You think he is looking to stay long-term? Like to move

here?' Seren had turned away and had been on her way back to the kitchen. She stopped and turned back, re-joining the conversation. 'Well, that's not going to happen. Unless one of you is feeling unwell.'

And there it was. The only way you could move to Unholy Island was if a place opened up. And people never moved away, at least not while breathing. Esme had never thought to ask what happened to the residents when they died. There was a tiny ancient graveyard next to the broken-down medieval church, but it didn't look like it had been used in centuries. She presumed they went to the mainland for burial or cremation. Unless islanders were put on a boat and ignited by a shot from a flaming arrow. Esme wouldn't have been surprised.

'I don't like it,' Fiona was saying. 'Nobody asks about moving here.'

'I did,' Esme said. She was the most recent resident, having arrived only seven years previously. She didn't like to think about that time, so she didn't, shutting the door in her mind and letting the latch fall with a click.

Fiona shot her a fond look. 'That was different.'

'I thought 'different' was the problem?' Esme didn't know why she was arguing. She didn't want a newcomer living on the island, either. She had no desire for change of any kind.

Fiona shook her head. 'The island chose you.'

'Who was before me? I mean, who was last to arrive before me?'

'There isn't a home here for him,' Fiona said, ignoring the question. She frowned, suddenly looking ten years older. 'Unless... No. Everyone is fine.'

Esme caught her meaning. 'Everything is fine, Fi. He will head off today. No harm done.'

Walking home from the pub, Esme caught sight of a

figure turning the corner ahead, disappearing down one of the wynds that led to the shore. It was a tall male figure with messy brown hair and a bulky backpack. She felt a thrill of alarm and hoped her reassuring words to Fiona had been true.

CHAPTER TWO

Along with Strand House and the associated mandate to run it as a bed and breakfast, Esme had inherited the title of Ward Keeper. Seemingly, a person of witch-like persuasion had held the position for centuries and the village had, thank Goddess, decided she fitted the bill.

When Esme had arrived on the island, Tobias had shown her the ward locations and run through the ritual. It had been on the tip of her tongue to ask him why he needed her to do them at all since he knew how, but she had wisely kept her mouth shut. She had wanted to be needed. Wanted a place on the island.

'Madame Le Grys always brought a flask of tea. Lapsang Souchong, I think, but I wouldn't swear to it. And I don't know if that was important or just because she liked a hot drink. This has to be done in all weathers, so it might have just been to keep her warm on a cold day. I've been doing it, anyway, just in case it's important.'

'You've been renewing the wards?'

Tobias nodded. 'Best I can. They don't respond as well to me, but it's better than nothing.'

'I'm sorry about Madame Le Grys.' Esme had already

expressed the sentiment, but now that they were standing together by the castle ruins on the north-east edge and Tobias was talking about his old neighbour, it felt appropriate to do so again.

He smiled in a wobbly way and she felt a new appreciation for the depth of his feelings. 'How long did you know her?'

Tobias looked out to the horizon. 'Long time.'

Esme had never considered herself a witch. Hadn't known they existed outside of fairy stories and Halloween costumes, but there was something about Unholy Island that helped you pass through the layers of disbelief remarkably quickly. And it wasn't as if supernatural powers were completely out of her field of experience. She had heard, naturally, about the ancient magical Families that supposedly still ran London, and her foster parents had an uncle who claimed distant kinship to one of them. He was a surprisingly good-looking man of advanced years, who seemed able to persuade much younger women to spend plenty of quality time with him. Of course, that could have been the patriarchy, his decent bank balance and the fact that there was something extremely magnetic about him. Charismatic. But Esme could easily believe there was a bit of the rumoured Pearl magic running through his veins.

Over the last seven years, Esme had developed her own routine for renewing the wards. She always brought a flask of tea – her own choice was Lady Grey with a little lemon juice – but she had added shortbread rounds and a sturdy rucksack to carry her supplies. She checked the castle ward, now. It was the last one. She had already checked the bay, the harbour and the liminal space where the causeway met the firmer land of the island proper.

Beneath the crumbled south wall of the castle, Esme found the ward site. The remains of the ritual were still visible, calming the unease that she had somehow forgotten to do it on the last full moon. She had been sure that she had done the ritual as usual but it was like anything you did regularly, like closing your front door or switching off the gas on the hob, once you tried to remember doing it your mind couldn't tell whether you were remembering the last time you did it or one of the countless other times you had performed the identical task. Esme, prone to distrusting herself at the best of times, had laid awake tying herself in knots over her faulty memory and possible flakiness. The relief washed over her, now, and she poured herself a celebratory cup of tea.

LUKE WALKED DOWN to the shore. The waves rolled in and the air was thick with moisture. A stiff breeze had picked up and he hoped it wasn't about to chuck it down. He still didn't trust the impulse that had brought him to Unholy Island. He knew it was rooted in desperation. His search had taken him through the Midlands, Yorkshire, around the borders of Scotland and much of Northumberland, but every trail had run cold. It was no excuse to give up, though. No excuse to come running away to a hidden island, a place that barely anybody seemed to know about and was turning out to be as unfriendly as one of those private gated communities he had seen on television. Perhaps that was it. Was it owned by a billionaire? Someone who wanted it to remain a certain way and strictly controlled the visitors who were and weren't allowed?

No, if that was the case, it would simply have a fence. A 'no entry' sign. And there would be a helipad for the billionaire. And a house made of gold and glass. Or one hidden inside a volcano. Luke smiled. It was possible that he was confusing billionaire with Bond villain.

He took a deep breath of salt-tinged air. His lead might be flimsy, but he would follow it nonetheless. If there was even the smallest chance that somebody on this strange rock knew something about his brother, he would stay until he had uncovered it. And if there was nothing to uncover? He would be no worse off.

The sea rushed in, licking Luke's hiking boots before pulling back. He stepped further up the beach and shaded his eyes against the bright glare of the sun. He had thought it was supposed to be dark up north. While the low cloud on the previous day had made him feel as if the sun was a myth made up by southern folk, today it was above the horizon in a pale blue sky and the light was clear and pure. Every detail of the shore seemed sharp and more real than he had seen before. Dark blue at the horizon, turning to broken up blue and white, turning to green and turquoise as the breakers rolled onto the sand.

Having asked about the accommodation in the pub and been told that the pub didn't have rooms and the only guest house on the island was closed, Luke knew it would be another night of camping unless he got back into his Ford Fiesta and returned to the mainland. He didn't know why he wasn't doing that. It wasn't as if he couldn't find somewhere to stay on the other side of the causeway. He could commute in and finish asking around about Lewis. Another few hours and he could be on his way north. Lewis had an old friend who had moved to Edinburgh. Luke had visited him early on in his search and kept in touch via WhatsApp, checking in semi-regularly on the off-chance the guy had forgotten to mention that Lewis had turned up alive and well. He could go there to make sure. Look the man in the eye while he ran through the same questions. He liked the city and a few days there would make a change.

Besides, the island was so small that he was fairly sure he had walked every inch of it already. There was an islet to the west, but he couldn't see Lewis hiding out there. Not without one of the islanders knowing about it, anyway. Of course, it was possible that they wouldn't have told him, but considering how much they seemed to hate him, he couldn't imagine them sheltering Lewis. They would be more likely to point Luke straight to him in the hopes that they would both leave.

The guy who had told him Lewis was hiding on a secret island 'up north' had probably been talking out of his arse, saying anything at all to get Luke to go away. The man's pink face, running with sweat, popped into his mind. He had been keen to end the conversation, desperate to get Luke to leave.

Luke thought of himself as unthreatening and bookish, having been told as much throughout his teens by his terrifying father and daredevil brother, but he had come to realise over the last ten years that those two men had slightly different scales of 'scary' than most people. Most people, Luke had discovered, were worried at the prospect of violence rather than resigned. Most people saw the size of him and were keen to keep on his good side. Never mind that he would prefer to settle down with a good crime novel than have a tiresome testosterone-fuelled stand-off. He just wanted to be left alone, to live a peaceful life with nothing unexpected and as much order as possible. The chaos of his teens and early twenties had put him off unpredictability for life.

Lewis, on the other hand, had a thirst for mayhem that remained undiminished. At least, as far as Luke knew.

Perhaps in the time he had been missing, his twin had discovered the joys of calm and order. He doubted it.

ESME KNOCKED on the door of the mayor's house. It wasn't the largest on the island, but it was definitely the nicest. A fine symmetrical building, like a child's drawing of a house, but with more windows and a generous wraparound garden.

It was the kind of house where you might expect a housekeeper to open the door, but Tobias wouldn't tolerate anybody in his domain for longer than the time it took to have a village meeting. And that was a stretch, so they usually held them at The Rising Moon.

'Come in,' he said, striding away from the door. He was wearing his customary outfit of ancient green tweed jacket, brown waistcoat and worn-out cord trousers, slightly baggy at the knees. Esme wondered if he had bought several identical outfits sometime in the nineteen-sixties, and was still determinedly rotating them throughout the week.

The living room looked like the study of a professor, with stacks of papers and books and journals covering every flat surface and much of the floor. A fire was blazing in the grate and Winter, Tobias's black lab, was snoozing in front of it. He thumped his tail in greeting, but didn't stir.

A pair of armchairs were pulled up close to the fire. One with a footstool and a small table, overflowing with more books, a spectacles case, and a heavy tumbler with the remains of some amber liquid. The other was at a slightly awkward angle and looked as if it had just been dragged into place.

'Sit. Warm up. It's a bitter day.'

It wasn't. Autumn was in full swing and the wind was brisk, but she hadn't even felt the need to put on her thinnest fleece hat. It wasn't like Tobias to feel the cold, and she peered closely, wondering if he was coming down with something.

'It's all right, I'm not cross.'

Esme frowned. Cross?

'The wards. You forgot to renew them last full moon. It's all right. If you do it now, it should work. Maybe not full strength, but we'll be quiet over the winter and we'll all do our bit in the spring to make sure visitors don't lollygag.'

'I didn't forget,' Esme said. 'I did the ritual as usual.'

Tobias shook his head. His eyes were crinkled in sympathy. 'We all make mistakes sometimes. And you haven't been here long, it's all still very new. Nobody expects perfection. You are one of us and you don't need to be afraid.'

'I'm not afraid,' Esme said, feeling a thrill of fear that made her words a lie. She folded her hands in her lap and forced her shoulders to relax a notch. 'I didn't make a mistake.'

His expression smoothed. 'Well, then. This young fellow will be on his way today, then. I told Matteo he was fretting over nothing.'

So Tobias had heard about the visitor. Heard that he was asking around the village for a place to stay. Asking wasn't the same as doing. Esme was surprised that Tobias was so jumpy.

They spoke for a few minutes about other matters, but Tobias returned to the subject of the cold weather again.

'Maybe I'm getting old,' he said, with a self-conscious half-smile. Winter picked up his head and looked at his master. He had white hairs on his muzzle, but his eyes were as clear as a dog half his age. Whatever age that was, Esme thought, realising she hadn't a clue.

. . .

ESME PICKED her way along the high tide line, stepping over the slippery seaweed and occasional dead crab. She had a black bin liner in one hand and was wearing thick gardening gloves. She collected the plastic rubbish that had washed up with the tide, some of it water-worn into grey anonymity and others bright and recognisable, as if they had just been dropped from their owner's hand. She apologised to the sea with a silent mantra as she worked. It was something that she did every so often after a high tide, when the water spat human rubbish onto the shore like a giant clearing its throat.

The mantra took only a small part of her mind and left the rest free to think about her day. She had finished cleaning up from her guests the previous afternoon and was intending to spend a few hours tidying up the garden before the winter. The paintwork on the wooden porch needed attention, too, and she wondered whether to tackle that first.

Her busy thoughts and sea-appeasing mantra were both cut off by the shocking sight of something that absolutely should not be there. A flash of dark green tent material. High up on the scrubby land beyond the high tide mark and tucked behind a line of waving marram grass.

Esme marched over to the tent, half-expecting it to disappear as she approached. To reveal itself to be a hallucination. A dream-vision. It did no such thing. It was a one-person hiking tent, wedge-shaped and slung low to the ground. The sides rippled in the breeze and the front zip was fully closed.

She hesitated. If there was a solid door she would have knocked, but since that was impossible, she dropped her bag of rubbish as noisily as she could and said 'hello' in a voice that wasn't as commanding as she had hoped. The wind whipped it away and left a reedy thin sound.

There was movement from within. Esme took a step back and waited while the sides of the small tent bulged and moved. The front unzipped and two legs appeared. The legs were swiftly followed by the rest of a man. He pinned back the tent flaps and looked up at her, elbows resting on his bent knees. 'Yes?'

He was wearing jogging bottoms, a navy guernsey jumper, and he pulled on a second pair of hiking socks as he waited for her to reply.

It was the figure she had seen in the village. The man who had been asking around the island for a place to stay. Her mind was stuttering over the impossibility of his presence. He had stayed a third night. This was his fourth day on Unholy Island. 'You can't be here.'

He concentrated on his socks, carefully adjusting the seam over the toes, and didn't answer for a moment.

Esme could see that his hair needed a wash. It was sandy brown, past his chin and straggly with salt-tinged air. His clothes looked clean enough, though, and there was no bad odour. He looked camping-scruffy, rather than long-term homeless. 'Did you hear me?'

He looked up, blue eyes boring straight into hers. 'Was there a question?'

Esme fought the urge to take a step back. This was her beach. 'You are trespassing.'

'This is public land,' he said. 'At least, I didn't see any signs.'

They didn't need signs because nobody had ever camped here before. At least, not as far as Esme was aware.

He reached into the tent and drew out a pair of battered leather walking boots and began lacing them on. 'I've been to a lot of unfriendly places, but everyone told me how welcoming people were in the north.' He looked up at her. 'Did you not get the memo?'

'You don't understand. Nobody stays here for more than two nights. It's not... allowed.' It shouldn't even be possible. The wards that protected the island should have given the man the unbreakable opinion that one night would be plenty on Unholy Island. If bad weather stopped a visitor from crossing the causeway or they had an unusually strong desire to stay longer, a second night's stay was permissible, if extremely rare. Three nights. Three nights simply should not have happened. The breeze picked up and whipped Esme's hair across her face, obscuring her view.

The man had finished lacing his boots and he unfolded from the ground, suddenly seeming far too close now that he was standing. Taller and broader, too. Esme allowed herself a step back, her heart hammering with a rush of fear. It's all right, she told herself. Still, she shot a quick glance to the scrubland, assessing her best path for escape. She was no athlete and would need to get away from the soft sand as quickly as possible to be able to put any distance between them at all.

'Why?'

That stopped Esme's whirling thoughts with another jolt of surprise. People didn't ask 'why'. Either something was very wrong with this man or something was wrong with the island. Which didn't bear thinking about. Perhaps he was simple-minded.

'Have you had trouble with campers? I don't leave a mess. I don't bother the wildlife.' His mouth quirked into something that was almost a smile. 'I follow the country code.'

He was being charming, Esme realised. Even with his salt-logged hair and unwashed hiking clothes, it probably would have worked. Probably it usually did. But Esme had lost her ability to be charmed by charm. That had been burned out of her, along with a few other things. 'This isn't right. I need to find out what is happening...' She trailed off, realising that the words should have stayed in her mind. 'You should head off today. The causeway will be passable between twelve and three.'

'I'm Luke,' the man said, holding out his hand. 'Nice to meet you.'

Esme turned away. There was no point meeting the man. He would have to leave in a couple of hours.

LUKE WATCHED the woman walk away from him. She had been cleaning up the beach and he could only assume that accounted for her bad mood. She must have seen him as the cause of yet more littering. Having seen the state that some campers left sites, he had some sympathy, but couldn't help feeling the sting of being painted with the same brush. Unfairness was never fun.

He felt the stirring of something else. Despite wind-reddened cheeks and being exceedingly pissed off, the woman had a strikingly pretty face, and he would quite like to look at it again. He watched as she walked away, her gait as she moved down the beach and the way the wind lifted her curly hair the only signs of her allure, given that she was wearing a long bulky coat and carrying a black bin liner. He shook his head. He had been on the road too long. Alone too long.

CHAPTER THREE

L indisfarne, also known as Holy Island, sits just off the coast of northern England. Visitors can gawp at the impressive remains of its ancient priory, a beacon of religious learning and salvation for many years, and the castle, built when Henry VIII demanded fortifications against the rowdy Scots.

Unholy Island sits a few miles northward, in an area that has been Scotland and then Northumberland and then Scotland again throughout recent history, but in ancient times was just the Old North. Unlike Holy Island, it escaped royal and monastic notice, and has endured without much external interference.

On an average day, you can see Holy Island from the mainland, with the distinctive shape of the castle rising on its rocky hill.

Unholy Island is only glimpsed when the air is clear and the sun is high in the sky. It seems to have its own weather system, staying almost permanently shrouded in mist. Even for those who live close to the causeway on the mainland, it is easy to forget it is there at all.

The island community is very small. Few people know about the island and those that do, those who bring delivery vans or visit to fix the water pipes or fibre broadband, don't really think about the place after they leave. It's not that they forget about it completely, it just passes from the front of their mind. In the case of the delivery drivers and the post office, this is a regular recurrence. A weekly knowing and then unknowing that becomes a familiar part of their mindscape and doesn't unduly trouble anybody.

There are tourists. Throughout the summer, a handful make the crossing. They walk the quiet beaches, watch the ringed plovers, skylarks and oystercatchers, birds which can still successfully nest as there aren't enough humans to trample their homes, and eat lunch in The Rising Moon. If the bookshop is open, they squeeze between the packed shelves and browse the used stock and usually come out with a small stack of books. They might buy some homemade tablet from the general store or a painting of the waves from the owner of Strand House, and as the sun crosses the sky and the tide begins to turn, lapping at the edges of the causeway, they get back into their cars and drive back to the mainland. The sea reclaims the island and the visitors eat their tablet, read their books, hang their new artwork, but never really think about Unholy Island again.

The village on Unholy Island is little more than a single street. There are short wynds leading from the main thoroughfare, stopping before the land slips into the sea. On the sheltered side there are sandy beaches and on the other, a scrubby lowland of tough grass and salt-loving wildflowers that leads to jagged black rocks. The track from the car park to the village has a wide grassy footpath running alongside. It avoids the broken-down walls and the kirkyard that are all that remain of the church that was built back in the 1300s. Seven hundred years of wild weather and human neglect have left it a ghostly ruin of what was once the bright hope of a community. Those who believe the darker stories about the island might see it as a symbol of the godlessness of the place. But it doesn't matter... They forget all about it when they leave.

THE TABLES in the pub had been pushed together to accommodate the residents in a makeshift committee meeting. They usually just leaned back in their chairs and called across the room from their various seats, so this made it more formal and underscored the seriousness of the topic.

Fiona and her husband Oliver had left Euan at home. They were chatting to Seren as she placed glasses of water and drams of whisky on the tables. Esme took a seat next to Hammer. He was the kind of man who ought to frighten her, with his massive frame, meaty hands and scarred face, but for some reason he didn't. When she had first arrived at Unholy Island he had been the first person she had met and it still seemed like a miracle to her that she had walked toward him and not run in the opposite direction.

The door opened, letting in a blast of cold air. Tobias, with Winter at his heels, walked in, closely followed by Matteo. At exactly half past the hour, Bee walked in. There was a slight lifting of tension as everyone realised that they would be spared either of the younger sisters. Bee was widely acknowledged to be the easiest to deal with. Acknowledged, at least, in silence. It wasn't something anybody would be stupid enough to say out loud.

The chat quietened as everyone took their seats. Seren locked the door of the pub and was the last to sit. A log in the open fireplace cracked and settled, shooting sparks up the chimney, and Winter padded from his place by Tobias's chair to settle on the worn rug in front of it.

'Where is he?'

'Now?' Esme looked at Fiona. 'How should I know?'

'You spoke to him.'

'We've all spoken to him.' Esme was not going to have this problem labelled her special project.

Tobias lifted his hands. 'Nobody is being blamed. These things happen from time to time. We are a closed community but we are not hermetically sealed. And perhaps there is a reason beyond our understanding for this boy's presence.'

'Why now?' Somebody muttered. Esme looked around the group but couldn't tell who had spoken.

'We should get Hammer to escort him off the island.'

There was a general murmur of agreement and Esme felt the room ease. She felt guilty at her own relief. A meeting like this likely occurred when she had arrived seven years ago and she didn't want to think about what her life might be like if they had turned her away. She swallowed hard. 'I don't know...'

Tobias gave her a sharp look and Fiona's eyes widened.

'You don't understand,' Seren said shortly. Her dark eyebrows were drawn low and her gaze didn't waver. 'You're new.'

A soft voice broke in. 'He stays.'

Everybody looked at Bee. She smiled implacably at the group. Her hands were clasped together on the table and white strands framed her face where they had escaped from her braid. 'Nobody can stay more than two nights, but he has managed it. That means something. It is no longer our call whether he stays longer.'

'The wards,' Tobias began, 'there must be a...'

'If the wards have failed, they were meant to fail. This

28

is not Esme's doing.' Bee nodded at Esme. 'This is something else.'

The room went silent then. Bee's tone on 'something else' made the hairs stand up on Esme's neck and she was pretty sure it had had the same effect on all of them.

Tobias sighed.

Hammer shrugged.

Seren frowned, but she picked up her whisky glass.

Fiona and Oliver had been looking at each other, communicating silently in the way of the long-married, but now they picked up their glasses.

Esme reached for her whisky just as Bee picked up hers.

Bee lifted her glass. 'The stranger stays.'

THE NEXT MORNING, Esme was in her kitchen, chatting to Jet while she made porridge and trying not to think about change and what it meant, when there was a knock on the back door. She was wearing her dressing gown over thick flannel pyjamas and sheepskin slippers, but she opened the door anyway. Everyone on the island had seen her in her nightwear before.

Not everyone.

Luke was standing on her back step, his rucksack in one hand and an easy smile. 'Hello again.'

Jet had been twining around her ankles, but he stalked over to the doorway and looked up at Luke as if assessing him.

'Can I help you?' Esme pulled the cord on her dressing gown, making sure it was tightly fastened.

'They said you had a room. For me.'

Esme shook her head. 'The season's over.' As soon as the words were out, she realised they were stupid. Luke was here. He was staying. Bee had said so. The chat in the pub after her decree had involved talk of where he would stay in the short term, where he might live if he became a permanent resident, but Esme realised now that she hadn't been paying enough attention. She couldn't remember now whether anything had been decided, and she certainly didn't remember volunteering.

'May I come in?'

Esme took a step back. 'I'm not...' She had been going to say 'decent' but she was swathed in more material than a polar explorer and there was a keen wind whipping outside. She noticed that the man in front of her may have been smiling, but he looked cold and tired and there was strain around his eyes. 'Of course,' she amended.

'Thank you.' He stepped into the kitchen and closed the door.

Esme retreated to the stove and stirred her breakfast. 'Would you like some porridge? Toast? I've got eggs.' When in doubt, focus on the catering.

He was bent down, untying his boots before stepping off the mat by the door. Jet was helping by pouncing on his laces like a kitten. 'I don't want to be any trouble.'

'It's no bother. Take a seat.'

The small table in the kitchen was tucked against the wall and Esme had never noticed how closely she moved around it while she was cooking. Of course, she was usually alone in here with Jet, her guests sitting in the dining room next door. She put the bread board with a loaf and knife in front of Luke, and added the butter dish and a pot of jam. 'You can start with that while you wait for your eggs. Poached? Scrambled? Fried? Boiled?' There was comfort in hosting, falling into the easy pattern of providing food.

'Fried, please.' Luke picked up the knife and started slicing.

Esme dished up her porridge, offering some to Luke, who shook his head. 'I'm not taking yours.'

'I always make too much,' Esme lied. She could measure portions by eye with perfect accuracy. It was one of the few things she was proud of.

'This and eggs will be perfect. Thank you.'

Esme fried the eggs while her porridge cooled and toasted the bread that Luke had cut. He had a piece with jam, and then buttered two more ready to top with his eggs. Esme already had a pot of tea going and she added some freshly boiled water and gave Luke a mug. The rhythm of cooking was soothing, and it wasn't until Esme sat opposite Luke and began to attend to her porridge that she realised she was too nervous to eat. There was a large man in her tiny kitchen. A large man with startling blue eyes and unwashed hair. A man whose clothes were giving off the unmistakable odour of damp with an undercurrent of male-ness. It wasn't a bad scent. In fact, part of her found it excit-ing. It was just the kind of exciting that reminded her of other things. Things that she wasn't even close to being ready to consider allowing into her safety zone. Plus, it was very early in the morning to be dealing with the urge to flee.

'What's your cat called?'

Esme looked down and realised that Jet, the hussy, was winding his way around Luke's ankles, probably hoping he would drop some food.

'Jet. Short for Jetsam.'

Luke raised an eyebrow. 'Unusual name.'

'I inherited him. Previous owner wasn't a big fan and said he was so objectionable someone must have thrown him overboard.'

He reached down and stroked Jet's head. Surprisingly, Jet allowed it.

'I don't expect this every day,' Luke said, when he had demolished his first piece of egg on toast.

It took Esme a beat to realise what he meant. He thought he was staying.

'And I'll work. I don't know how much you charge out of season, but I'll help out. On top of paying cash, I mean. I'm not looking for charity.'

Esme felt like she had missed an essential part of the conversation. 'I'm sorry,' she said. 'I'm shut for the season.'

He closed his eyes briefly. It was a small moment of defeat and she felt an unexpected guilt. Which was ridiculous. She owed this man nothing.

Luke's blue eyes were open and his charming smile back in place. 'Bee. The woman from the big house at the point?'

Esme nodded to show she knew who Luke meant.

'She told me you would let me a room.'

Well, that was that, then. Esme shoved down her panic and hoped it didn't show. 'How long are you planning to stay?'

'I don't know. A week or two. Maybe longer.'

Esme ignored the swooping of her stomach. She couldn't share her home for that long. She dug her nails into her palm. 'Why?'

Luke ran a crust of toast around his plate, picking up the last of the egg yolk. 'I like to travel,' he said, not meeting her eyes. 'Meet new people.'

Cursing her stupid bed and breakfast and its surplus of rooms, but most of all cursing Bee, Esme nodded. 'Right. Well. Let's say five days to start with. I've never had a guest for longer than two nights before and it might not work out. Fair?'

'Fair,' he said, wiping his hands on his jeans before holding one out.

Esme hesitated before shaking his hand. It was warm and enveloped hers in a way that set her fight or flight into overdrive, but she managed to take a slow breath and not have a full panic attack. So that was something.

CHAPTER FOUR

When Bee crossed the threshold to her home, she knew immediately that her sisters were out. There was an emptiness to the house. She hadn't long returned from her summer activities, travelling the mainland, reading fortunes and stockpiling money and experience. Enough life and energy to see her and her sisters through the long island winter.

She had met a son of The River Man and extracted a promise from the head of the Crow Family. Unexpected boons from an already successful season.

The back room of the house was probably meant to be a dining room originally, but it served as the Three Sisters' workroom. A narrow pine table sat against one wall, packed shelves ranging above it. The tent that she took with the fair, travelling from site to site along with the carnival booths, fairground rides and food trucks, was decorated with velvet cushions and coloured glass lanterns. This room had subtle lighting that was controlled via dimmer switches, potted plants, and minimal pale wooden furniture.

Three large mirrors arranged in a semi-circle dominated the middle of the room. They were foxed with age, the silver patina stretching across their surfaces so that reflections were strangely dark. Bee stepped into the centre point. Her sisters appeared in the mirrors to her right and left.

'There is a new soul here,' Diana said from the right-hand mirror. Her sun-kissed skin glowed with vitality and her plaited hair was held back from her face with a silk scarf.

'Yes,' Bee confirmed. 'A man.'

'Delicious,' Lucy said, licking her red lips.

'What does it mean?'

Diana shook her head. 'I don't want to look.'

'Scaredy cat,' Lucy said in an annoying sing-song voice.

'At least winter is coming,' Bee cut in, trying to forestall an argument. 'Tobias has woken up. The island is strong.'

'Not that strong if it let a newcomer in.'

Bee shook her head, admonishing Diana. 'The wards are fine. Which means he is meant to be here.'

'You have too much faith in the ward witch,' Lucy said. 'She's very green.'

Bee looked at her youngest sister. Her black eyes were as unforgiving as always. 'Green isn't bad. Besides, she has strength we haven't seen yet.'

'If you say so, sister,' Lucy said. She lowered her gaze as if deferring to Bee's age and wisdom, but Bee wasn't fooled. Lucy was unpredictable. Which, coming from Bee's perspective, really meant something.

'We will look if you really want to,' Diana said, placating them both.

Bee felt a thrill of fear. She no longer wanted to peer at the newcomer's fate. 'We will wait,' she said.

. . .

AT THE OTHER end of the village, in Strand House, the room Esme showed Luke was larger than he expected, and decorated in a more neutral style than he associated with rural guesthouses. He had stayed in several dated shockers over the last year. Wallpaper that made you hallucinate, or piles of floral cushions and cutesy sayings stencilled on the walls. This room had white walls, crisp white bedding on the black iron-framed bed, and a large (and slightly disturbing) oil painting of a grey and turbulent sea placed in the middle of the opposite wall. He was extremely happy to discover that it had an ensuite shower room. He didn't mind wandering the halls looking for a bathroom, but he had the impression that it would make his new landlady uncomfortable. He had seen the way she went very still around him and couldn't help but think it wasn't just shyness.

That had been the best breakfast he could remember, though. It hadn't been anything unusual, but every item had been the most delicious version he had ever tasted – the most perfect eggs, the toastiest toast, the butteriest butter. That was probably the effect of barely eating over the last couple of days. Hunger truly was the best seasoning.

He couldn't fall into comforts, he reminded himself. He wasn't here on holiday. He wasn't here to make friends and eat delicious breakfasts. He was here to find his brother. And if this trail ran as cold as the others, he would move on. Something he felt his new landlady would be pretty pleased about.

The question remained, though. Were they all being unfriendly because they were a tiny island community and didn't like strangers, or were they hiding something?

There was a knock on the door. He opened it to find Esme holding a stack of blue towels. She passed them to him. 'The Rising Moon does decent food. If you want to meet folk, that's the place to go early evening.'

'What about late evening?'

'If you're looking for a party scene, you are definitely in the wrong place.'

Esme's offended look stayed with him. He didn't seem to be able to keep his foot out of his mouth around his new landlady.

ESME HAD to get out of the house. She needed the fresh air and the calming view of the sea. It was too early for day trippers and she expected to have the bay mostly to herself, and she was almost right. The figure hirpling over the shoreline was wearing her distinctive Breton rain coat. It was bright yellow and several sizes too large for the tiny human inside.

'Morning,' Esme said when she was close enough to Alvis.

The woman peered out from under the voluminous hood. She seemed distracted but managed a brief smile, pushing at the errant strands of her grey bobbed hair that were blown by the breeze. 'Have you seen that new fella?'

'Yes,' Esme said. 'Bee sent him round to mine. I've got to put him up for a few days.'

Alvis's face collapsed into a multitude of wrinkles as she frowned. 'I don't like it.'

'I know,' Esme said. 'I've already heard about it from Tobias. I swear it's not my fault. I haven't neglected the wards...'

'I know that,' Alvis interrupted.

Esme didn't have time to enjoy a glow of confidence before Alvis added, 'I checked'.

'Well, then.'

'And I found this,' Alvis pulled the thick winter glove from one hand and dipped into a coat pocket.

It looked like a piece of sea glass, but much darker than any she had seen. It was a deep blue, almost black, but with a lustre. Esme was already forming the words 'that's pretty' when Alvis tipped the glass into Esme's palm and she felt the weight of it. Not glass. Or, not *just* glass. It was the size and shape of a paperweight, but was clearly not man-made. There was a warmth to it, too, but that could have been from Alvis's body heat.

'What is it?'

Alvis pursed her lips and shook her head. 'I need to do some research. Do you get anything from it?'

Esme didn't want to sound stupid, so she didn't mention the peculiar warmth or that she could see colours moving within the dark surface. It was probably her eyes playing tricks.

'Oh well. Give me a couple of days and I'll hopefully have an answer.'

Esme passed the object back and Alvis slipped it back into the deep pocket of her raincoat. She saw that the older woman was worrying at her lower lip. 'You look concerned.'

Alvis nodded. 'That'll be because I am. And you should be, too.'

Right then. That was reassuring.

The wind was brisk and it whipped a little cold rain into Luke's face as he made his way along the main street. He passed a house with a metal verdigris door knocker in the shape of an octopus, and another with glass fishing floats stacked in the porch.

He had walked out along Shell Bay, wanting to stretch

his legs before his appointment, but had decided to cut back through the village when the weather turned. The sea had gone from inviting blue-green waves to thrashing grey surf in a matter of minutes.

Esme had given him directions and the time of his appointment, and he walked up the path to the mayor's front door with five minutes to spare. He wasn't one for authority and had considered refusing the meeting, expecting some variation of 'don't make trouble' from a crusty codger with a ceremonial necklace and an inflated sense of self-importance, but he had his own agenda. He would interview every resident, kick over every rock, and he may as well get started.

The tall man who opened the front door of North House was dressed in ancient-looking tweed in shades of green and brown. He greeted Luke with more warmth than anybody else on the island so far and hurried him inside 'before the heat escapes'. Turning and walking across a wide hallway and into a room that turned out to be a cosy library-like room with a blazing fire, piles of books and papers and a massive black dog, he noted that the mayor had clearly been strong in his youth. His posture and gait still held the remains of that strength, despite his white hair and knotted hands.

Luke looked out of the small window, which showed the front garden. The glass was thick and traced with frost. Luke blinked. It hadn't been icy outside.

'Over here,' the mayor said. 'Have a seat.'

Luke didn't ask about the frost on the window. He had grown up with stranger things and had idle questions beaten out of him. Now he rationed his questions. Made them count.

The mayor was settling in one of a pair of armchairs near the fire. There was a tray with a decanter of amber liquid and two glasses on a side table, and he waved a hand in its direction. 'Help yourself if you would like a drink.'

'I'm fine, thanks.'

The mayor nodded as if he had expected the refusal.

'You settling in at Esme's?'

'Yes, sir.' Luke sat in the chair opposite and concentrated on appearing trustworthy. 'She's been very accommodating.'

The mayor shot him a sharp look. 'Don't mess with that woman.'

'I have no intention of messing with anyone,' Luke said. It was mostly true. If there was someone on this rock that had something to do with his brother's disappearance... Well, then. That would change things.

'Good.'

A short silence. The mayor drew together his impressive eyebrows and seemed to regroup. 'What do you plan to occupy yourself with? Now that you're here?'

Luke looked at the man and wondered whether he should just come out with it. He dismissed the idea immediately. Rule one of rooting out information was to keep your cards close to your chest. Only reveal what you absolutely had to reveal. Don't give away information for free. That was a fool's game. 'I'm looking for someone.' The words popped out anyway.

The mayor raised his eyebrows. 'Here?'

Luke shook his head, wondering what was wrong with his brain. 'I've been looking. It's all I've been doing for the last eighteen months. And I just... I don't know.' His mouth, mercifully, stopped moving while he tried frantically to work out what had possessed him to be so honest. Tobias had a calm and trustworthy face, but still. That was no excuse.

'You're tired,' the mayor said.

41

It felt like an admission of guilt. Like he was letting his brother down all over again, but he couldn't lie. He didn't have the energy. 'I'm done in. Yeah.'

'Grief is exhausting,' the mayor said. He held up a hand before Luke could object. 'I don't mean that your loved one is dead, but if they are missing you have been worrying and grieving their absence and probably starting to grieve their loss, as if that will insulate you from what you fear you might find.'

'My brother is alive,' Luke said stoutly.

A pause. 'I'm sure you're right.'

A log cracked in the fire. Luke watched the flames for a moment, gathering himself. He didn't usually talk about his brother, but there was something about the mayor, this room, that invited confidence. 'I haven't found a trace. Of him, I mean. Of where he's gone. The leads I had initially went nowhere. There's been nothing to follow for months and I've been wandering, really. I keep thinking I should stop. Go home and get back to work. Be normal. But I can't.'

The mayor stood up from his chair and crossed to the tray. He unstopped the decanter and poured two measures. He passed one to Luke and then resumed his position in the chair.

Luke stared into the glass. It was late afternoon and the sky visible through the living room window had shaded from pearl grey to black. He knew the days were shorter in the north at this time of year, but it still surprised him. Made him feel further from home than he had before. He took a sip from the glass. Smoke from a homely hearth. Heat from the fire. Ancient peat under a sky filled with a million shining stars.

He raised his gaze and found the old man watching him over the rim of his own glass. His expression was thoughtful and... Something else. Something Luke couldn't identify. Suddenly, he felt uneasy. He stood, placing the glass carefully back on the tray. 'Thank you for your hospitality, Mayor.'

'Call me Tobias.'

He wondered, again, what had possessed him to be honest. Just because the mayor was doing an excellent 'kindly old gent' routine was no reason to forget everything he had ever learned about human nature. 'I would appreciate it if you didn't... talk to other people about what I've said. I don't usually tell people about my brother. I don't know why I told you.'

'Of course.'

'Well,' Luke stood awkwardly for a moment. 'Don't get up,' he said, despite Tobias giving no indication that he intended to do so.

'My door is always open,' Tobias said as Luke made his way from the room.

Luke paused at the door. 'Thank you.'

'What's your brother's name?'

'Lewis.'

Tobias inclined his head. 'It is a terrible thing to lose a twin.'

It wasn't until Luke was almost back to Strand House that he realised he hadn't told the mayor that Lewis was his twin.

CHAPTER FIVE

L uke stared at the ceiling for a moment of confusion. His brain had expected canvas a few inches from his face and it took him a second to remember that he was in Esme Gray's spare bedroom. Well, her guest bedroom. It was, apparently, a bed and breakfast, but there had been no sign out front and it wasn't listed anywhere online. Which shouldn't have surprised him as there wasn't much about the island online at all. A weird blank where visitor guides and reviews and photos ought to be.

He heard a creak outside his door and imagined Esme walking down the landing. Her bedroom must be on the same level as the guest rooms. He imagined her in a dressing gown, very little on underneath, and then realised that his hand was on part of his anatomy. He had just woken up. It was automatic. A routine bodily reaction. He moved his hand away, feeling weirdly guilty, and sat up. He was going to behave impeccably in the hopes that Esme let him stay longer than the stated five days.

Of course, perhaps he wouldn't want to stay longer. He might get a new clue. A whisper of what had happened to Lewis. Something that would send him in a new direction with refreshed purpose. Or maybe even he would just find him. Alive and well. Cleaning tables in the pub. For a moment, he allowed himself to daydream. Lewis's smile. An infuriating 'what's the big deal?' expression. Luke's eyes stung with tears as his body remembered what it was like to be near his sibling. The sense of being complete rather than a half-alive broken thing. It was a strange mixture of longing and fear. He might never be completely whole without his twin, but he was a great deal safer.

Getting dressed in the cool air, he pushed the thoughts firmly down. At least they had distracted him from his morning boner.

Esme didn't like the blow-in from the mainland. She didn't like that he was looking for somebody, and she didn't like the unsettled feeling that seemed to have permeated her community. She might not have been an experienced or powerful witch, but she was adept at picking up undercurrents, and the emotions swirling around the island were complex and strong.

Esme went into the dining room and tried to ignore the way her heart rate kicked up at the sight of the mainlander. He looked out of place in the small room, his frame too big for the compact table in the window. There was no need to be frightened, she reminded herself, ignoring the part of her agitation that felt more *interested* than alarmed. She decided to set aside her confusing feelings and cut to the chase. 'Are you leaving today?'

Luke looked up from his bacon and eggs, and a frown passed quickly across his face. 'I wasn't planning on it.'

'Causeway is open from three until six today.' Truthfully, it would be safe to cross for a couple of hours either side of those times, but it was always best to be cautious.

Islanders always gave mainlanders the most conservative estimates for the causeway and used their own judgement for themselves.

He looked around the empty room. 'I would have thought you would be glad of the extra income.'

'I'm not.' She underlined her words by turning down the dial on the oil heater. If he was cold, he wouldn't linger over his food.

Luke put his knife and fork down. 'Why run a bed and breakfast if you don't want guests?'

'Somebody has to.'

His mouth quirked into a smile. 'Is that on your website? Visit Strand House Bed and Breakfast. Somebody has to?'

She wasn't going to respond to his teasing tone. 'You're upsetting people. Nobody stays more than two nights.'

He leaned back in his chair. 'Are you even aware of how ridiculous that sounds?'

'I'm not the one being dense.'

'Dense, is it?' He tilted his head as if she was being obtuse.

'Thick,' Esme supplied helpfully.

He laughed, showing white teeth and dangerous dimples. Dimples on a man that looked like a Viking god. That wasn't playing fair.

'Seriously, though,' she tried again. 'There is nothing to do here. It's bad enough in the summer, but at this time of year...' She gestured to the grey sky visible through the window.

'Are you sure you're not running the tourist board too?'

'People don't come here. And they definitely don't stay.' Okay, so she no longer sounded detached, emotion had crept into her voice and she was in serious danger of crying in frustration. She didn't know why he was bothering her so much, but she had to get a hold of herself.

'That doesn't make any sense.' He sat forward and picked up his cutlery, preparing to resume his breakfast.

She hesitated, searching for the right words. The magic phrase that would convince him to pack up his rucksack and take his disruptive fine self back to the mainland and out of her life. Before she could think of it, he spoke instead.

'There is one thing about me you should know. I don't do well with orders.'

For a moment the air was thick with tension, and Esme took a step back.

Luke seemed to sense her discomfort and he smiled reassuringly, then tried to change the subject. 'What's the deal with the guy in the shop?'

'The deal?'

'He doesn't speak.'

'No.'

'Well?'

'That's the deal.' Esme knew that Matteo was capable of speaking and that he chose not to, but she wasn't going to volunteer that information to a near-stranger.

Luke had his eyes raised to the ceiling as if he was calling for strength. But when he refocused on her, his gaze was warm and gentle. 'You don't give much away, you know that?'

'Thank you,' Esme replied.

THERE WASN'T much call for policing on the island and it was too small and too remote for the official channels on the mainland to have much of an interest. Hammer was the local stand in. Tobias may have been the mayor, but

Hammer was the muscle. The enforcer. If a tourist wandered where they weren't welcome or Oliver got rowdy in The Rising Moon after one too many beers, Hammer stepped in. Truth was, muscle wasn't really required. A word or even just a long look was usually all that was needed. He might not have loved what he saw on the rare occasions he looked in a mirror, but it was bloody effective.

Now there was a newcomer. He was sitting in the corner of the pub, a half-drunk pint and a meal on the table, and he had returned Hammer's long look with a bland expression. Hammer was impressed. Either the guy was simple in the head or he was hard as nails.

NOBODY COULD ACCUSE Unholy Island of being tropical, but when Luke stepped out of The Rising Moon both the sky and the sea were an inviting deep blue, with a few white fluffy clouds for contrast. The air was cool, but the ever-present breeze was at an all-time low and Luke tilted his face to the sky and enjoyed the sun on his skin. It was nice to be out of the pub, too, with the woman who had banged his plate onto the table with more force than was necessary and the massive guy with the lumpy, scarred face, who had glared at him from the corner of the room for the duration of his meal.

He was on a mission to find his way around the entire island. There was a basic map that Esme kept in a plastic folder in the dining room, but Luke wanted to know all of it. Every street and lane, every path and secret way. He had always been the same. If he stayed in a place for any longer than a couple of nights, he felt the urge to map it thoroughly. To know it.

Besides, this place had been confounding him. Luke

had an excellent sense of direction and the kind of mind that absorbed spatial information. By this point, he would usually have a complete mental picture of his environment, but there was something about Unholy Island that resisted understanding. He knew that the village was tiny, and that the streets were absolutely not moving around in the night to reconfigure themselves by the following morning, but still... It was most disconcerting.

You are distracted by Esme, a small voice from the back of his mind piped up. He told it to shut up. He was not a teenager and was perfectly capable of compartmentalising. Just because his libido appeared to have woken up after a long slumber, did not mean he was suddenly incapable of functioning in all other areas of his life. Besides. It was just libido. It would burn itself out. Or they would get together and that would solve it. Scratch the itch, so to speak. His mind stuttered as he imagined for a moment what that would be like.

He walked away from The Rising Moon toward the edge of the village where Bee's imposing house stood. Turning down to the right, he expected Crow's Nest Lane, a pretty row of white-washed houses, but instead the black and white sign read Widdershins Wynd. Luke didn't remember walking down this lane which, again, had to be impossible. The island was not big. The village was a village. He had been here for four days now, and had to have walked every street.

The cottages on the wynd were the same old grey stone as the rest of the village, but the ground was cobbled and too narrow for cars. One cottage had external steps leading up to the second floor and the stonework was painted white. There were colourful plant pots clustered in front of the steps and wooden window boxes finished in navy blue.

A couple of houses further down and the wynd seemed

to get even narrower. The sea ahead was a slice of blue between the buildings. Unexpectedly, he discovered a bookshop. Or, at least, he thought it was a bookshop. The door was shut tightly and there was no sign outside, but the two front windows were packed with books, many laid out as if to entice browsers.

Peering in at the titles, many of which were obscured as the books were cloth bound with faded lettering, he caught movement from behind the display. Perhaps it was about to open? He waited, cupping his hands around his face in order to see inside, and trying to look like a hopeful customer. After a few minutes, he tried the door. As he expected, it was locked. He waited a bit longer, in case that action had alerted whoever was inside to his interest. When nobody came bustling to the door to unlock it, he walked on. Another friendly business on this strange, closed-off island. The question of how a place so small supported a bookshop was superseded by the larger question of how a shop survived when it wasn't open on a Saturday. Another small mystery to add to his growing list of questions about this place.

Walking down to the shore, he realised that he felt lighter inside. His curiosity about the island made a welcome change from the grinding reality of looking for Lewis and the miserable uncertainty of the previous five hundred days.

Don't get too comfortable, he warned himself, automatically. But then the sun came out from behind the clouds and lit a dazzling path on the waves and he forgot that he didn't deserve a moment of happiness.

THE HARBOUR on Holy Island was low slung and muddy, the island easing from land to water in a slow gradation.

When the tide was out, the large expanse of mud ensnared boats moored too closely. It also had the rotting remains of a jetty. A leftover from its days as part of the lime trade and now used primarily as a photographic prop by the thousands of visitors. Those comparing the islands would agree that Unholy Island's harbour was no less muddy, but definitely on a smaller scale. And there were no signs of a past that involved large-scale trade. There were, however, a couple of upturned herring boats which had been repurposed into sheds.

If anybody on this strange island would know something about his missing brother, he would lay money on it being the scary-looking guy from the pub at lunchtime. He had eyed him in a way that would no doubt have had most people pissing themselves. Luke had grown up with a father who was a mean drunk, a brother who liked to fight for fun, and had spent his life dodging trouble or, when that was impossible, going in fists flying. He didn't think he would win in a fight with the man from the pub, but he wasn't afraid of pain and that helped. Threats lost their bite when you didn't much care if they were carried out.

The woman who had served him his pie and chips, Seren, had told him that the man was called Hammer and that he could be found in his boat. The tide was in and there were three small boats in the harbour. Luke put his hand to shield his eyes from the low sun and looked across the water. He couldn't see any signs of life on the boats and, besides, he didn't know how he would get out to them even if he did see Hammer. She didn't seem to be joking about his unusual name, so Luke figured he would have to take her at her word. He would probably avoid using it to the man's face, though, until he'd heard somebody else use it. He wouldn't put the islanders past having some fun with a 'mainlander'. He turned back inland. He would have to find the man later. Hope that he hadn't been marched off the island by the unfriendly locals before then.

Movement by the upturned herring boats caught his eye as he turned to walk back to the village. A door opened and a large figure appeared from within, back first. Luke was sure it was the man from the pub and that was confirmed as he emerged fully.

He was carrying a plastic waste sack and he lifted the lid of the dustbin to the side of the upturned boat and dropped it inside.

He walked over before he could lose his nerve. 'I wanted to ask you some questions.' Luke had the feeling that small talk would be wasted on the man, so he may as well jump right in.

The man turned. He looked no-less intimidating that the last time Luke had seen him. Well over six-feet tall, broad, and packed with muscle, and topped with a face that only a mother could love. 'Did you now?'

'Easier to answer and I'll fuck off out of your hair.'

Hammer didn't move and his expression didn't change. Two could play at that game. Luke took a slow breath and let stillness flow through his body. He knew his expression was blandly neutral and he kept it that way. The two men waited like this for more than a couple of minutes. The breeze dropped and there was a little warmth in the air. Gulls wheeled above, calling in their harsh voices, and there was a rustle from some unseen creature in the nearby gorse. Luke felt perfectly relaxed as he watched Hammer watch him. He felt he would wait all day. All day and all night and the next after that.

Then it hit him.

Somewhere along the line, pretending to be relaxed had turned into genuine calm. He was relaxed because he had no real hope that this man would have any information, any leads on his brother. He was relaxed because he was hopeless. His brother was gone and he was going through the motions of his search. Spinning his wheels because he didn't know how to stop. He felt his face twist. A failure of his calm exterior. He had lost the waiting match with Hammer, but he no longer cared. Part of him had admitted that his search was pointless. Part of him, for a moment, had let his brother die. He looked away, out to sea, and contemplated walking into the waves. Even that thought felt neutral. Everything was grey. The sky and the sea and the ground. What did any of it matter?

'I have been here for years,' Hammer said, surprising him. 'No trouble.'

He looked back at the man. His hands hung loose at his sides in readiness for movement, but Luke wasn't getting as strong a 'fuck off' vibe as he had a moment ago. 'What about when you're not on the island?'

Hammer shrugged.

'You spend time on the mainland, I assume. You can't be here,' he waved to encompass the muddy bay and the island as a whole, 'all the time. Surely.'

'Why do you say that?'

Luke shook his head. 'I don't know. You don't seem the type for the quiet life.' Luke's last lead had been an old acquaintance of Lewis's, who said that he had last seen Lewis when something bad had gone down in Newcastle. He swore blind that Lewis had walked away from the trouble, but that he had been muttering about an island beyond Lindisfarne. Somewhere that nobody knew about. Somewhere quiet to lie low for a while. Luke had never known his brother to lie low for more than a day or two, let alone volunteer to visit somewhere remote and quiet and small. Still, he was here, now. And it was his only direction. He may as well ask the resident hard case.

Hammer tilted his head, seeming to appraise Luke. 'You don't know me, pal.' Then he turned and disappeared back inside his boat shed, shutting the door with finality.

SITTING BY HIS WOODSTOVE, Hammer sipped tea from an enamel mug and pondered the newcomer. He hadn't been wrong to suggest that Hammer didn't spend all of his time on the island. In point of fact, he travelled with the Three Sisters on their spring and summer tour, providing security, but he hadn't felt like volunteering that information. What was it to this stranger, anyway? Was he asking just because of the way Hammer looked – like worse trouble on a very bad day – or did he know something? There were a lot of things in Hammer's past that he wasn't too proud of and a few loose ends that might come unravelled. It wasn't anything that worried him day to day, but he still didn't enjoy the thought of the hassle. Whatever the newcomer thought of him, he did relish the quiet life. He'd had the alternative and this was better. Hammer pocketed his knife and stretched, feeling his spine pop and his bad shoulder grind. Souvenirs from his life before. Quiet was definitely better and he would do whatever it took to keep it.

CHAPTER SIX

The causeway opened at eleven the next day and a lone car made the crossing. It was a young couple with an eighteen-month-old. They packed her starfish limbs into a padded rain suit and then loaded the struggling child into a backpack carrier. The husband shouldered the lot and the wife took a backpack of her own filled with nappies, packed lunch, snacks, toys, muslin cloths and two complete changes of clothes for the baby. If they took in the deserted car park and the stiff breeze that was coming from the sea and had second thoughts about their outing, neither voiced it.

By lunch time they had walked past the ruined church and down to the beach marked Shell Bay on the map. The baby had eaten sand, gone through one set of spare clothes, and had fallen asleep for approximately three minutes after a comfort feed. The couple had taken turns to stare at the water or close their eyes, feeling the air clear their tired minds and weary spirits. They made their way to the village for the last hour before the causeway became impassable and bought takeaway coffees from Seren at The Rising Moon. Alvis in the bookshop made them put the cups down on the counter while they browsed. The baby held chubby arms out to Alvis as if reuniting with a long-lost friend. Amused (and exhausted) the couple accepted the old woman's offer to watch the baby while they looked around unencumbered. As a result, the baby had a short nap on Alvis's lap as she sat in her comfy chair and the young couple bought a stack of paperbacks.

Once the door had shut, Alvis pottered about the shop. The baby had lost a pale-yellow cotton mitten. She put it in the lost property box that she kept under the counter, but knew that if the couple didn't come back within the next hour or so, they never would. She took a duster and wiped down the shelves in the crime fiction section and was just thinking about making a hot drink and returning to her research when Fiona walked in with her son Euan.

Euan was a fifteen-year-old with an unusually self-contained air about him. Alvis didn't know if he took after Fiona and her particular ability, or whether it sometimes skipped a generation, and she had never thought to ask. She smiled in a welcoming way and told him about the new Manga title that had come in. He ducked his head and didn't answer, and then sloped off to the back of the shop.

Alvis raised an eyebrow and Fiona shrugged. 'It's his age.'

In her day, young ones showed respect to their elders. Well-brought-up ones, anyway. She decided not to voice this opinion for the sake of island harmony. Alvis knew that when you lived in close proximity to others, it was better to pick your battles and bite your tongue. 'Did you want a tea?'

'I'm fine, thanks. Go ahead and make yourself one, though.'

'In a bit,' Alvis said. She had the sense that Fiona wanted to talk.

'Did you want me to do your hair soon? It's gone a bit straggly.'

Alvis touched her bobbed hair and thought that Fiona was going to offend somebody one of these days with that bluntness, but luckily she wasn't so delicate. In truth, Fiona wasn't very talented as a stylist, but she stopped people from having to go to the mainland. Besides, she knew that Fiona needed the cash she got from tending to the islanders' hair. Her husband, Oliver, did something to do with stocks and shares on his computer. Alvis didn't understand it and therefore didn't trust it. She wasn't surprised that Fiona was looking for cash to supplement the household income.

After Fiona and Euan had gone and the causeway had closed, having funnelled the visitors safely back to the mainland, Alvis returned to her books. She regarded the strange lump of glass for a few minutes before settling into her reading chair to see what she could find. So far, her best guess was a polished piece of flint or obsidian. Back in less-enlightened times it was called a hag stone, and the myth ran that it could either reveal a person's true nature or fix it in place, stopping them from ever changing, depending on which story you believed.

LUKE THOUGHT that he had met everybody on the island, but then Esme had mentioned the Three Sisters. Apparently, Bee was one of the sisters and they lived together in the house at the far end of the village.

Knocking on a cottage door in the middle of the day shouldn't have felt like a particularly scary activity, but Luke's system was on high alert. He could feel the hairs on the back of his neck lifted and there was a tingling in his fingers that suggested surging adrenaline. Calm down, he told himself. *There is nothing to fear here.* Bee was forth-right and intimidating, but she was also a very small, silver-haired woman. Her sisters had to be of similar age, so he definitely wasn't going to be in physical danger.

The door opened, bringing a waft of warm scented air and the sound of Ella Fitzgerald singing. Luke realised that his mouth was hanging open as he took in the sight of the woman standing inside the doorway. She wasn't much shorter than him, which was unusual in itself, and she had thick dark hair which was pulled back from her face with a red silk scarf. 'You'd better come in,' she said, and the sound of her voice made him want to obey. To make her happy. To be near her.

'I'm Luke,' he said, closing the door and following the woman into a large room. He was dimly aware that it was an open-plan space and it was filled with plants and cushions and candles.

'You're looking for my sister, I assume.'

Luke was trying to fight through fog to have a coherent thought. The scent in the room was overwhelmingly green. He wasn't one for noticing perfumes, but this was chlorophyll and wood sap, underlaid with something warm and comforting. Amber. Maybe the sweetness of caramel or vanilla. It was making his head spin.

The woman gave him a slightly pitying smile. 'I'll go and get her. Stay here.'

The last words were spoken firmly and Luke realised that he had taken several steps towards the woman, as if making to follow. With an act of will, he forced his feet to plant to the floor.

Once the woman had left, the scent in the room seemed to recede and his mind began to clear.

Bee appeared, her silver hair braided along the sides of her head in a way that looked unnecessarily complicated and loose at the back. It reminded him of the pictures from the book of Norse legends he had been given as a boy. She was wearing denim dungarees with a long-sleeved black T-shirt underneath and bare feet. Seeing her familiar, lined face was a relief. Luke felt like he could finally take a proper breath. But it brought fresh confusion, too. The other woman had light brown skin and couldn't have been more than forty at the absolute limit. Bee was beautiful and extremely youthful, but had to have been over sixty. Their different skin colouring solved some of the mystery – they were half-siblings or adopted – but the age difference was certainly unusual. Although, Luke couldn't help thinking that they looked alike. If you ignored the difference in skin tone, they definitely looked related. His head was spinning and he felt like he needed to lie down quite urgently.

Bee gave him an assessing look. 'You need to eat some-thing.' She crossed to the kitchen area and plucked an orange from the bowl on the counter. Quartering it with a sharp knife and placing the pieces onto a plate, she passed it to Luke. 'You'll feel better in a moment.'

Luke took the plate automatically and ploughed through the fruit, sucking each quarter like a man with chronic scurvy. Gradually, he realised that the room was no longer tilting and that his thoughts had cleared properly. His face was sticky with juice and he wiped it with the back of his hand.

Bee took the plate of rinds and motioned for him to sit on one of the floor cushions. He stayed standing, wanting to be ready to bolt. Luke had thought the island was odd, had come here for answers, but now felt that his wisest course of action would be to back away slowly and hope that he hadn't inadvertently offended any member of this household.

'So you met Diana,' Bee said, conversationally. She

stepped closer and patted his arm. 'Don't feel bad. You did very well, really.'

'I did?'

She seemed to consider. 'Not *very* well, perhaps. But not too badly. I've certainly seen worse.'

'Is she your sister?'

Bee smiled. 'Of course.'

'And three of you live here?'

'So many questions. Yes, we are the Three Sisters. The clue is in the name.'

'Right.' The thick green sap smell was still in the background, but there was something else mingling with it now. Wood smoke, perhaps, although he couldn't see a log burner.

'What can I do for you today?' Bee sank onto the floor in a cross-legged pose and looked up at him. With her head tilted to one side and her eyes bright and assessing, she looked like a curious bird.

Luke had intended to ask Bee whether she had ever met Lewis, but the question was stuck in his throat.

'I should probably warn you,' she continued. 'Questions are free if you don't expect an answer, but otherwise they cost. I won't look ahead unless it's painfully specific or uselessly vague and either way it costs more.'

'Um.'

Another head tilt. 'Do you even know why you're here?'

'I'm looking for my brother. Lewis. He disappeared eighteen months ago and I'm worried he might be dead.' Luke's eyes widened in shock. He hadn't meant to say any of that.

'Since the island has let you stay for longer than two nights, I will waive payment for one question.'

'Is Lewis on the island?'

'Come here,' Bee said, reaching out a hand.

He went closer, automatically holding his own hand out to shake hers. Like they were going to make a deal. Instead, she touched the back of his hand with one finger, eyes closed.

'I've never met your brother.'

'Is he here, though? I've looked everywhere, I think, this place isn't that big, but...'

'You've had your one question.'

Luke wanted to say 'but you didn't answer it', but something stopped him. The good sense that had kept him whole and breathing for the last thirty-odd years, perhaps.

ESME WAS ABOUT to cross the high street when Bee called to her. She was wearing a navy fisherman's smock and her hair was in two braids wrapped around her head in a style that looked chic and Scandinavian. If Esme had tried that, she would have looked unhinged.

'You probably hate me right now,' Bee said conversationally.

'Not hate...' Esme realised she had crossed her arms in front of her body and forced herself to let them drop.

'It'll be good for you.'

She was used to having guests so it shouldn't have made any difference. She had never accepted a booking from a lone man before, though. She didn't see how waking up with panic fluttering in her chest could be good for her.

'He's here for a reason,' Bee said. 'And he needed to stay with you. I don't know why, yet, but that much was clear.'

'Okay,' Esme said. There wasn't much else she could say. Bee had a way of knowing things. And when she told you something you didn't argue. Besides, she had told the

63

man he had five days of shelter and she wouldn't go back on her own word, either. She still didn't know what had possessed her to make the offer.

Bee touched her arm and waited until Esme met her gaze. 'You are safe.'

Esme nodded, more from politeness and the instinct to agree with the kind-but-terrifying woman.

Bee smiled as if she could see through Esme's scepticism, see right through her skull and into her most private thoughts, in fact. 'It is safe for him to stay in your house. You know that if you look inside yourself. When are you going to start trusting yourself again?'

Esme's mouth went dry. It wasn't herself she didn't trust, it was other people. Mainly men, but not exclusively. She didn't trust other people and that was the problem. Esme wasn't about to contradict Bee out loud, though. That meant conflict. Which led to terror. And a lack of oxygen in an ever-tightening chest.

Bee patted her again, as if she were a pet. 'You'll get there,' she said cheerfully, and walked away.

CHAPTER SEVEN

Esme wasn't watching her guest dig over her vegetable plot. She was working in the kitchen and was only glancing out of the window every now and then to see how he was getting on with the task. She didn't know why he had offered to work in her garden, but she wasn't about to turn down manual labour. Digging over the beds wasn't exactly fun.

What she definitely wasn't doing was watching his muscles flex in his arms or the way his shoulders moved. She wasn't feeling her breath catch at the sight of his profile as he straightened. Or noticing that when he leaned back to stretch, she could feel the answering tug of her own muscles. Something had woken up and she needed it to go back to sleep. Those kinds of feelings were dangerous.

Jetsam let out an offended screech. He had been twining around her ankles and was obviously bored of waiting for her attention. Esme crouched down and stroked between his eyes with a finger. She ran her hand over his head and under his chin and he pushed into her hand. 'I'm not distracted,' she told the cat. 'I haven't forgotten.'

The cat gazed at her with clear disbelief.

'I haven't. I'm getting ready to go. I'm just...' She glanced up as the back door opened.

'May I have some water?' Luke asked, bending to untie his laces.

Esme straightened up. 'I'll get it.'

He took the proffered glass and downed it gratefully.

Esme watched his Adam's apple bob as he swallowed, mesmerised for a moment by the line of his neck. She felt Jetsam's head butt into her right calf. 'I know,' she said, irritation creeping in.

Luke frowned at her. 'Sorry? What?'

'Not you.' Esme looked down at Jetsam. Was talking to her cat normal-weird or weird-weird? Not that it mattered. It didn't matter what this man thought of her. It only mattered that she did her job, and kept her place on the island. Where she was safe.

'I've got a question,' Luke said, handing back the empty glass. 'Why is it called Unholy Island?'

Esme transferred her attention from her cat to Luke. 'What do you mean?'

'I Googled it. Its real name is Mallachtach. Hard to say, but it sounds a bit nicer.'

'It means 'cursed', so not really.'

'Oh.'

'The mainlanders said this place was unholy, barbaric, dangerous. The islanders decided they didn't really mind and adopted the nickname.'

'I can relate,' Luke said with a smile. 'But it's not? Unholy, I mean.'

Esme gave him a long look. 'Do we dance widdershins in the moonlight and drink the blood of newborns? No.'

'I didn't mean now... I meant historically. Sometimes

66

place names do have their roots in fact. Like 'shelter of trees' or 'river'.'

'This is fact,' Esme said flatly. 'Ignorance. Fear. Prejudice. Persecution.'

Luke closed his mouth. Wisely.

'Anyway, thank you for your help.' Her voice was stiff. 'Are you after a reduction on your bill?'

'I've got money. Don't worry. I can pay up front.'

'That's all right,' Esme said. If he tried to skip out on the bill, Hammer would explain the error of his ways. Or they would just let Luke go and he would, at least, have left the island. It wasn't as happy a thought as it ought to have been.

He was watching her with a wary expression. 'So, what else are we doing in the garden today?'

'You're off the hook,' Esme said after a moment. 'I've got an appointment.'

OUTSIDE, the wind was brisk and she zipped her coat before walking along the front path and into the village. The Three Sisters lived at the far end, where the village trailed away to rough grassland, sloping down to meet a stony beach, black rocks and the wildest, least sheltered part of the North Sea.

She knocked on the red door on the side of the house. It was white-washed stone with exterior steps that led to the upper floor. A collection of plant pots was clustered on each step and along the base of the building, filled with spiky plants and metal spinners made from scrap metal.

Bee opened the door and Esme allowed herself to relax. She was never sure which of the sisters she would be meeting when she came for her weekly class, but Bee was definitely her preference.

'He's still here, then,' Bee said, not bothering with anything as pedestrian as 'hello'.

Esme was shedding her coat as quickly as possible and hanging it on the peg beside the door. The sisters liked their home warm. Good for doing yoga, Bee asserted, and given the woman was as lithe and bendy as a woman half her age, Esme wasn't going to argue.

'Come on, then.'

Esme followed Bee into the main room of the house. The walls had been knocked down where possible to create a room which seemed larger and lighter than ought to be possible from the outside of the building. Lush greenery hung from planters suspended from ceiling beams and rose up from large ceramic pots in every corner. A pedestal held a gigantic fern that exploded out in every direction with delicate pale fronds, like frothing green water from a fountain. The windows that looked onto the headland were clear glass, but the ones which faced the village were filled with colourful stained glass in blues and greens. Not a picture that Esme had ever been able to recognise, but an abstract pattern that was both soothing and jarring at the same time. Much like the sea on the opposite side.

'Have you been practising?' Bee sank down onto a floor cushion in a perfect cross-legged pose.

Esme followed in a slightly less graceful manner. Her form had definitely improved over the last seven years, but her limbs still refused to behave as Bee's did. 'Yes. Trying to.'

Bee fixed her with a stare. 'Don't make me quote Yoda.'

Esme opened her mouth to say that it was hard to practise when she so clearly wasn't making any improvement. Her lotus pose might have come along, but her witchery had stalled out at renewing the wards and the occasional burst of intuition. The sort that was so shrouded in metaphor as to be utterly useless. Luckily, good sense caught up before the words left her throat. Bee had a no-nonsense brand of kindness that wasn't above sharp phrases when required. And Esme knew she loathed her defeatist attitude. *How can you expect to get better when you don't expect to get better?*

'Let's begin,' Bee said. 'Close your eyes.'

Esme obeyed. She listened to Bee going through the preliminary meditation, bringing their awareness to their bodies, their breath, their senses. Her mind refused to focus, random thoughts and worries crowding out Bee's steady voice. Suddenly, in the same calm and dreamy tone as she had instructed Esme to focus on the sounds she could hear both far and near, Bee said, 'if you don't focus I will get Lucy'.

Esme cracked an eye open in alarm. Bee was smiling slightly, eyes closed, posture perfect. 'I'll tr... do better.' When she returned to the meditation, she pushed away every stray thought, she breathed in and out as Bee instructed and slowly, very slowly, felt some of the tension flow from her muscles and a calm space open a little in her mind. And then she noticed that it was working and that made her think about all the things she was successfully not thinking about and the window of calm snapped shut like a Venus Flytrap.

Expecting an admonishment or, worse, Bee to rise from her position and go and call her terrifying sister, Esme opened her eyes. She wasn't in the same room. She was in a small bedroom, curtains shut tightly but with daylight leaking around the edges. There was a lumpy figure in the single bed, obscured by a duvet pulled high over the head. It might not have been a person at all, just a long pile of clothing or pillows, but Esme knew there was somebody under the duvet. There was that unmistakable sense of an occupied room, as distinct from an unoccupied one as night and day. She didn't recognise the room, so she was surprised when the duvet shifted and revealed a familiar face. Luke.

She blinked in surprise and then found herself back in the house of the Three Sisters, sitting on the floor and her stomach rolling in an ominous way. She shot upright and over to the kitchen area just in time to lose her breakfast into the sink. 'Sorry,' she managed, running the water and wiping her mouth. 'Sorry.'

'Finally,' Bee said drily. 'Progress.'

LATER, with a cup of peppermint tea and a ginger biscuit in hand, Esme felt halfway human again. Bee was chopping carrots for soup with a massive knife on a wooden butcher's block. Esme could only see her back and the motion of her chopping arm and couldn't tell from that whether Bee was angry or not.

'I'm sorry about that,' she tried.

'Don't be,' Bee said, turning around and flashing a smile at Esme. 'You had a breakthrough today.'

Esme's stomach was still delicate and she wasn't at all sure that she liked the kind of breakthrough that was accompanied by chunder, but still. It was something. And Bee was smiling at her, so it wasn't all bad.

'Are you ready to talk about it?'

Esme had just bitten into the ginger biscuit and her system seemed to be rebelling, so she concentrated on chewing, swallowing and not choking.

'It's like dreaming,' Bee said encouragingly. 'Speaking out loud helps to solidify the vision. It doesn't even have to be to another person. You can tell yourself, but do it out loud if you can. And as soon as possible after the vision.'

Esme took a sip of the peppermint tea to wash the biscuit down. The vision already felt dreamlike and she was beginning to doubt what she had seen. It had looked like Luke, but maybe she had just been thinking about him. Subconsciously. 'It was a house. A bedroom I didn't recognise,' she said. 'And there was a person in the bed, but all I could see was the duvet and a shape.'

'But you knew it was a person?'

Esme nodded. She wasn't going to tell Bee it had been Luke. What if it was just a pathetic fantasy leaking out of her brain?

Bee nodded briskly. 'That's good. Next time, try to stay with the vision. See if you can look around. Over time, you'll find you can control things a bit, maybe even interact.'

'How will I know I'm not just dreaming?' Esme asked.

'Practice.'

'Right.'

CHAPTER EIGHT

L uke opened the unlocked back door to Strand House. He would need to ask for a key for when Esme was out. He also needed to give her the safety talk about locking her doors, even when she was home. This was a small community and she probably felt safe, but she lived alone and there was no such thing as being too careful. A moment later, he remembered that it was none of his business. It wasn't his job to look after everybody he met, especially not when he had ballsed it up so comprehensively. He couldn't even keep his twin safe, so why the fuck should he think he could protect anybody else?

The kitchen was empty apart from the resident enormous black cat. It was sprawled in front of the range cooker, green eyes fixed on Luke. He bent to take off his boots, feeling strangely vulnerable when he couldn't see the cat, as if it might jump up and attack.

There was a thump from the room next door and Esme's voice, muffled.

The door was open and he followed the noise into the dining room.

'For fat snake.' Esme had her hands on her hips and

was glaring at the small wood-burning stove that sat in the middle of the outside wall.

'What?'

'Bar steward.'

He looked at her like she had lost her mind. Which, to be fair, might have been accurate. 'I'm trying not to swear.'

'Okay.'

'So I'm trying out phrases that are similar to say to see if they have the same effect.'

'And do they?'

'Not so far.' She turned back to the stove and adjusted a vent on the top. 'Fuck it.'

The phone rang. It was a landline attached to the wall of the dining room and looked like it had been installed in the eighties. Esme listened and then said. 'I'll be right there.'

'I've got to go.' she was moving through the room with purpose.

'What's wrong?'

'Seren burned her hand. I'm sure it's fine, but I need to check on her.' Esme threw this over her shoulder as she left the room. She returned moments later with a large green bag with a red cross on the side.

'Do you need help?'

'I don't think so,' Esme replied.

That didn't sound definite and Luke was painfully aware that he needed to gain some good favour with Esme and the islanders, so he followed her to the pub.

It was empty inside, and Esme walked straight around the bar and through the swing door that separated the pub from the kitchen.

Seren was sitting on the floor of the kitchen, with her hand in a bowl of water. 'I can't bear to take it out,' she said immediately. She was pale despite her sun-golden skin and

Luke could see pain written in the tightness around her eyes.

'That's okay,' Esme said. She went straight to the sink and washed her hands thoroughly. 'Have you had any pain killers, yet?'

'No.' Seren answered Esme but was staring at Luke. He felt suddenly very aware that he had tagged along where he hadn't been expressly invited.

'Are you any good with stoves?' Seren asked suddenly.

'In what way?'

She smiled grimly. 'I would like to say the bloody thing is faulty and I need you to fix it, but I just made a stupid mistake. Not sure I'm going to be in a fit state for the dinner rush, though. Need a willing pair of hands.'

'I can cook,' Luke said, wondering what he was letting himself in for.

'There's stuff in the freezer. It'll mainly be reheating on the stove and in the microwave.'

'I can do that,' Esme said. She cut her eyes in Luke's direction. 'You don't have to...'

'I'm happy to pitch in,' Luke said. He was shocked to discover it was true.

'I'll pay you,' Seren said.

Luke opened his mouth to say 'that's all right', assuming it would be the right thing to do. And gain him more favour in Esme's eyes.

Instead, Esme spoke over him. 'Free dinners for a week.'

'A work week,' Seren countered. 'And you both clear up the kitchen tonight. Nothing left out for me to clean.'

'Done,' Esme said. She had finished washing her hands and looked at Luke almost shyly, as if she had momentarily forgotten he was there. 'If that's okay with you?'

'Absolutely.'

'Good.' Esme was in front of Seren now. 'I'm going to need another bowl of cold water. You can put some ice cubes in it. And a clean tea towel. They're in the top drawer next to the sink.'

Happy to have something to do, Luke went on his errand while Esme coaxed Seren to lift her hand out of the water long enough for her to examine the burns.

Having decided they were second degree, not third, and that Seren hadn't done nerve damage (that had involved Esme poking the pads of her fingers with a cocktail stick and Seren swearing loudly, tears leaking from her eyes), Esme told Seren to take painkillers every four hours for the first couple of days and to use the bowl of ice water as much as she liked.

Walking away from the pub, Luke asked the questions that had been building up. 'Are you a doctor?'

She shook her head. 'I started training as a nurse, back in the day, but didn't get to qualify.' Her face clouded.

'Shouldn't she go to hospital?' He wanted to take the words back as soon as they were out.

Esme shot him a sharp look. 'There isn't anything else they would do. I have checked for nerve damage and these sorts of burns are best left to the air to heal. Especially since there are already blisters. As long as they don't break too early and she keeps her hands clean, the risk of infection is low. Burns to the pads of the fingers hurt like nothing else, but they do heal very quickly. The skin on fingers renews faster than other skin.'

'So you're the island's medic as well as running the bed and breakfast?'

'And I tend the...' Esme stopped speaking abruptly. Then she continued. 'Yes. We all wear lots of hats. It's the only way on an island. Fiona cuts hair, Hammer can fix just about anything, Oliver gives financial advice.'

Luke wondered what she had been going to say before she had stopped herself. 'I thought it would be different. With the causeway.'

'It is, but the weather makes the causeway impassable on a fairly regular basis. And we're all here because we don't particularly like spending time on the mainland. We're a very closed community.'

Well, that was an understatement.

HAMMER WAS WORKING on his wood carving. He had a stove with a steel chimney that vented through the centre of the upturned herring boat he had renovated into a small home. He had a curtained alcove with a platform bed with built-in storage underneath and a small kitchen area with a sink and a stove connected to a gas canister that sat in a shed bolted onto the side of the boat, like the world's smallest extension. If anybody asked, he would emphasise that he had built his boathouse well before the craze for tiny homes had hit, but nobody ever questioned his life choices. There were advantages to looking the way he did.

He picked up his knife and pondered the newcomer. The piece he had been working on was a bear standing on her hind legs. He had the rough shape and was now working on the detail. He almost slipped and severed an ear-in-progress, realising that his head wasn't calm enough for the task. He put it down before he could ruin several hours of labour.

Somebody banged on the door, making him glad he had already put down his knife. Standing outside in the dusk, as if summoned by Hammer's thoughts, was the good-looking mainlander.

. . .

'I'm not looking to make trouble,' Luke said. He had been acting too much like he was on holiday and he needed to get back on task. His brother was out there, somewhere, and he wasn't going to find him while spending all his time trying to get on Esme Gray's good side. 'I'm just looking for someone.'

'And I don't care one way or the other. It's all the same to me.'

Luke respected Hammer's need for a front. Reputation was useful. He had witnessed that with his brother, as Lewis gained a name for himself. 'My brother. Lewis Taylor. Have you heard of him, or not?'

'Not.'

'Fine. Is this the part where you tell me to get off the island?'

'If you like.'

'It's what everybody else is saying. Especially at the bed and breakfast. I don't know why she is letting me stay when she clearly doesn't want...'

'Leave her alone.'

The menace in Hammer's tone was unmistakable and Luke felt the hairs on the back of his neck stand up. 'I'm not going to...'

'You're not going to do anything at all when it comes to that woman.'

The devilry that dogged his family, especially his twin brother, was something that Luke prided himself at avoiding on the whole. It was hard not to attack back with someone like Hammer, though, and Luke allowed himself a wide smile. 'I'm helping her in the pub tonight. Make sure you tip well.'

CHAPTER NINE

Esme tied her unruly hair into a ponytail and then twisted it into a bun. She always wore sturdy shoes, but she chose her comfiest trainers in preparation for being on her feet for hours.

Working in the kitchen of The Rising Moon was a new experience. It was Seren's domain and it felt sacrilegious to be rummaging through her drawers, looking for equipment. Soon, however, the pressure of providing food obliterated the strangeness, and Esme and Luke fell into a rhythm. It was an easy rhythm and they worked well together. Based, it had to be noted, on Luke doing exactly whatever Esme told him to do.

Whirling around each other to plate up five venison stews in a row, Luke wondered out loud how on earth Seren managed the place on her own when she had a full house.

'We all know not to come in when there are tourists, or to stagger our times a bit, so Seren doesn't get overwhelmed. And Euan helps out on summer weekends.'

'In the kitchen?' Luke couldn't imagine the silent fifteen-year-old managing front of house duties.

'Mostly. He pulls a good pint, though.' Esme shot him a wry smile. 'Don't tell the police.'

Luke mimed zipping his lips.

Esme took the first three plates out, balancing one on her wrist and bumping through the swing door to the pub like she had been waitressing for years.

The dinner rush wasn't bad, in all honesty, but Luke was glad to sit down with his reheated stew at half eight and he had a new respect for Seren's work ethic. Especially as he contemplated the devastation of dirty plates, pots and dishes that covered the counter tops.

Esme came back in with the last pile of dirty dishes and put them with the others. 'I've told them they have to finish their drinks and go home. The deal wasn't to serve drinks to closing time, so that should be the last of it. I've told people to put their glasses on the tray on the bar when they finish.'

'I've got our food ready,' Luke said. 'Thought we could tackle that lot after.'

'Good plan,' Esme said, joining him. 'We could eat in the pub, you know.'

'Do you want to?' Luke made to pick up the bowls and cutlery. There were two stools and he had pulled them out in front of a small area of clear countertop. He had created it by piling dishes in a teetering tower and balancing them on top of the dishwasher.

She shook her head. 'No. I'm a mess and too tired to talk.'

Taking the hint, he turned his attention to his food. He thought briefly about protesting that she looked fine, but wasn't sure he ought to comment on her appearance. After the first bite, he realised he was ravenous and focused on shovelling the stuff in.

Once they had eaten, Esme put on the small radio and

they got to work, rinsing dishes and cutlery for the dish-washer, putting the tray of dirty glasses from behind the bar into the glass-cleaner, and then filling the sink with soapy water to do the pots, knives, and microwave dishes. As everything had been reheated, there was nothing oily or burnt to deal with and, with the music playing, it took half the time Luke had expected.

'Thank you,' Esme said, once the counters were wiped down.

'Happy to help,' Luke said, hating that he sounded formal. He wasn't usually such a mess around women and didn't know why he couldn't get his act together with Esme.

'You can head off,' she said after an awkward pause.

'I was going to walk you home.'

She laughed, the brief sound escaping before she clamped a hand over her mouth. 'I'm going to have a drink with Fiona. But thanks.'

'It's dark,' he said, doubling down on his idiocy. Since when did showing gentleman-like concern become a laughing matter?

'I have a torch,' Esme said, no longer laughing. 'And I know every person here. Except you.'

'Right. Message received.' He had been aiming for a jokey tone, but knew as soon as the words were out that he hadn't managed it.

Going over the conversation in his head as he walked back to the bed and breakfast he was pretty sure of one thing – he wasn't about to sweep Esme Gray off her feet with his suave flirting skills. Perhaps the island really was cursed.

. . .

Back at Strand House, Luke opened a bottle of wine he had bought in the silent man's shop and poured himself a glass. He didn't feel right sitting in the kitchen or the living room, but he thought it might be all right to use the dining room. He had eaten there before, at least, and it seemed like the most 'public' space of the guest house. He could have gone up to drink in his bedroom, but that felt sad.

He picked up a paperback from the bookcase and read while he sipped his wine, pretending that he wasn't really waiting for Esme.

She walked in an hour later. He heard her at the back door, greeting the cat in warm tones. He put the book back onto the bookcase and was hovering awkwardly near the stairs when Esme appeared from the kitchen.

She stopped in surprise.

'Sorry,' he said.

'No,' she shook her head. 'It's fine. I just forgot you were here.'

Not what he hoped for.

He nodded at his empty glass. 'I'll wash that up.'

'You don't have to go to your room,' Esme said, not looking entirely sure. 'I mean, you're welcome to use downstairs.'

'I don't want to get in your way.' What he meant was, he didn't want to do anything to cause her to throw him out. After his useless chat with the man called Hammer and his disturbing one with the mayor, Luke didn't feel he had got any answers, and he wasn't in a hurry to move on from Unholy Island.

Esme shrugged. 'Knowing you're here means I won't relax properly anyway. Doesn't matter whether you are hidden away or not.'

He took his foot off the bottom step of the stairs and turned to look at her properly.

'Sorry,' she pulled at the cuff of her over-sized sweat-shirt. 'That sounded rude. I don't mind you here this week. I just meant you're welcome to use the rooms downstairs. And thank you, again, for your help this evening.'

'Is this a good time to mention that I am happy to share the wine?'

'Yes,' Esme smiled properly. 'Excellent timing.' She turned back to the kitchen and Luke followed.

He got a second wine glass from the cupboard while Esme emptied a packet of salted cashews into a bowl.

'Living room?'

'Sure.'

He followed her into a short hallway to a snug room with an unusual blue wood burner set below a chunky wooden beam. The fireplace and hearth were lined with dark turquoise tiles and the burner was ornate metalwork. He stepped closer and read the name 'Sylvie' picked out in art déco script on the top.

'Ah, yes. I will need to negotiate with Sylvie soon. But it's not quite cold enough to bother, yet.'

'Unusual piece.'

'I inherited her,' Esme said. 'Along with everything else in the house.'

Luke was about to express his condolences for her loss, but she carried on, pouring glasses of wine while she spoke.

'Well, everything except the studio. That was a junk room. I cleared it out and moved in my equipment.'

'You paint?'

'The sea,' Esme stopped, as if embarrassed. 'It's just a hobby.'

'The painting in my room, is that one of yours?'

'Yes,' Esme seemed suddenly very interested in her wine. 'That probably seems egotistical, but...'

'Why would that be egotistical?' Luke was genuinely confused. If he had a gift like that, he would be thrilled to hang his work wherever he could find a space.

'I... I'm not sure how to explain it.' She took a gulp of wine and nudged the bowl of nuts closer to Luke. 'So. What makes you so determined to stay on Unholy Island?'

Well, that was blunt. He took a handful of cashews to buy some time.

'We haven't been particularly welcoming. I should apologise.'

Which wasn't the same as actually apologising. Interesting. He had several lies ready but, just as he had with Tobias and Bee, Luke found himself telling the truth. 'I'm looking for someone.'

'A particular someone?'

Esme's expression was careful and she had gone very still. He could feel the waves of tension roll from her like waves on the beach. 'My brother,' he said. Again, he hadn't meant to, but had wanted to do anything to alleviate that awful, guarded expression on Esme's face.

She visibly relaxed. Terrible poker face, he thought.

'My brother went missing eighteen months ago. I started looking for him about two months after that.'

'You assumed he was coming back? At first, I mean.'

'At first, I didn't realise he was missing. I didn't see him every day or anything. And he's an adult, with his own life.'

'I wasn't accusing you of anything,' Esme said gently.

'No.' Luke shook his head, trying to clear the fug of guilt and anger that rose up whenever he thought about Lewis. 'I know. It's just...'

'You feel responsible.'

It was Luke's turn to go still. 'What makes you say that?'

She shrugged. 'It's what we do, isn't it? With loved ones. Feel responsible for everything they go through, even though it's not our fault.'

'Do you have siblings?'

'No.' Esme got up abruptly. 'I forgot the water.'

Luke looked around the room while she was gone, wondering how he had put his foot in his mouth this time.

In the kitchen, Esme sat at the table and bent forward. With the smooth wood pressing gently on her forehead and her eyes closed, she took several slow breaths. What was she thinking? Why had she engaged Luke in conversation? Shared wine? She was behaving like a girl with a crush, when she was no longer a girl and had no business entertaining any thoughts in that arena. No more men. It wasn't as if she had officially sworn off the opposite sex, hadn't needed to do anything so formal. In her mind, it was just simply the most obvious course of action. Only a lunatic would countenance anything else.

She felt a dull thump as Jet leapt onto the table. A moment later, his body pushed along her arm. She lifted her head and found herself eye to eye with the only male she truly trusted. 'What am I doing?' She asked the cat.

Jet looked into her eyes without blinking. After a moment, she pushed to her feet and filled a glass jug with water. With a couple of tumblers in the other hand, she squared her shoulders and went back to the living room.

Luke was sitting on the sofa, wine glass in hand. 'I'm sorry.'

Esme busied herself with pouring water into the tumblers. Then she closed the thick curtains against the dark night and curled up in the armchair underneath the window.

'I didn't mean to upset you.' His voice was low. The vibrations of it seemed to go right through her body and she shifted slightly. The vision she had seen of him in that unknown bedroom leaped into her mind. In that vision, she had felt uneasy. A thrill of fear. But here, with Luke physically in the same room, the time when her instincts should most definitely be making her panic, she felt a different kind of nervous energy. Excitement.

'You didn't.'

'I think I did. And I'm sorry. The last thing I want to do is to disturb you.'

It was a strange choice of words, but apt. And the problem was, he did disturb her. Esme felt like something dormant that had been poked into life. Her calcified surface shifting and cracking. 'Why here?' She asked, determined to keep the conversation away from her and her life and family. Or lack of.

'I heard a rumour,' he said. 'Flimsy reason. And it doesn't ring true.'

'How so?'

'My brother is not the hiding away type.'

'You think this is a place to hide?'

'Isn't it?'

Esme looked away. The island was a place to hide, but more than that it was a place where nobody stayed. Except the chosen few. That this man was still here was confusing. It had to mean something, but nobody seemed to know what. And his reason for looking here made no sense, but his reason for staying made even less. 'Your brother can't be here,' she said, wincing as she realised how harsh that sounded. 'I don't mean to be blunt, but nobody stays for longer than a night or two. I'm sure enough other people have told you that by now, so you know it's not just me being odd. Even if your brother had visited the island, he would be long gone by now.'

He put his wine glass down on the table and leaned back against the cushions. His broad frame dwarfed the small sofa, which was a wooden-framed model made sometime in the nineteen-sixties when people were evidently shorter than today. Esme imagined what it would be like to climb onto his lap, to feel those arms around her body, his hands firm against her back, and took a large sip of her wine. She imagined she had flushed bright red.

Just when she thought he wasn't going to respond, he spoke in a low voice. 'I have been moving around for months, sometimes aimlessly, sometimes because I'd heard something about Lewis or was visiting one of his friends. Anyone I could think of with any connection to him. This is the first time I haven't felt the urge to move on.'

'You must be tired.' She meant of travelling, of searching, and of worrying, but he took it as a hint to leave her in peace.

He got to his feet in a sudden movement. 'Yeah, it's getting late. I'll head up. Thanks for the drink. Night.'

'You brought it,' Esme said, but she was speaking to thin air as he had bolted from the room.

CHAPTER TEN

On Monday, Luke tried the bookshop again. Esme had said it was open all week and that he had just been unlucky before. The lights were definitely on inside the shop as he approached from the opposite side of the road, but when he tried to open the front door it was, once again, locked tight. Then the lights went out. Alvis must have just left through the back of the shop or, perhaps, gone upstairs to her living quarters. Logically, he knew that she hadn't been watching him approach and that the locking of the door and turning out of the lights was pure coincidence. Not personal, he told himself firmly. This strange place was definitely getting to him, though, as he couldn't help feeling a little hurt as he peered through the window. He had always loved a good bookshop and felt like a kid with his face pressed against the window of a sweetshop.

He didn't know why he wanted to go in so badly, but he did. He hadn't seen Alvis at the pub at dinner yet, but that didn't mean she wouldn't show up. Esme said that she definitely ate there on occasion, just not as regularly as most of the islanders. 'Alvis is a loner,' Esme said. 'Which is saying something around here.'

Luke had been thinking the same thing, but he kept his face strictly neutral. Things seemed to be going much better with Esme and he had no desire to rock the boat.

AFTER A FEW NIGHTS of sleep in the comfortable room at the top of Strand House and plenty of hot food from both Esme and The Rising Moon, Luke felt somewhat restored. He had always been resilient and now that the exhaustion had receded, he began to wonder what had made him decide to stay in this place. He needed to keep looking for Lewis and Unholy Island was a distraction. Having admitted that to himself, he expected to feel his usual restlessness, the driving force that had kept him moving for over a year. Part of him wanted to stay distracted, though. To take a break. And, he argued, it wasn't as if he had any leads. He had nowhere to go, nowhere to look. Lewis was as lost today as he had been eighteen months ago. The feeling that he had experienced outside Hammer's boat shed washed back over him. The sense that Lewis was dead and that he had been kidding himself otherwise. The certainty that he should just stop looking. Could he stop? If all he would find was death?

It was a bright day with a clear sky and the sea looking more blue than grey. Luke laced up his boots and set out for a walk around the west side of the island. Beyond the village there was a sandy bay carved in a sickle shape before the land tapered into the scrappy northernmost point of the island. That was where a wicked collection of rocks jutted out into the North Sea, a natural defence against boats.

He stopped in at the shop to buy a filled roll and a

bottle of Coke. He had been into the shop on every day since his first, trying to make small talk and smiling as much as he could without appearing unhinged. Today, Matteo almost smiled back. The expression was tiny and brief, but for that split second it transformed his face. He looked ten years younger and his handsome visage became magnetic.

'I'm heading down to the bay on the other side of the harbour,' Luke said. He raised his roll and drink. 'Picnic.'

Matteo reached for his pen and paper.

Leaning slightly, Luke read the words. *Coire Bay*.

'Right,' he said. 'Okay.' He tapped his head to indicate that he was storing this precious nugget of information. He knew from Esme that when an islander volunteered something, however obvious or banal it appeared, he needed to act like it was a gift.

Matteo wrote again. *Means cauldron. Not safe to swim, unless you can hold your breath for a really long time.*

A joke. He glanced and realised that Matteo was smiling with his eyes now. A proper sardonic smile. Progress.

THE SOUND of the waves on the beach and the gulls wheeling and calling gave him a nostalgic feeling. Childhood holidays by the sea, his mother unpacking sandwiches from Tupperware containers and Lewis crouching over the channel they invariably dug. A straight trench leading from the sea to the dry sand of their temporary encampment. They sometimes added a castle, but always created the channel. As if they were both already digging escape routes, even then.

Of the two brothers, Luke was the one who ought to have gone missing. He had been telling anybody who would listen that he needed a change, that he needed to work out what he was doing with his life. Lewis had shown no sign. He was living with his girlfriend and had seemed more settled that he had ever before. The worst of his wild years seemed to be behind him, and he was no longer picking random fights or turning up at Luke's flat at four in the morning on a cocktail of drugs, wanting to pace the floor and tell Luke 'how things were'.

His girlfriend, Freya, swore that everything was good between them and Luke hadn't found anything to suggest otherwise. She had been convincingly distraught when he had disappeared, anyway, and her friends had all expressed relief that Lewis had moved on because they didn't think he was good for Freya, which also had the ring of truth. Freya was with someone else now, but Luke didn't blame her. She and Lewis had only been together for six months. Living together had been more a matter of financial convenience than anything else and Luke wasn't about to pretend that his brother was some kind of saint. He wouldn't have been easy to be with, to live with.

But he was his blood. His twin. His mirror image and the other half of his soul. He couldn't just forget that Lewis was missing and carry on with his work and his routine. He couldn't keep going running around the same route three mornings a week or spend Fridays at the pub, go hiking with friends, the cinema on Sunday afternoons. Life couldn't just carry on. The world couldn't just keep on being. It was unbearable, but somehow that fact wasn't enough to make it stop. So instead, he searched. First, it gave him purpose. Something to hold on to and a way to fill his time and his thoughts, to keep the sadness and fear at bay. Now he couldn't remember how to do anything else, how to be any other way.

Maybe this place would shake him from his routine. If

he could stay here for a week. Two weeks. Maybe then he could go home and restart his life. Or go somewhere new and start again. Perhaps what he needed was a full stop. Punctuation at the end of a chapter.

Deep in thought, he hadn't been paying attention to his surroundings. The beach and the sea and the sky just a wide-open backdrop. Now he was nearing the northern end of the bay and could see gigantic black rocks curving ahead. The edge of the sand was a gentle rise to higher ground with gentle dunes covered in marram grass, but here it was higher.

There was something that didn't belong. Blue-grey waves, pale blue sky, white sand, black rocks. And something bright yellow.

CHAPTER ELEVEN

After the first second of incomprehension, Luke knew what he was looking at. The bright yellow was a raincoat. The reason it was there, rippling in the stiff coastal breeze, was because it belonged to a body. And that body was lying motionless on a large flat rock, between two larger jagged rocks.

Lewis didn't own a yellow raincoat and the curled figure was too small. Still, his brain stuttered for a moment, having imagined every scenario of finding his brother, including finding his corpse in a lonely place. Birds in the sky, bare earth, and all the breath that had once animated his living flesh carried away on the wind.

His mobile phone was in his hand, the impulse to call for help dashed by the lack of signal. He held up his phone, but the bars remained empty.

A figure appeared on the path above the beach. He recognised Esme's hat and bulky coat and raised both arms to wave, shouting for good measure although he wasn't sure if his voice was stolen away by the wicked air. The breeze had got ideas above its station and was now whipping his hair into his face and roaring in his ears.

Esme must have picked up on his panic, or perhaps she could see the yellow coat from her vantage point, because she made her way down from the dunes at a good clip. She was almost running as she arrived at the rocks and her face was pink from the exertion and the wind.

'What is...' Esme's question died on her lips and she took a step closer to the black rocks. She looked back over her shoulder. Her expression was stricken and Luke realised that she recognised the person. The body.

'Who is it?'

Esme was shaking her head as she picked her way closer and she didn't answer.

He stepped up to hold out a hand, thinking to steady her or to... Well, he didn't really know. Just that he didn't want Esme to be upset or to have to see a dead person that she seemed to know.

'No, no, no.'

He realised she was chanting under her breath as she moved, but that her footing was sure. She reached the figure and bent over it, looking. Her hand dipped down and he realised that she was touching the figure's skin, feeling for a pulse, for breath. Signs of life.

He ought to have done that straight away and he felt like a fool. He swallowed. 'Is she dead?'

Esme straightened. 'Yes. We need to get someone.' She looked back at him, eyes wide, but not seeing him. She was having a conversation with herself. 'Do we still call an ambulance? No. It's too late. She's gone. But I don't know what I'm supposed to...' She stopped, put a hand on her chest and seemed to struggle to take a breath. 'I'll get Tobias. He'll know what needs to be done. Will you wait with her?'

'Of course,' Luke said immediately. He still wanted to reach out to Esme, to put an arm around her. He kept himself still, not wanting to overstep propriety or alarm her. There was something very self-contained about the woman. 'Or I'll go and get Tobias. Whichever you prefer.'

'I'll go,' Esme said, sounding more certain. She turned and looked out to sea, shielding her eyes. After a few seconds she muttered. 'Better get a move on.'

'What?' Luke wasn't sure if he'd heard her correctly.

'I'll call Tobias as soon as I get signal, should just have to get up onto the main path. Won't be long.'

'It's fine,' Luke said. 'I'll wait.' Then he wanted to kick himself. He had sounded like he was doing a favour, not the bare minimum of what any halfway decent human being would do in the circumstances. Luckily, Esme was too preoccupied to notice.

'Storm's coming,' she said, looking back out to sea.

He turned and followed her gaze, about to contradict her. The sky was blue, after all. A grey smudge on the horizon was moving fast. Getting bigger and darker as he watched. 'Are you sure?'

Esme didn't bother to answer, just turned and began marching across the sand toward the path.

LATER, in The Rising Moon with a mug of sweetened tea, Luke realised that he was in a state of shock. Seren had been speaking to him for a few minutes and he hadn't heard a single word. He shook his head. 'Sorry.'

'That's all right,' she touched his shoulder. 'I'll get you a sandwich.'

The thought of food made his stomach turn over and then, a moment later, he realised he was hungry. Luke had been on the beach, standing sentinel over the woman for almost an hour by the time Esme came back. In that time the weather had turned, just as Esme had predicted. The grey smudge on the horizon had turned into a mass of dark clouds and a wild wind had sprung up from the north, plucking at his clothes and whipping his face until his nose was red and his eyes ran.

He was warm now, in the pub, but his insides still felt chilled. And his mind was sluggish. When he closed his eyes, he saw images of the yellow raincoat, white hair spread on black rock, and the churning sea in a staccato slide show.

He didn't know why he was so affected. He had never met the woman on the shore. And she was clearly very old. Yes, it wasn't lovely to find a dead person, but it would be natural causes. Or close enough. A fall onto those rocks, maybe a simple foot-slip or the result of a stroke or heart attack. A quick death in old age, while walking in the fresh salty air with the sound of the sea roaring in her ears. There were worse ways to go.

Seren was back with a fresh mug of tea and a plate. The sandwich was made with fresh white bread and it contained thick slices of salty ham, tangy mustard and crisp lettuce. He took a bite and closed his eyes. It was possibly the best sandwich he had ever eaten.

Seren was watching him. 'Good?'

He swallowed and nodded. 'Really good. Amazing. Thank you.'

She smiled a little sadly. 'Death food always tastes the best.'

Luke didn't know how to respond to that. Instead, he said, 'I'm sorry for your loss.'

Seren patted his shoulder again. 'Eat up.'

TOBIAS WATCHED the storm rage outside through his living room window as he paced the floor. The weather had sprung from nowhere as if in response to the death of Alvis. After so many years on Unholy Island he wasn't even a little bit tempted to call it coincidence. The island, or something that lived on it, was expressing its fury at the loss of one of its own.

Also, intentionally or not, Tobias didn't know, but the weather was preventing the long arm of the law from reaching the island. He had spoken to DS Robinson at the Berwick station and she had confirmed that Tobias needed to do his best to secure the scene with a tarpaulin, and then to leave well alone. She was very firm on the latter point. 'It's wild out there and I don't want another body on my list.'

Putting aside the questionable manners of a mainlander lecturing an islander on the dangers of stormy weather, Tobias accepted that the detective sergeant had a point. The wind, never shy, was whipping around the island like it wanted to rip it from the seabed.

Tobias looked at the phone in his hand and, after a slight hesitation, called Esme. She sounded flustered and he wondered whether she was going to hold up through this crisis. Esme was the newest member of the island community and was largely untested. She had taken to caring for the wards, and was good at welcoming the transient visitors. Far better than anybody else on the island, and light years ahead of her predecessor – a tiny, furious woman who had allowed people into Strand House with a vinegary resentment that had kept all but the most determined and thick-skinned away. On second thoughts, Tobias reflected, Madame Le Grys had been perfect.

'We're going to bring her inside,' Esme said.

Tobias's attention snapped back to the conversation. 'I beg your pardon?'

'Seren said we can't leave her out there and she's right,'

Esme continued. 'Hammer is down there now with Matteo and Fiona. They're bringing her home. The bookshop, I guess. But I'm not sure. I'm supposed to be organising a place for her to rest but I'm not sure where would be best.'

Tobias pinched the bridge of his nose where a headache was beginning. 'We're not supposed to disturb the scene, DS Robinson was very clear...'

'With all due respect, Mayor, you are outnumbered. Something you can tell the police whenever they manage to get here.'

IN THE END, it was decided to bring Alvis to the pub. The back room had the chairs pushed around the edge and a board was laid on top of a couple of tables to form a platform. When it had come down to it, nobody had felt able to unlock the bookshop and walk in without Alvis. This way, the village could sit with their fallen friend, and sip a pint or knock a shot at the same time.

Hammer had carried Alvis from the beach, the wind ripping at his clothes and the rain driving into his eyes. The path from Coire Bay to the village was running with water and even with his sure footing and good boots, he almost went over at one point. Luckily Alvis was a small woman and he had been able to carry her in a front cradle-hold. Over the shoulder would have been easier, still, but would have appeared less respectful to the islanders who had gathered to witness her arrival at The Rising Moon.

Seren had put lamps into the back room so that the main overhead light could be left switched off and pushed the chairs against the walls. She had unplugged the Space Invaders machine. Esme was stretching a tartan blanket out on the pushed-together tables in the middle. It wasn't as if Alvis would be able to feel the material, but he supposed Esme knew what she was doing. Perhaps she thought a sheet of plywood on top of a table that usually held pints of beer ought to be transformed before it could hold a person. Or perhaps she was thinking of soaking up the fluids that might begin to leak from the body. Hammer wasn't entirely clear on when that would start to happen.

After he had laid her on the checked blanket, Alvis looked smaller than ever. He shook out his arms a little self-consciously and Esme reached up to pat his shoulder. 'Thank you,' she said. 'You should get a hot drink. You must be frozen.'

She bent to a shopping bag on the floor and produced a towel, handing it to him. She picked up another and began to gently dry Alvis's face and hair. Hammer had raised the hood on her coat as best he could, but it had moved while he was walking and her grey hair was plastered to her pink scalp.

'Will do,' he said absently, his attention caught by Alvis's hands. They were mostly covered by the sleeves of her yellow raincoat, but the knuckles and fingertips of her right hand were visible.

Hammer wasn't one for rituals and wasn't overly bothered by either the concept or the reality of death. One day you went dark and, as far as he could tell, it was just the same as the day before you were born. A blank. Nothing to know, nothing to worry about, and nothing to grieve.

Still, despite being a man with particular experience in the area, he still never really managed to be zen about murder. It shouldn't be up to another human being to decide on the day the lights flicked out. It was bad enough when it was bad men doing bad things, at least there was an element of culpability to it, but this... Alvis had never done anything much and certainly nothing to warrant this attack. He bent over the body and examined what was visible on the fully clothed woman. He knew from Esme that she had hit the back of her head, presumably when she fell, but he gently lifted and turned each of her hands in turn, noting defensive wounds. Either Alvis had been in a separate scuffle, or somebody had helped her fall over on the rocks. As far as he knew, Alvis had led a quiet life. But they all had pasts, that's why they were on this island. The question was, had Alvis's caught up with her?

CHAPTER TWELVE

The mayor knew that it was his responsibility to maintain order on the island. With the storm still raging, there was no chance of a boat landing safely, which meant that the police from the mainland would not arrive until the causeway cleared at midday the next day at the earliest.

The body was in The Rising Moon and a rota had been drawn up to ensure Alvis was never left alone. It hadn't been difficult, as Alvis had been well liked. Even Lucy, who generally hated everybody, had been seen to smile in her presence. It was good that she wasn't around much and didn't seem to be aware of the situation. He wasn't sure how she would react. He made a mental note to check-in with Bee about her youngest sister.

The island had been a sanctuary for the more unusual members of society for as long as Tobias could remember. He had woken up on this patch of salt-scoured earth and it was his to watch over. That had been a great deal easier before the people had arrived, but he had found early on that he couldn't turn them away. Not those in need. Not those chosen by the island itself.

As the wind howled around the outside of the pub, rattling the windows, and rain battered the glass, the islanders took turns sitting with Alvis and in the main room to eat, have a drink, or talk quietly. They didn't look like a random collection of misfits. To Tobias, they looked like his community. His flock. They were shocked and sad, of course, but he could almost see the comfort that the islanders were drawing from being with one another.

Nobody seemed keen to leave the pub and it wasn't just because of the lashing rain. The newcomer was sitting next to Esme, his body curved toward her as he listened to her speak. Tobias walked around the room and offered a few words of comfort. Fiona surprised him with a quick, hard hug.

Esme got up and went to the backroom to sit with Alvis. Tobias joined her for a few minutes, wanting to check on their second-newest resident. Seven years was the blink of an eye as far as Tobias was concerned, and he wasn't sure how she would cope with this first loss. He made stilted conversation until he realised that the Ward Witch wanted to hold vigil alone.

In the main room of the pub, Luke felt awkward sitting alone now that Esme had gone to sit with Alvis. He wondered whether he should leave. But he wanted to wait for Esme, to walk her back to the house. It wasn't a matter of outdated chivalry, just good sense. The storm was still raging and the winds had to be gale-force. It was practical to stick together. Besides, a woman of Esme's size might get blown right off the island and into the sea if he wasn't there to hold on to her.

He got up and went to the bar, more for something to do than because he wanted a drink. Seren pulled him a pint and waved away his offer of payment. 'Not tonight,' she said. 'On the house.'

Tobias appeared from the back room and spoke quietly to him. 'There's going to be a lot of this tonight.' He indicated Luke's pint. 'Soon the conversation is going to get onto details. Can I rely on your discretion?'

Luke cut his eyes to the mayor. He wondered what the man thought he had seen. He had noticed scrapes on Alvis's hands and had wondered what they meant. Tobias being jumpy might mean he had seen them and believed the worst. Or, he just wanted to keep speculation to a minimum. 'Of course.'

'Good.'

Tobias's gaze shifted and Luke realised that somebody had approached. He turned to find Matteo holding his notebook open. He had written a question: *How did she die?*

'I don't know,' Luke said, willing himself not to glance at Tobias. He didn't want it to look like they had just been having a secret conversation about Alvis. The islanders didn't need another reason to resent or mistrust him.

Matteo flipped the page and wrote: *You found her?*

'Yes.'

Matteo raised one eyebrow in a perfect 'so what the fuck?' expression.

Luke shrugged. 'I don't know any more than you, man.'

'If there is anything untoward, the police will investigate,' Tobias said.

Matteo wrote for a moment. *That's not good either.*

'We will all cooperate.' Tobias raised his voice to cut through the quiet chatter. 'If the good people of the Northumbria Police deem it necessary to investigate the circumstances of our friend Alvis's death, we will all cooperate fully with that investigation. Is that understood?'

There were murmurs that sounded like agreement and a couple of reluctant head nods.

'Why would there be an investigation?' Fiona asked. Her voice carrying clearly across the room. 'Wasn't it natural?' The last word hung in the air.

'Almost certainly,' Tobias said briskly. 'Alvis wasn't a young woman. It was just her time.'

'We don't know that,' Seren said, unhelpfully. 'She could have slipped.'

Hammer had been sitting quietly in the corner of the room, but he chose this moment to chip in. 'Or she was pushed.'

Luke felt the atmosphere in the room shift.

Hammer was scowling in his direction, so he wasn't entirely surprised when he added. 'We hadn't had a death on the island for years. Now he shows up and Alvis is gone.'

'Coincidence,' Luke said. 'People die. And, as Tobias pointed out, she was old. It's not exactly unexpected.'

'Careful,' Tobias said. He looked around. 'You all need to be careful. This isn't a respectful way to be speaking. Our friend lies through there,' he indicated the back room, 'and we should be contemplating her life, remembering her kindness and wisdom.'

Luke wondered if it was his imagination, or had the storm got louder?

People shuffled in their seats, looking away from Tobias and each other. Luke thought that would be an end to it and that someone would break the tension and change the subject.

'Alvis would want us to find the truth,' Fiona said. She wasn't speaking loudly, but the room was quiet and it carried.

'I'll save you all some time,' Luke said, standing up and

looking around the room. 'I didn't hurt Alvis. I certainly didn't kill her. I never even met the woman. Never been anywhere near her until today.'

'You found her, though?' Seren asked.

'I was walking on the beach and I found her. Yes. She was already dead. Almost immediately after, I saw Esme on the top path and waved to her. I can go and get her, she'll tell you.'

'Leave her be,' Tobias said sharply. 'She is paying her respects.'

Luke sat down. Defeated. He couldn't argue his way out of this. Either the people on the island would believe he hadn't hurt Alvis or they wouldn't. His words weren't going to sway them one way or the other. He felt the old feeling of injustice. He was always assumed to be guilty, was cut from the same cloth as his twin and was, therefore, assumed to share Lewis's personality, preferred pastimes and lack of ethics. For the first time in a few days, he wondered what the hell he was doing on Unholy Island. He ought to just leave.

CHAPTER THIRTEEN

After he finished his pint, trying to ignore the suspicious looks and the circle of empty chairs around where he was sitting, Luke went through to the back room to speak to Esme. He didn't relish the thought of seeing Alvis again, but thought that nothing could be worse than what he had already experienced. Stumbling across her on the beach and then standing sentinel while Esme got help. Her small body on the rock with the gulls wheeling and calling above, her half-closed eyes, and the heavy emptiness that had seemed to emanate from her life-less form.

Laid out on the table in the backroom of the pub, Alvis ought to have seemed out of place. Surreal. But somebody had lit candles and turned off the overhead lights and in the flickering glow, the room was transformed to something meditative. Almost holy.

'Are you ready to go home? I'm happy to wait, but I'll sit in here. It's getting heated next door.'

Esme looked at him with eyes that were far away. She had been deep in thought and seemed to be struggling to focus on his words.

'Fiona says she is next on the rota and is ready to take over whenever you want. Sitting in here, I mean.'

'Heated?' Esme said eventually.

'Yeah,' he ducked his head, hating that Esme was going to find out whether he told her or not. 'A few of them think I had something to do with Alvis...'

'Them?'

'I didn't,' he said. 'You know that, right? I would never... And I literally never met the woman. I have absolutely no reason to hurt her.'

A shutter had fallen behind Esme's eyes. 'Reason doesn't usually come into it.'

'You don't think...'

Esme looked away. 'I don't know what I'm thinking right now. I'm just sitting with Alvis, trying to take it all in.'

'Sorry. Yes. Sorry.'

'You don't have to wait for me,' she said, still not looking at him. 'You go can go back.'

'It's wild out there, still. I thought it would be safer if we walked together.'

'I'll stay here tonight. Seren has a spare room. Or I might stay with Alvis.'

Luke knew he had been dismissed. The injustice bubbled up, mixing with past frustrations. 'Right, well. I will go. Before that lot form a lynch mob. Guilty until proven otherwise. I am an incomer, after all.'

'Yes,' Esme spoke coldly. 'You are a complete stranger. And my friend is dead.'

His anger rushed away as quickly as it had come. He flushed with shame. He was attacking the one person who least deserved it. And she was right. The islanders might have every reason to fear strangers. He knew as little about them as they knew about him. He started to apologise, but Esme wouldn't look at him and he knew he was just making things worse. Forcing his presence on her when she clearly didn't want him around, so he left.

AFTER A FEW HOURS, the noise from the main room of the pub quietened down. Seren brought Esme a mug of tea and told her to take a break. 'You've done your time. You can go home and get some sleep if you want.'

Esme shook her head. She was the island's Ward Witch and she would watch over Alvis on this first terrible night. Besides, she didn't want to be anywhere near Luke Taylor until she had sorted out her jumbled thoughts.

'I'll sit with her for a bit,' Seren said. 'If that's okay.'

'Of course.' Esme was going to take her tea to the main room, but swerved and went outside instead. She didn't want to be with the others and the blast of fresh air would help to wake her up. It was past midnight and the cosy warmth of the pub had dulled her senses.

It was colder outside than she had anticipated. Listening to the storm from inside the pub had given her a conceptual understanding of the weather, but now the air and rain were giving a harsh practical lesson. Within seconds, her fingers were numb, despite her thick gloves, and she felt as if the wind was cutting straight through her layers of clothes. Still, it felt right to be uncomfortable. Alvis had been lying out there on the beach, all alone. She wondered how long it had taken her to die. Whether she had been afraid.

Bee appeared, saying something. Her voice was snatched away by the storm, but she tried again, yelling into Esme's ear. 'What are you doing out here?'

'It's fine. Just rain.' Esme's lips felt clumsy with the cold. She ignored the gale that was buffeting her, making it difficult to stay upright. She was standing in what she imagined would be the shelter of the pub, but the wind hadn't got the memo. The fresh air was so cold that she couldn't feel her face and the rain felt like tiny blades.

'Inside,' Bee shouted into her ear, gripping her arm with authority.

Esme thought about resisting, but realised that she had begun to shiver. And her whole body hurt. She let Bee hustle her back into the pub.

'What the hell?' Seren said from across the room. 'I'll get a towel.'

Moments later, she threw one at Esme, who failed to catch it. Her arms didn't seem to want to obey commands. Bee scooped it from the floor and began vigorously drying Esme's sopping hair. She had no idea until that moment just how wet she had got. She had only been outside for a minute or two. It was ridiculous. She wondered what state Luke was in and whether he had made it to Strand House safely, then pushed the thought firmly away. He could look after himself.

'You're frozen.' Bee's hand touched her cheek briefly and it felt like a brand. The heat of her skin against her chilled face.

'I'm okay.' Even as she spoke, she felt her whole body shudder, as if it had finally noticed how cold she actually was. Or Bee had conjured it with her words. She radiated power and Esme had no idea of what she could actually do.

Once Esme was settled next to the open fire, Bee went to the bar. She returned with two hot chocolates and two tumblers of whisky.

'I don't really...'

'Drink up,' Bee said, knocking her own back in one swallow. 'And then you can tell me exactly what is going on. We can't afford to lose you to hypothermia.'

Esme felt tears pricking her eyes and she blinked, hoping Bee wouldn't notice her weakness.

'I'm waiting,' Bee said, a touch of asperity in her tone.

Esme sipped her whisky, pulling a face at the taste. The burning warmth in her throat seemed to thaw out her core, though, so she took another bigger taste. 'I don't know.'

'Lie. Try again.'

Esme picked up her hot chocolate and wrapped her fingers around the mug. 'I just keep on worrying that I'm doing something wrong. Or that I did something wrong and that's why Alvis... I don't know.'

'You didn't hurt Alvis. It's not your fault.'

Esme wanted to ask 'but what if it is?' but she didn't want to hear the answer. Couldn't bear to have Bee confirm that she was a substandard Ward Witch and that the islanders wished that they still had Madame Le Grys.

Bee knocked back her whisky and then picked up her hot chocolate. She was watching Esme as if trying to decide whether to speak and it made Esme's insides contract.

'Everyone gets things wrong. You can't expect perfection all the time. And nobody expects it of you.'

'But what if I messed up the protection? What if that hurt Alvis somehow?' The words were out.

'That's not what happened,' Bee said. 'And you should know that. You should be able to feel it.'

Esme felt tears stinging her eyes. She didn't want to reveal just how little she trusted herself.

'It will come with time,' Bee said.

Esme swallowed hard. She couldn't admit that there was another deeper and darker fear that ran beneath her concern over Alvis. It wasn't logical. Nobody had suggested that her position was performance related or that she would be asked to leave at any point. The fact that she had inherited the position of Ward Witch and the guest house all in one package should have allayed her fears. It was the most secure set up imaginable. If that didn't close the yawning pit of terror, then what would? And the last thing she wanted was to sound ungrateful. Unholy Island had saved her life.

Bee was watching her, waiting.

'I just... I just can't stop feeling like this is temporary. It's nobody's fault. Just my own.'

'We learn our fears.'

Well, that was true. But how did you unlearn them?

CHAPTER FOURTEEN

Tobias didn't often drive, but he took his ancient Land Rover down to the edge of the causeway to meet DS Kerry Robinson. As expected, the police car was struggling with the mud that rose up between the end of the causeway and the start of the island proper. It was usually completely passable during the hours around a low tide, but after the stormy weather and increased rain it was a quagmire.

'I can't leave the car here,' Robinson said, her voice swallowed by the wind.

'I'll send someone down with a tow bar.' Tobias opened the door for the police officer and she climbed into the passenger seat.

Once they were bumping back toward firm ground, she shot him an accusatory look. 'You knew I would get stuck.'

'Suspecting is not the same as knowing. Thought that's something they taught you at police school.'

'Touché.' She grinned at him. 'It's been too long, Toby.'

He shook his head in mock irritation. 'Don't call me Toby.'

Robinson had been with the Northumbria police for

over twenty years, a span of time she considered significant.

'And how are you, boy?' Robinson twisted in her seat to address Winter, who was sitting in the back. The dog immediately hopped down from his place and pressed his body between the front seats so that he could accept the head rub that was his due.

Tobias parked on the main street outside The Rising Moon. The sky was blue with streaks of white cloud and a low winter sun shining through the coloured glass floats which hung in knotted ropes outside the pub entrance.

'I'm fine to go straight to the site,' Robinson said, misunderstanding. 'I've already had my coffee. I'm not allowed more than one these days or I don't sleep.' She pulled a self-deprecating smile. 'Getting old.'

'You're not old,' Tobias said. It was better than the thought that had leapt to his mind. *You're barely out of childhood.* Tobias was old. He knew what that phrase really meant. He watched people wither and die when, in his opinion, they had hardly started true adulthood.

'And she's in here.'

'What?' Robinson said, her good humour vanishing in an instant.

Tobias opened the door for her without answering.

Seren was cleaning the coffee machine behind the bar and she nodded to Tobias. He ushered DS Robinson through to the back room.

Alvis was exactly where he had left her, which made sense. Tobias still felt a small pulse of relief. Unholy Island was a strange place, even by his standards, and you just never knew.

It was Oliver's turn to sit with Alvis and he was tucked into the corner, as far away from her body as he could get while still being in the room. He was folded in on himself and he looked extremely relieved to have company. 'You're here, then,' he said, jumping up. 'I'll get on, if that's okay.'

'That's fine,' Tobias said.

'I have a few questions,' DS Robinson said firmly, eyeballing the man.

'You can interview Oliver later,' Tobias said, just as firmly. 'Elsewhere.' He glanced at Alvis's body.

'Yes,' Robinson said after a beat. 'That will be acceptable.'

Oliver didn't need to be told twice. He escaped from the room at lightning speed.

Tobias watched him go, wondering at the man's squeamishness. He supposed Alvis might very well be the first dead body the man had ever seen.

'So,' Robinson said, walking around the tables that had been pushed together to hold Alvis's body. 'Do you want to explain to me why this poor unfortunate is lying in the back room of a pub and not, for example, in situ? Where I expressly indicated she ought to remain?'

'We weren't leaving her out in the storm all night.'

Robinson had her hands on her hips and she wasn't hiding her irritation. 'You can't disturb a scene when you don't know what has happened. As you well know. I told you to secure it with tarpaulins. I understand that nobody could be asked to stand guard, but I do think that as the de facto leader of this community, you should have set a better example...' Robinson trailed off.

Tobias waited politely. He knew that DS Robinson had a job to do, and that job involved rules and regulations and a certain form of words that had to be said at certain times. It was much like the renewing of the wards or the other magic that Esme would be able to do once she fully embraced her role. There were orders to things and necessary actions. There was no point in being annoyed with DS

Robinson, just as there was no point in her being annoyed with him.

DS Robinson didn't seem to share his philosophical outlook. She paused in her pacing, hands on hips and blew out an irritated breath. 'Tobias. Seriously. This woman has been the victim of a crime and you can't just contravene procedure. Whoever is responsible could end up walking free because the investigation wasn't handled correctly. Break a rule here or there, and the case gets broken, too. I've seen murderers walk free because of filing errors. Why can't you listen to me?'

'Crime?'

Robinson took a long inhale, closing her eyes for a moment. When she spoke next, she was calm. 'This woman fought before she died.' Catching his expression, she put a hand on his arm. 'I'm sorry.'

'You're sure? Don't you need...' He was going to say 'an expert' but then he realised that DS Robinson wouldn't have said something that she wasn't certain of. And that he trusted her opinion. Just because he didn't like it was no reason to call her judgement into question.

'Here,' Robinson pointed at Alvis's hands. They lay palm up on the table, the fingers lightly curled. She had short fingernails, no polish. And there were scrapes. Tobias hadn't noticed them before and he didn't know why.

'Defensive wounds,' Robinson was saying. 'The injury to the back of her head could have been sustained when she hit the ground, but it could also have been from a blow. We need the pathologist's report for that.'

Tobias looked at the scrapes on Alvis's fingers, the places where the skin had ripped and bled. Now they were mottled blue-ish black where the blood had settled, the first signs of hypostasis setting in as the body moved toward

118

rigor mortis. He moved to one of the chairs at the side of the room and sat down heavily.

'Did Alvis have any enemies?'

Tobias ripped his gaze from the hands of the woman he had known for sixty years. 'Enemies? No.'

'I'm sorry,' Robinson said with genuine sympathy. 'I wouldn't usually speak so candidly, but I've had dealings with Unholy Island before.'

'I remember,' Tobias said quietly.

'And I know that I trust you. That's not something they teach you and it's not something you're supposed to admit to in the modern policing framework,' Robinson shot him a conspiratorial smile, 'but I know you look after this community and that you will want to help me catch whoever did this. Bring them to justice.'

Tobias managed not to smile at that. The earnestness of the DS was endearing and so was her notion that something as prosaic as the human legal system could get anywhere close to justice for Alvis. If she had, indeed, been killed.

'Anyone she didn't get on with?'

'I don't know what you mean.' He had always had the sense that DS Robinson was a good person, which was why he had chosen her as the liaison between the island and the mainland. It didn't mean that she couldn't make trouble for him, though.

The police officer tried again. 'Petty grievances. Squabbles. Even a small falling out can lead to...'

'This is a tightknit community. Everyone gets on.'

Robinson gave a short laugh. 'Now I know you're lying. That's not possible.'

Tobias closed his eyes. 'You said it yourself. Small grievances can lead to big consequences, so we don't allow them to fester. If there is a disagreement, it is resolved

119

quickly and equably. We pull together, not apart.' He felt a shiver of uncertainty as he spoke. He could see the scepticism on the mainlander's face. Was he deluding himself? Had he spent so much time around people that he was beginning to fall into their weaknesses, chief of which was self-delusion?

'Tell me about those small grievances,' DS Robinson said. 'Who had one with Alvis?'

'Nobody,' he said immediately, ignoring the ice that ran down his spine.

DS ROBINSON STAYED for lunch in the Rising Moon. She didn't have much choice as, although she told Seren clearly that she was working, using the main room as an interview space to question the islanders, Seren ignored the directive not to provide food and brought her a meal anyway. And it would have been a waste of food not to eat the delicious homemade tomato and chilli soup and cheese toastie.

In a couple of hours, she had spoken to everybody from the village. One advantage of an insular community was that everybody was pretty easy to locate. And they all seemed to be aware that Robinson was there and what she needed. They all gave similar responses that raised no suspicion, except for their bland sameness. That was the disadvantage to a place like this – word travelled and you couldn't get a fresh, unbiased story from anybody.

One resident, Esme Gray, had seemed nervous, but that might not indicate anything other than an anxious personality. Or, it could be that she had had a bad experience with authority in her past. Robinson made a note to run her name through the system.

Tobias stopped in, ready to escort Robinson down to

the causeway to collect her car. 'I suppose there will be more of your lot.'

Robinson shrugged. 'Maybe. Maybe not.'

He shot her a curious look. 'I thought you said Alvis's passing was suspicious?'

'I did and it is,' Robinson said. 'But we're stretched thin and I don't see them sending a unit. Coroner will collect the body in,' she consulted her watch, 'well, half an hour ago according to their email, and it will go on the pile.'

'I beg your pardon?'

'Sorry,' Robinson pulled an apologetic face. 'Bad choice of words. The case will go on the pile, not the body. Not your friend. Sorry.'

'I see.' And he did. Alvis was an old woman. She had no family and there was no obvious suspect or motive for her death. DS Robinson had explained to him in the past that the Northumbria police covered Sunderland and Newcastle as well as a huge swathe of countryside, packed with villages and towns and lonely farmhouses, all of which had their share of domestic violence, substance abuse, theft, and arson. Every year budgets were cut and policing became spottier. Detective work was focused on cases with a chance of prosecution or high-profile deaths. Alvis didn't fit any of those criteria and, just to cap things off, she had died in a place that most people didn't know existed. Even DS Robinson, his mainland contact for law enforcement for the last fifteen years, struggled to remember the island in between her visits. Even with the notes she had scribbled in her notebook and the case number the system had spat out when she had logged Tobias's call, DS Robinson would find her mind going strangely blank whenever she thought of Alvis's death.

'They should be here now,' Robinson said. 'And the

causeway is clear. They must have got backed up. It might be tomorrow, I'm afraid.'

'That's fine,' Tobias said. He was already making alternative plans in case the coroner failed to materialise later in the week. There was a small burial ground next to the ruins of the church. He didn't relish the digging, but was pretty sure Hammer would lend a hand for the right price.

DS Robinson had got out of the Land Rover and was looking out at the causeway, one hand shielding her eyes from the low sun. 'It's strange to see it from this direction,' she said. 'It feels more solid than it does looking the other way. More like a proper road.'

'Trick of the light,' Tobias said. And an effect of the wards. They discouraged the flow of people coming onto the island and encouraged people in the opposite direction.

'I am sorry about Alvis.' Robinson turned back and laid a hand briefly on Tobias's arm. 'And the delay.'

'Not a problem,' Tobias said. He didn't bother to say anything else, knowing that DS Robinson was already starting to forget their conversation.

'I'll see you next time,' Robinson said, her feet carrying her towards her police issued vehicle.

'Next time,' Tobias said, holding a hand up in a goodbye salute. He got into his Land Rover once the officer had driven far enough on the softer ground to join the solid road. Turning back to the island, he drove into the darkening day, secure in the knowledge that the wards were holding and that Alvis was theirs to honour as they saw fit. Alvis belonged to the island and if DS Robinson was right and she had been murdered, island justice would be done.

CHAPTER FIFTEEN

Hammer was carving a figure from a piece of cherry wood by his stove when Tobias knocked on the metal door.

'Copper's gone, then.'

Tobias nodded, stepping inside with Winter close on his heels. The dog made straight for the wood stove and lay down in front of it. 'All clear.'

Tobias made a show of admiring Hammer's carvings and the interior of the shed. Hammer had made a shelving unit from driftwood since Tobias had last visited and he spent a good few minutes studying it.

Hammer waited patiently for him to get to the point of his visit. He thought that Tobias looked older today, the lines in his face seemed deeper and there was extra stiffness to his movements.

'She spoke to everyone in the village.'

'Everyone she knows about,' Hammer responded.

'Quite.'

There was a short silence while Tobias seemed to be gathering himself.

Hammer shaved another tiny strip of wood from the cub he was carving. A companion piece to the mother bear he had already finished. The small figure was fiddly to work with, but his fingers had always been more dexterous than they looked. His hands were big and scarred from years of violence, but he could form, if not beauty, then something pleasant, from them, too. And that was good. A little balm on his ravaged soul. He didn't kid himself that it would make any difference in the big reckoning of his life, but luckily enough he was an atheist and didn't expect any such judgement day. Bad people had to be punished in this life or not at all.

'Kerry... DS Robinson. She said that Alvis didn't die of natural causes. She doesn't think it was an accident.'

Hammer put the cub and his whittling knife down. He didn't want to make a mistake while he was distracted.

'I don't know if it will result in any further investigation. I doubt it, but I can't be certain. I'll warn you if I hear anything or if we get visitors.'

Hammer nodded his thanks. He had been very careful to go off-grid even before he had landed on Unholy Island. Here, he had no registered address. He bought most things in person using cash or a barter system, and his Amazon orders went to Tobias's house. DS Robinson had spoken to everybody in the village who allowed themselves to be recorded in some way.

'You don't seem surprised,' Tobias said, watching Hammer carefully.

'About Alvis? That's because I'm not.'

'You already knew it wasn't just old age.' A statement, not a question.

'Her hands were scuffed up,' Hammer confirmed. 'I wasn't certain, but...' he trailed off, wondering how much detail to go into. People could be squeamish about these things. He knew Tobias wasn't exactly normal people, but he had known Alvis for a long time. He might not want to hear too much about how his old friend had died.

'It leaves us with a problem.'

Hammer thought about saying 'it leaves you with a problem'. He liked Tobias, but he was the de facto head of the island and Hammer had never played well with authority figures.

'Will you help me?'

If Hammer allowed himself to reveal his feelings so plainly, he would have sighed. Instead, he tilted his chin and regarded the mayor for a beat, considering. 'What's it worth?'

'What do you want? Cash?'

'That'll do.' Hammer didn't care how much, he just wasn't going to get involved for nothing. It was a principle of his. Keep relationships neat and transactional, then everybody knows where they stand. He wouldn't want Tobias mistaking him for a friend. And it kept things clean and simple. Esme popped into his mind, her face streaked with tears and her body hunched over, cradling her broken arm. He had helped her immediately. No transaction. No fee. He pushed the thought away. Everyone is allowed an off day.

'Of course,' Tobias said, the warmth in his blue eyes fading. 'I could be paying the culprit to help me find the murderer. That would be awkward.'

'Very,' Hammer agreed. He was still thinking about Esme Gray and the way she had looked on that first meeting, seven years ago, and he couldn't be bothered to rise to the insult. Besides, it wasn't really an insult. Just a fact. The mayor was taking a chance that he hadn't bumped off Alvis, given that he was the most qualified person to find the wrongdoer. Takes one to know one and all that.

'Where will you begin?'

Hammer stood up and stretched, cracking his spine so loudly that the mayor's dog looked up from his snooze. 'I'll keep you posted.' The thing about a murder on a place this small, with a storm that had followed, keeping the place cut off from the mainland. The killer had to still be on the island.

HAMMER STOOD on the shore at sunset and ran through the possible suspects. Alvis had been well liked, but people had been wary of her, too. Wariness could lead to hatred. People didn't like what scared them.

So who was capable of murder? The Three Sisters. Probably Tobias, although he had no motive. Fiona's kid. There was something unusual, there, but that wasn't exactly news in a place like Unholy Island.

And, of course, it might not be murder. Could have been an argument that went too far. A warning that resulted in accidental death. That opened the field. Lots of people were capable of shoving a person in anger. Not realising how easy it could be to snuff out a person's life. All it took was an awkward fall. A pre-existing condition. Hammer knew well enough what could happen in the heat of the moment. And how fragile human life really was.

He contemplated Euan. Fiona's boy was still outwardly a child, but he was fifteen. The age when hormones and fury and horniness reigned supreme. Maybe it was his imagination, but the kid *had* seemed different lately. Calmer. More contained. Hammer had put it down to growing up and mastering the baser impulses, but perhaps there was another explanation. Perhaps he was allowing those impulses a new outlet.

And then there was the newcomer. It might be simplistic to look to the new guy as the likely culprit, but it was tempting. Especially to Hammer, who had an instinctive dislike of the man's good looks and quiet confidence. But the fact remained that he had no motive to kill Alvis. He would dig into the man's past, just to make certain, but as far as Hammer could see he had nothing to gain by doing so.

Luke was clearing debris in the garden of Strand House. The storm had dropped all kinds of rubbish across the island and broken a few fences, but the place was otherwise unscathed. On the morning after, there was a gentle breeze and a bright blue sky. The landscape was practically whistling to show its innocence, as if it would never dream of doing anything as violent as it had the night before. 'We've weathered far worse,' Esme had said when he had asked about damage, but she seemed to appreciate his offer to help tidy up. Although she looked and sounded exhausted, so it was hard to tell.

He had just dropped a sea-smoothed piece of plastic into a bin bag when Esme came out of the front door. She hadn't long been home, having stayed at the pub all night. He wasn't sure how things stood between them. There was every chance she believed he had hurt Alvis. Or, at the very least, that she would take Alvis's death as a sign that he was trouble. He was fuzzy as to how he could be blamed for a very old woman he had never met having a heart attack, but logic didn't seem to be an obstacle for the islanders.

'Bee just called,' Esme said, surprising him. 'She wants you to meet her at the bookshop.'

He shielded his eyes from the sun which had risen

behind the cottage and was shining into his face. 'Did she say why?'

'Nope,' Esme said. 'But when Bee calls, you'd better go running.'

He put a rock on top of the half-filled bin bag to make sure it didn't blow away if the wind returned, and went indoors to wash up. Five minutes later he was walking along the main street and telling himself that he wasn't afraid of being late for Bee.

She was waiting for him outside the bookshop and smiled as he approached. He felt his shoulders relax a notch. Partly because she looked genuinely pleased to see him, and that made a pleasant change, but also because she was alone. He wasn't in a hurry to meet her sister again.

'I have news.' Bee wasn't one for small talk and she launched into an explanation of the island's need for a bookshop.

'I'm sure someone will want to buy the place,' he said, hoping to be reassuring. In truth, he wasn't sure whether it would be a quick sale. He still didn't understand how the place had made money and thought it would need to be an independently wealthy person who, somehow, also wanted to work in a shop. It was more likely that the buyer would turn the shop into a holiday home. He also didn't understand why Bee had called on him for the conversation.

'You are going to move in.'

'Sorry, what?' Luke only half-caught the words and didn't think he could have heard Bee correctly.

Bee tilted her head and looked at him with kind patience. Like he was a slow child. 'The island needs the bookshop. Alvis is dead. You have arrived here for a reason. You are going to run the bookshop.'

'I don't understand.'

'I don't think I can put it any more clearly.'

'I can't afford to buy this,' he gestured to the shop. 'I could pay rent, probably, maybe, depending on how much it is. If there is a place to live, too. But I've never run a business.' And he didn't know if he wanted to, either.

'Alvis left the shop to you. It has accommodation. You can choose the opening hours, but I suggest you keep to the existing schedule.'

Luke's brain was not processing the conversation. It made no sense. 'But I never even met Alvis.'

'I know,' Bee said. 'Alvis must have had her reasons.'

The thing about the island was that it invited acceptance. Part of Luke's brain was already calm, already adjusting to this new information. The island needed someone to run the bookshop and, really, did he have anything better to do?

'Shall we go in?' Bee produced a set of keys.

'I wanted to come here,' he indicated the bookshop, 'but it was always closed.'

Bee pursed her lips, looking suddenly uncertain. 'Really?'

He nodded. 'Yeah... I wondered how Alvis kept a business going when she was never open.'

'That could be a problem...' She shook herself. 'I'm sure it will be fine.' She smiled brightly and turned the key in the lock.

Luke waited for Bee to go ahead, but she stepped to the side.

'After you,' he said, gesturing for her to enter first. He might not have had a good upbringing, but he had manners. And common sense. There was something about Bee that made him anxious to stay on her good side.

She shook her head. 'You need to first-foot.'

He was about to say 'that's a new year thing' but he caught sight of movement inside the shop and it distracted him. It felt as if he was being beckoned and before his brain had caught up, his feet had moved over the threshold and into the dark of the bookshop. Shelves rose on either side, creating a narrow corridor which doglegged to the right. Within steps, the daylight was swallowed up and he pulled his phone out to use the flashlight. He looked over his shoulder. The doorway seemed further away than it ought to be and Bee was silhouetted in the rectangle of light.

'Go on.' She made a shooing gesture with her hands.

Turning back to the darkness ahead, the light from his phone played over the spines of books and wooden shelves. He took the corner and found himself in a square space, hemmed with more bookshelves. The shelves were packed tightly, books wedged on top of rows, filling every available space, and they reached upward to an unseen ceiling. Something stopped Luke from aiming his torchlight high enough to see where they ended.

There was a counter made from more shelving, with an old cash register and an avalanche of books on top. Walking around the side, Luke found a stool and behind that, in the front corner of the room next to the window that looked out to the street, a low-slung comfy chair in dark red velvet. Next to the chair there was a pile of thick antique-looking books. There was one on the seat, too, splayed open to a page of watercolour illustrations of what looked like rocks.

An opening in the back corner promised more shelving. The shop seemed to stretch further back than expected. It was a warren. A Tardis.

A tiny scraping noise.

Luke stopped moving and held the beam of light from his phone onto the counter. He half-expected to see a mouse, but there was nothing there. 'Bee?' He raised his voice, but it was swallowed by the reams of paper and yards of wood.

Why hadn't she followed?

The scraping noise happened again. It was behind him this time and he turned quickly. The wall of bookshelves was still there. He didn't know why he thought that. Of course it was still there. His head was swimming and he suddenly felt as though he couldn't take a full breath. He consciously made himself inhale. The smell was classic second-hand bookshop - wood and still air and old paper. A slight note of vanilla that always made Luke hungry. It was clean, though. Remarkably little dust for a packed place.

He retraced his footsteps until he could see the entrance. It was back where it ought to be and took less time than it had to get to the main room. Another strange thought that he didn't allow himself to dwell upon. 'Are you coming in?'

Bee lifted one foot and then paused. 'How do you feel?'

'Fine,' he said. 'Why?'

'No reason.' She put her foot down gingerly, crossing the entranceway as if expecting something to happen.

'What's wrong?'

Bee held out the bunch of keys, all business. 'These are yours now. Look around. Make yourself at home.'

She flinched slightly as she said the last word. It was a tiny movement, but unmistakable. His fingers closed around the keys. 'What aren't you telling me?'

'It's just strange to be here without Alvis.'

He felt a flood of guilt. 'Of course. I'm sorry.'

'Come to the Rising Moon later. We'll all be there for dinner and you're very welcome.'

'Thank you,' he said, surprised.

'You're an islander now,' she said. Her smile was

lopsided and she still seemed tense, but he appreciated the effort.

Once Bee had left, closing the front door behind her, Luke realised he should have asked her where the light switches were. He walked back to the front room, finding that he no longer needed his torch. The sun must have appeared and there was now enough light coming through the window to see. It was a bookshop. He felt something ease in his shoulders and he almost laughed at himself for being spooked earlier.

He explored the downstairs, through the short shelf-lined passageway to another square space with an opening through the bookcases to yet another nook. This one had a wooden set of steps and a worn red rug on the floor, its edges curling in a trip-hazard kind of way. He was just thinking about public liability insurance and the potential for court action when he saw a handwritten sign with blocky black text fixed to a shelf at eye height. 'Patrons browse at their own risk.'

The heady experience of being surrounded by so much paper and ink had to be to blame for him realising, belatedly, that there was soft lighting in these back rooms. The bulbs had to be well hidden as they weren't obvious and he had yet to find anything resembling a light switch. He put his phone back into his pocket and continued through the small spaces until he reached what had to be the back wall of the building. This appeared to be the non-fiction section with large, illustrated tomes on art, history, geography and science, as well as smaller volumes covering philosophy, psychology, theology, and palm reading. A large red cloth-bound book looked important and antique. Luke squinted to make out the faded gold writing on a spine. It said 'Jams,

Jellies and Preserves'. Next to it, there was a worn paperback with the title 'Prophecy Cards for Beginners'.

On the shelf above, there was another hand-written sign in the same blocky black writing as the other sign. Luke had to read it twice, despite the handy picture of a mouthful of sharp teeth that accompanied the words. 'Shoplifters will be eaten.'

CHAPTER SIXTEEN

Tobias didn't usually play detective, but this was the kind of tragedy that could poison a community. And it was his community, his responsibility. Now that the weather had calmed down and the waves were no longer crashing up on the beach like the snapping jaws of some ravenous beast, Hammer was combing the beach for whatever signs or clues he might be able to glean. Tobias decided to leave him to it and turned his attention to the islanders instead.

Fiona and Oliver's house was a white-washed cottage attached to The Rising Moon in the centre of the village.

Oliver opened the door and he scowled when he saw Tobias, probably guessing that it wasn't a social call. 'This isn't a good time.'

Tobias spread his hands in a gesture of peace. 'I just want to check in on you. It's an upsetting time for all of us.'

'We're fine,' Oliver said brusquely. He made to close the door.

'May I give this to Fiona?' Tobias had anticipated this reception and had come prepared. He held out a paperback. 'I think she'll like it.'

Oliver made to pluck the book from Tobias's grip, but he moved his hand.

'I'll give it to her,' Oliver said, no longer even pretending to be friendly.

'Is that the mayor?' Fiona appeared behind her husband in the narrow hallway. 'Don't keep him on the step. You're letting all the heat out. You want a tea, Tobias?'

'Thank you,' Tobias said, stepping toward the entrance. For a moment, it seemed as if Oliver wasn't going to move, but then he stepped back and let Tobias into the cottage.

Sitting in their small living room, the wood burner glowing in the hearth and a mug of tea in hand, Tobias knew that he had to get straight to business. Oliver was going to find a reason to cut the visit short. That was if he didn't take a swing at Tobias first. He was standing by the door, glowering.

Fiona ignored her husband's mood and chatted to Tobias. They had always got along well and she was the kindly sort of woman who 'accidentally' made too much food on a regular basis and brought pies and soups and the occasional fruit cake round to Tobias.

'It's a terrible thing,' she was saying now, shaking her head.

'It is,' Tobias agreed.

'You should have been out there looking last night,' Oliver said.

'Not with the weather,' Fiona cut in, shocked. 'It wasn't safe.'

'I would have done it,' Oliver said. 'If I was mayor.'

Tobias ignored this. He held a hand out and felt the fur on Winter's head. It was comforting. He didn't want to upset Fiona. But Oliver wasn't wrong in one aspect. However unpleasant the job, he was the mayor and he had a responsibility to get answers.

'Nobody should be out there,' Fiona said. She glared at her husband and he ducked his head.

'Well,' he said. 'I just think...'

'Would you like some cake?' Fiona jumped up, cutting off her husband mid flow.

'Yes, please,' Tobias said.

'I'll get it,' Oliver said, clearly wanting to make up ground with Fiona.

Tobias assumed he had walked in on a marital dispute. Oliver wasn't the warmest of the islanders, but he wasn't usually so openly hostile. He had known this couple for many years and they always seemed to make up quickly. Small disagreements never seemed to grow into big arguments, and he had certainly never heard either of them raise their voices. Not even when Euan was small and running circles around Fiona. Once Oliver had left the room, Tobias steeled himself. 'How is Euan doing?'

Fiona stiffened a little. 'He's fine. Shocked, like the rest of us.'

'Is he?' Tobias had meant to keep his tone mild, but he must have misjudged it as it was his turn for one of Fiona's sharp looks.

'Of course,' she said.

He nodded in agreement. 'I hope he's not too distressed.'

'It's a very upsetting thing,' Fiona said.

Tobias patted Winter, taking the opportunity to break eye contact with Fiona. 'How is he in general? Not too bored I hope?' There weren't any other young people on the island, and Tobias knew that Fiona worried about Euan's social development and happiness. At least, she had used to worry about it. Tobias couldn't remember the last time she had confided in him regarding her son. He had believed himself to be the only one who knew Fiona's true nature, but perhaps she had confided in somebody else, someone who could better understand the difficulties of living in the human world.

Fiona was sitting on the edge of her seat, her legs not just crossed, but twisted in a corkscrew. Her hands were clasped in her lap, fingers tightly interlinked. 'Fine,' she said after a brief pause. She forced a laugh. 'You know teenagers. Hard to know what they're thinking.'

Tobias nodded as if he did know. He couldn't remember being a teenager himself. Had a feeling they hadn't been invented when he had been young. 'Is he in his room?'

'Yes. Of course.' Another forced laugh. 'Hardly ever comes out.'

Tobias pushed himself upright, hands on his thighs for leverage, and ignored the cracking from his knees. 'I'll just pop my head in, say hello.'

'You don't have to,' Fiona began, looking up at him with a pleading look.

'You stay here,' Tobias said to Winter, who had also risen. This was partly because Fiona's hand had drifted to pat Winter's coat and he knew it was a relaxing activity, and partly because he didn't like the way Euan looked at his dog. If he was going through the change then it wasn't his fault, but Tobias didn't want to take any chances where Winter was concerned.

The house was a single-storey cottage with rooms off a central hallway, the living room at the front and the kitchen at the back with bedrooms sandwiched in between. He found Euan's door and knocked. There was no reply. He knew that Oliver wasn't going to be much longer in the kitchen and didn't want to lose his chance, so he knocked once more to give fair warning and opened the door.

Euan was sitting in the middle of the floor, cross-legged. He didn't look surprised to see Tobias. He wasn't wearing headphones and would certainly have heard Tobias knocking and simply chosen not to answer. Not unusual in a teen, perhaps, but not friendly.

'May I?' Tobias stepped into the room and closed the door, ignoring the primeval sense that told him not to trap himself with this creature. He is a boy, he reminded himself, not much more than a child. He couldn't let prejudice cloud his judgement. Still, the skin on the back of his neck was crawling.

The room had dark blue walls with a few posters. Japanese cartoons, a horror film franchise, and a tasteful framed image of the solar system which Tobias assumed was Fiona's doing. Weights in the corner, an unusually neat desk with a laptop and a lamp, and a log-pattern patchwork quilt in blues and greys on the single bed completed the décor. Tobias realised that Euan was watching him look around, and he managed a smile. 'I like your room.'

'Swap you.'

'Sorry?'

'For your massive house.'

'Oh, right,' Tobias attempted a chuckle. 'Yes. Well. I just wanted to see how you were doing. How is everything?'

'Everything?' Euan cocked his head. For a split second, his eyes seemed pure black, with no whites showing at all.

'You must be upset. I mean, we're all upset. I just thought you might want to talk about it.'

'About the body?' Euan became animated. 'Did you see it? I haven't been allowed. I heard her skull was all bashed in. Like a broken egg. Did you see the bone?'

Tobias's stomach turned over. 'About your feelings. I thought you might want to talk about... Feelings.'

139

Euan instantly reverted to his usual inert state and fell silent.

Tobias eyed the floor. He wasn't going to join the kid down there. He didn't trust himself to be able to get up again in a hurry. Instead, he perched on the end of the bed. Tried to look relaxed and open, despite the discomfort that was lodged in his stomach and the urge to flee that was hammering at the base of his skull. 'We all liked Alvis,' he tried. 'It's a shock for something like this to happen.'

Nothing. Euan was blank again. He wasn't meeting Tobias's gaze, just staring at the carpet in front of his crossed legs.

'How are things in general? How is school?' Euan had been home schooled his whole life, but he did a handful of courses online and Tobias had the vague notion that he would go to the mainland at the end of the academic year to sit his exams.

Euan shrugged with the smallest movement possible to still be classed as a shrug.

'You're not worried about your exams, I hope?'

'They're a piece of piss. Only doing them because mum says I have to.'

'Your mum says you spend a lot of time at home.' He had been going to say 'in your room' but changed the words in time to something that sounded less judgemental.

Euan didn't respond.

'You used to like the beach. I suppose you were a lot younger then.'

'If you want to know whether I was on the north shore yesterday, you can just ask.'

Tobias's hands reflexively tightened on his knees. 'Very well. Did you go to the north shore yesterday? I am asking everyone.'

'Mum did. She's there every morning. Well, almost

every morning. Unless she's sick or there is something happening early, like when the septic tank needs to be pumped.'

Fiona put her head around the door, a dangerous glint in her eye. 'Your cake is waiting, Mayor. And Euan needs to do his homework.'

Tobias stood up. He hadn't missed that Euan hadn't answered his question, but he also knew when to bow to Fiona's authority.

CHAPTER SEVENTEEN

E sme put the bedding into the machine and cleaned Luke's room, throwing the window wide open to change the air. The storm had passed and the sky was a blameless blue. The causeway would open that afternoon and the coroner would arrive from the mainland to collect Alvis.

Esme knew she ought to be relieved to have her home to herself again, the quiet winter season stretching out in all its glorious emptiness, but she wasn't as pleased as she expected. Dutifully, she went into her studio and worked on a piece for a couple of hours. It was one of those unsatisfying sessions in which she spent most of her time redoing a mistake she had made at the beginning, and her mind never quite sunk into the flow state of creation. There was part of her still listening for sounds in the house. Part of her expecting Luke to walk in and offer her a cup of tea.

Downstairs, brewing chamomile tea, she conceded that Alvis was probably on her mind, too. She had been very old. Definitely the age when people said 'she's had a good innings'. But this was Unholy Island and Alvis was a long-term resident. The rules here were different and Esme had learned that you couldn't make assumptions. According to Tobias, who had been here the longest of them all, Alvis had taken over the bookshop in the sixties and hadn't been a young woman at the time. But that didn't mean it had been 'her time' to go.

Jetsam was sitting on the table watching her with his green eyes. 'Tobias said we should stay away,' she told him.

A slow blink.

Esme put down her mug and pushed back from the table. Her boots were by the back door and her supplies were packed into her daysack, ready for the next full moon. She added a joyless cereal bar from the cupboard, the remains of the supplies she kept in for guests who wanted a 'grab and go' breakfast, and slipped out of the door into a crisp day. The November sun was still low in the sky despite it being late morning, and gulls were wheeling overhead.

The path down to Coire Bay was lined with bramble bushes and greeny-blue knotgrass. The last of the autumn fruit dotted the hedgerow, but the storm had stripped the honeysuckle of its final blooms. The spit of rocks at the far end of the curved bay was called New Moon Hollow. At least, that was what Esme called it. The name had come to her when she had first cast the wards.

She had been so scared that first time. The air had been mild, a summer's full moon lighting the path to the rocks and the sea shushing over the sand like a soothing lullaby. She had been in a trance, still dazed from weeks of barely sleeping and the fear of fleeing her old life. It was as if the sky and the sea and the land had known she needed calm and safety and had been as accommodating as possible to welcome her.

The fear that had been living rent-free in her guts and chest and mind had still been doing its best to trip her up, but she had found the hollow in between the rocks. It was just as Tobias had described. There was a small hearth made from a circle of blackened stones and she had placed dry wood gathered from the shore and lit a fire, then renewed the ward, her breathing shallow and her heart pounding.

Each ward required the same things: a stone, a shell, a piece of bone and a drop of blood. These days it was habitual. She carried a sharp needle in her pack to pierce her thumb or finger and antiseptic cream for when she was finished. She squeezed a red droplet onto a stone gathered from the bay, and heard a clear chime when it touched the salt-rimed surface. She didn't hear it through her ears, of course, and she knew it wasn't a real sound. Instead, she felt it inside, somewhere that must have been her soul. That ringing sound was more sensation, more *knowing* than it was an auditory phenomenon, and it was the signal that the ritual was complete. She trusted it now, after doing it so many times.

It had been Alvis, she remembered now, who had confirmed that she had done it correctly that first time. Esme had been back at the house, fretting over whether she had messed up her new responsibility. Whether that meant she didn't belong on the island or, worse, that she might be ousted from it. The voice that she had so thoroughly internalised from years of abuse spoke in cutting tones. *You are useless, you must have fucked it up the way that you fuck up everything you can't be trusted everybody knows that that's why you don't have any friends nobody can rely on you you're flaky and stupid and...*

The knocking on the back door had interrupted the flow of bile, sending her heart rate further into the stratosphere. Chest tight and sweat breaking out across her forehead and back, Esme had opened the door to discover a small and heavily wrinkled woman carrying a stack of murder mystery paperbacks.

'Hello?' Esme hated the way she sounded. So uncertain and yet so haughty. *Too big for your boots.*

The woman smiled. 'I brought you some reading material.' She hoisted the stack of books.

'I don't...' Esme had been going to say that she didn't read, but then she remembered just in time that she could, now. If she wanted. He hadn't liked her reading, as it took her attention away from him. But he wasn't here now. She swallowed the words down and forced a smile. 'Thank you. That's very...'

'You can pay me later,' the woman said. 'Or just bring them back to the shop.'

Before Esme knew what was happening, her hands were holding the pleasing weight of the books and the woman was in the kitchen that still didn't feel like her own and was filling the kettle with water.

'I'm Esme,' Esme said. She thought that she had met all the residents of the island, but she didn't remember this woman.

'Alvis.' She was busy with the teapot and a packet of tea leaves she produced from her tunic pocket and didn't turn around. 'Book keeper.'

That didn't sound right. Bookkeeping was accounts, not running a bookshop, but Esme wasn't about to correct the woman. Alvis. She accepted the mug of tea, which gave off an exotic smoky aroma. She couldn't resist dipping her face closer and breathing deeply. 'What's this?'

'Gunpowder tea. You're just back, then.'

'Back?'

Alvis gave her a long look over the rim of her own mug. 'The wards. You just did them.'

'Yes.' Esme sipped the tea and felt the knots loosen.

She breathed in and felt the air fill her lungs, not get caught halfway. 'At least. I think so. I think I did it right.'

Alvis paused, her head cocked as if listening. Then she nodded. 'You did. Well done.'

STANDING on the beach in the stiff winter breeze and remembering Alvis in life, Esme's eyes filled with tears. They stung her cold cheeks and she wiped them away as quickly as they fell. Alvis might have been a little odd, but she had been kind to Esme at a time when she had needed it. Tilting her head to look up at the pale blue sky, Esme sent out good thoughts to Alvis's soul, wherever it might be. For a witch, she wasn't especially spiritual and had no idea what happened after death, but she knew that thoughts had power and that sending out love and good wishes was never a bad idea.

Esme found the place where Luke had found Alvis. It was near the beach ward, something that had been bothering her. As if the island had let down one of its own. Which was hardly fair. Whether something sinister had happened or whether Alvis had died of natural causes, it was hardly the island's fault. She hoped it had been natural causes and that DS Robinson was wrong. It was better to think that an elderly woman's heart had just decided it was time to have a rest. That it had given up as she walked along the shore, breathing fresh air and seeing the view she loved. Esme presumed she had loved it. Alvis had certainly taken a walk along the beach on most mornings before opening the bookshop.

The rocks were shades of grey and from a distance they looked smooth and rounded. Inviting. Up close, the reality was more complex, with the jaggy remains of limpets, small pools filled with cold and slimy seaweed, and unexpected crevasses just waiting to trap your foot and cause a twisted ankle. Beyond the corner where Esme tended to the beach ward, the rocks reached out toward the sea. When the tide was low, you could walk around it easily, but when the water came in, it rushed and roared until it covered half of the outcrop with churning, deadly waves. Alvis had been out when the tide was low, she had no reason to be picking her way over the rocks.

Esme found the flattish stone that had held Alvis's last moments. The brown stain at one end could be the remains of her blood. Her head had cracked on the rock and had bled copiously, as scalp wounds tended to do, but it seemed unlikely that anything would be left after the scourging storm. Esme closed her eyes at the image of a checked tea towel coming away from her own head, soaked in bright red. She shook her head lightly, clearing the past. She refocused on the grey expanse of rock. Of course, it might also be some old staining from seaweed or similar. Or a natural colouration of the rock itself. A chemical pigment like haematite running through the grey basalt.

Esme bent over to examine it and felt an answering pull in the pulse of her neck and wrists. Blood, then. This wasn't so strange. Alvis had fallen. She had hit her head. Head wounds bled. What was bothering her? Esme allowed her gaze to roam over the flat rock that had held Alvis's body. She looked at the jagged rocks that surrounded it and the glimpses of sand and sky beyond. She took deep slow breaths until her mind was calm and there was an ease through her body and she looked again.

Nothing. Bee had told her that if she practised calming her mind, she would see more than other people. Normal people. Esme wasn't convinced. It was hard to imagine that she would be any more successful as a witch than she had been at anything else.

Don't give up so easily.

That sounded like Alvis. Her voice was so clear in Esme's mind and she felt a rush of guilt. Her friend was dead and she was letting her lack of confidence stop her from finding out why. A spurt of fear, fiery and cleansing, raced through her blood. Bee had asked her when she was going to start trusting herself again, when she was going to accept that she had good instincts, better than most normal people, in fact. Esme pushed down the habitual flare of panic. She was scared. She was sick of being scared. The fear had hollowed her out inside so that she no longer had a core. But maybe she could find it? Maybe it was still there somewhere, buried deep where she felt it was safe. But Alvis hadn't been safe here on the island and Esme had one question to answer. Was she going to sit back and let Alvis's death remain unsolved? Fold her death into the story of fear she had been telling herself? Or was she going to step up and do something about it? The island was her home and it was safe because of the people who lived here. That included her.

She looked at the flat grey rock with the ominous, awful blood stain, and imagined a blank screen in the corner of her vision. She ignored the fear that gnawed on her guts, turning her stomach hollow and cold. She was the Ward Witch. She protected the island and she couldn't help but feel that Alvis's death meant that protection had failed.

She forced herself to look at that small screen in the corner of her mind. Not her whole vision, that would be too much. The small rectangle in the corner was manageable, though. Like a tab on her computer screen that she could close at any time. Or a small canvas, prepped with gesso and ready for an image to be brought to life in safe, controllable paint.

She let the shape grow a little, making it more visible. She breathed in and out like Bee had taught her. The blank rectangle filled with dark blues and greens, the colours of the sea. A line of white froth confirmed it, rolling to the bottom corner of the canvas and out of sight. Esme relaxed, just for a second, and in that moment the image on the canvas changed. It was a shining piece of glass clutched in Alvis's hand. Esme jumped back in surprise and the image vanished. The blank rectangle had gone, too, and all Esme could see was the rocks, the sand and the sea that was in front of her.

CHAPTER EIGHTEEN

Tobias had visited Hammer and told him that he had had a very unsatisfactory chat with Euan. 'Maybe he sees me as an authority figure. Maybe he will open up to you. You're more...' The perpetually tweed-clad Tobias had paused before saying 'cool'. Hammer shuddered at the memory. It had been like watching a fish try to ride a bicycle.

As it happened, Hammer couldn't find Fiona or Euan. Oliver informed him that they had gone to the mainland to buy clothes. 'Another growth spurt,' he said. 'You know what kids are like.' Like it was a bad habit that Euan would eventually overcome.

Hammer waited at the front door, not moving, until Oliver was forced to invite him inside.

The cottage was clean, but cluttered. Oliver had clearly just been sitting on the sofa as there was a half-drunk mug of coffee on the side table, and an obvious dent in the cushions with the TV remote abandoned on the seat.

'How's business?' Hammer nodded at the desk in the corner of the living room, where Oliver had clearly not just been working. The computer was the hub of Oliver's business empire, but it looked a little old to Hammer's uneducated eye. He knew that Oliver did something involving stocks or hedges or one of those fancy financial terms which told the average Joe exactly fuck all. Which was the point.

Oliver was fidgeting, clearly not comfortable with having company. Or maybe it was Hammer in particular. That certainly wasn't unusual. If Tobias was the de facto leader, he was the de facto enforcer. And that made everyone nervous around him, even the innocent.

'Fine. Good.' He picked up his mug and then put it down again without drinking. 'You know.'

Hammer didn't, so he didn't nod.

'Climate is tricky at the moment,' Oliver said vaguely. 'Do you want a coffee or...'

'How about family life?' Hammer asked. 'All roses and sunshine?'

Oliver went still. 'Why? What has he done?'

'Who?'

A beat. 'Euan.'

'Nothing, as far as I know. It was just a general enquiry.'

'I find that hard to believe. Anything goes wrong, everybody looks at Euan. Just because he's a teenager. A kid.'

'What about Fiona? How is she?'

'You added marriage counselling to your remit?'

Hammer smiled thinly. 'Hardly.'

Oliver let out a short laugh. A pressure valve letting out steam.

'Any problems with anybody. Arguments. That kind of thing.'

Oliver shook his head. 'I know what you want. You want me to say I had a problem with Alvis. Give you a neat reason for her death. But I didn't. I hardly knew the woman.' He gestured at the book-free living room. 'Not a big reader.'

'Why do you think I need a reason for her death?' This was the problem with a tightknit community, secrets were practically impossible. But if the news was out that Alvis's death was suspicious, it was going to make his job a little harder.

Oliver snorted. 'Everyone knows she was... You know. And of course you come straight here. Accusing Euan even though you haven't got a shred of evidence. Even though he's just a kid.'

Although the added pressure might prove useful. Oliver going from cagey to losing his shit being case in point. He had just confirmed that Hammer should still be keeping Euan firmly at the top of his list. 'I didn't ask about Euan,' he said mildly. 'As far as I know, he had very little to do with Alvis and no reason to hurt her.'

Matteo opened the shop from nine until twelve, closed for a long lunch, and then opened from three to five every day except Sundays, so it wasn't difficult to find him. What was less straightforward was getting a conversation flowing. With one person writing down their answers, it was much harder to have a casual chat. Luckily enough, casual chats weren't really Hammer's style anyway. 'This is a courtesy visit,' he said as his opener. 'The mayor has given me the job of finding out what happened to Alvis and I wanted to let you know. It's going to get messy, small place like this. People are going to start pointing fingers, you know that. Everyone is in shock at the moment, but that won't last. When it breaks, it will all kick off. So. If there was anything you wanted to tell me, now's the time.' It was a long speech

153

in Hammer-terms, so he reflected that Matteo's silent stare might have been getting to him more than he let on.

Matteo didn't move for a moment and then he bent over his notepad, pen moving quickly. *You know what happened. Fall. Old age.*

Hammer looked at the man directly in the eyes. 'I don't think either of us believe that. You want to try again?'

Matteo's eyes widened. He bent over his paper and then slid it across for Hammer to read. *Murder?*

Hammer nodded.

Matteo swallowed hard and turned back to his notepad. He held it up. *Had to be outsider.*

There were no visitors staying when Alvis died. It had been too early for the causeway and Esme's guest house had been empty. Apart from the new guy. He met Matteo's gaze and nodded his understanding. 'Only problem is, I don't see why he would do it. I don't like the guy, but he doesn't seem completely deranged. Do you know if he spoke to Alvis? He says not, but if he was lying about that...'

Matteo shrugged, looking uncomfortable. He bent over his pad and wrote: *Bookshop?*

'What?'

Matteo wrote again. *He's moved in.*

HAMMER WANTED to believe it had been Luke. He was a stranger and the thing that had changed most recently on the island. And he didn't like the way the younger man's gaze followed Esme. Or the way she looked back at him. He was handsome and Hammer wasn't above admitting to himself that this put his back up in itself. That Luke had won life's lottery was an instant source of irritation, and he itched for a reason to eject him from the island. But good looks and charm didn't make the man a killer. As Matteo had indicated, he also had something to gain. The bookshop. Problem was, Hammer knew that Luke hadn't known that he would inherit the shop. And it wasn't as if he could sell the place and cash in. It was a role with an attached accommodation, not a windfall. It was interesting that Matteo had been so quick to point the finger, although not incriminating in itself.

THAT EVENING, Luke walked into the Rising Moon and found it packed to full capacity. He picked out Esme first. She was sitting with Fiona and Euan and seemed to be deep in conversation. She must have felt his gaze, though, as she turned around and smiled at him. He felt the usual loosening in his chest, as if she let him take a full breath. It came with a strange tightening in his stomach that he wasn't going to examine. All signs from Esme had been strictly 'friendship' and he wasn't going to make a nuisance of himself, stomach-excitement or not.

There was a spare seat at the table in the middle of the room, in between Hammer and Bee. They were, hands down, the two most intimidating residents on the island, but Luke was hungry. Besides, he had a question for Bee.

'Evening,' he said.

'Seren's got venison casserole or fish pie, she just hasn't had time to update the board.'

'What are you having?'

'Venison,' Bee said, licking her lips in a surprisingly feral manner.

Luke shifted in his seat, suddenly uncomfortable. For some reason he recalled the sign in the bookshop. All those teeth.

'Fish.' The rumbling voice came from his other side. He turned to greet Hammer.

'It's got chorizo in it.'

'Right,' Luke said. Was this a test? Would his choice reveal his loyalty to a particular person? Or worse, declare his general trustworthiness. 'It's hard to choose, Seren's food is so good.'

Hammer smiled in a genuine expression of happiness. It was spoiled slightly by the missing teeth, and it disappeared as quickly as it had appeared. Luke made a mental note. The terrifying man-mountain really liked his food.

'What will you have?'

Seren was by his right elbow. He looked up. 'Fish pie, please.'

'So, new boy,' Hammer said, leaning forward in a way that could not be mistaken for friendliness. 'What's your story?'

The conversation on either side dipped in shock. Luke had the distinct impression that Hammer had just made an island faux pas. And he didn't seem to care.

'I've been travelling around for the last while.'

'Working?'

'A bit,' Luke said. 'Here and there.'

'We all help out here. What special skills do you bring?'

'He can dig over a veg plot,' Esme volunteered, clearly trying to help him out.

'So you can use a spade. Bravo.'

Most people had finished their meals and a couple had pushed back their chairs as if about to leave. Luke stood up, deciding to tackle the subject head-on.

'I wanted to say something. To everyone.'

Esme smiled at him encouragingly and Hammer clenched his fists.

'Thank you for letting me stay. And I know many of you might be suspicious of me, especially with what has happened... With Alvis passing away. I didn't know Alvis, but I'm sorry for your loss. I feel bad because I am benefiting from it. I came here expecting to stay a week or so and then move on. Instead, I've found I want to stay and so being able to, and then being given a position and a place to live is beyond... Well. I don't want anybody here to think that I'm not grateful or that I don't take it seriously.'

ONCE THAT WAS DEALT WITH, he listened to the conversation for a while. Tobias was talking about a sealed crate that had been washed up on the west shore. Bee had already started on her venison and was halfway done when Seren gave him his plate. The smell was too enticing and it had been a long time since his lunchtime sandwich, so he dug in with gusto.

He was just trying to work out how to bring the subject up with Bee without sounding ungrateful, when she gave him an opening.

Wiping her mouth with the paper serviette that had been wrapped around her cutlery, Bee tilted her head and asked him how he had been settling into the bookshop.

'Good,' he said promptly. 'Good. Really good.'

She smiled as if she knew there was something else coming.

'I haven't found... You said there was a living space.' He tried to make his voice go up into a question at the end, worrying that he sounded too accusatory.

'I would bunk down in the shop for now, if I were you. Baby steps.'

Well, that made no sense.

'You've got your camping equipment, right? Therm-a-

Rest mat on the floor, sleeping bag and a lantern, you'll snug as a bug in a rug.' Bee seemed to think for a moment. 'I wouldn't recommend using a stove, though. No flames.'

That made sense. Lot of paper in a bookshop. Luke could see a blazing inferno of ink and glued bindings, wooden shelves turning to charred wood and the paper to ash, him trapped in the centre of the warren. He shuddered.

Bee was watching him with bright, assessing eyes. She nodded sharply. 'I'm sure you will get along just fine.'

Luke had drunk two pints with his dinner and now that he was standing outside the bookshop he wondered whether there was a downstairs toilet for customers or whether he needed to wander down the beach to pee. He took a deep breath and unlocked the front door. As he stepped into the dark of the shop, soft lights flicked on and lit the passageway of bookshelves. The lights had to be on a motion-sensor, he decided, without really believing it. Wilful ignorance had never really been his style.

He looked around the shop, trying to work out if the passageways and small rooms were in the same configuration. It felt as if the space had altered, but he hadn't got familiar enough to be certain. Whatever the case, he found a door that he hadn't noticed earlier and found it opened into a tiny office space. A kettle and mugs were balanced on top of a fridge and a rickety wooden table covered in books was shoved against the opposite wall and, between these two the heady delight of a door with a handwritten sign. W.C. No Smoking. No Reading. No Shenanigans.

Having relieved himself and washed his hands, Luke wondered whether to make a mug of tea or to just settle down for the night.

The lights seemed dimmer and warmer in most of the shop, with a brighter glow in the front room shining onto the red velvet chair in the corner. It looked like the ideal spot to do some reading. Unrolling his mat, he wedged it between the chair and the counter with the cash register. He moved the stool to the other corner of the room, out of the way, and shook out his sleeping bag onto the mat. There weren't any curtains so there was nothing he could do about the light that would come through the front window in the morning, or the fact that anybody walking outside would see the interior of the shop lit up. Realising how visible he would be to a curious passer-by with their face pressed against the window, he decided against getting fully undressed and just stripped down to T-shirt and boxers before getting into the bag. Lying in the softly lit room, the bookshelves reaching high above, he tried to imagine himself calm and sleepy. He wasn't, though. A couple of beers were no match for the sheer weirdness of the situation. And he still hadn't found a light switch. Without wanting to examine the impulse too closely, he spoke out loud. 'I'm going to sleep, now.'

There was a shift in the air, barely perceptible, and the lights went out.

CHAPTER NINETEEN

Esme brewed her morning tea while Jetsam sat on the kitchen table, washing himself. She would never have guessed that she would miss having a lone man staying in her home, but the place felt unaccountably empty in a way that it had never done before. It was still early and the view through the window showed the bright line of the coming sun along the horizon.

Esme hadn't felt anything for a man for over seven years. She had appreciated good looks, of course, she wasn't dead, but everything had been safely theoretical. Crushes on actors being the extent of her hormonal urges. She often wished she wasn't as solidly heterosexual as she seemed to be, that way she might actually be able to have another relationship. As it was, the thought of getting anywhere near to a real-life man was unthinkable. Any attraction immediately drowned in an ocean of terror.

Now, with an attraction to a real-life human for the first time since her disastrous marriage, the man in question was under suspicion of murder. Or manslaughter, at least. She didn't believe it. No, it was more than that. Esme had a bone-deep certainty that Luke was not a killer, that he had not hurt Alvis.

Her intuition was firing, her instincts awake and screaming. Problem was, she still didn't know whether to trust them. She might be certain that Luke wasn't dangerous, but she had stayed with Ryan, thinking that he would change. She couldn't allow herself to make a mistake like that again. Especially now that she was responsible for the islanders, too.

LUKE WOKE up to the sound of knocking. He sat up immediately, heart pounding, and his head spun for a few seconds. With a couple of blinks, the disjointed view resolved itself. Wooden shelves packed with books. His sleeping bag. The window with a figure outside. He was on the floor of the bookshop. On Unholy Island.

He unzipped the sleeping bag and clambered upright, glad he hadn't slept naked. He pulled on a pair of joggers and rubbed his face with his hand, trying to wake himself up. The figure outside turned out to be Matteo, the silent man from the shop. He was carrying a paperback copy of *The Remains of the Day* and he frowned at Luke and tapped his watch.

Luke checked the time. It was almost ten. He couldn't remember the last time he had slept so long or so well. He rubbed a hand over his face. 'What time does this place usually open?'

Matteo gave him a questioning look and moved inside. Luke felt like the bookshelves had shifted again and it felt somehow more spacious inside the front part of the shop. Sunshine was streaming in, showing dust motes, and Luke could almost swear the shop was stretching in the morning light. He shook his head. Too much sleep obviously sent him off-balance.

Matteo had disappeared further into the shop and Luke took the opportunity to tidy away his sleeping bag and to put the kettle on. With a mug of instant coffee in hand, he returned to the front part of the shop and discovered a couple of people browsing the shelves (fiction A-H) there. He didn't recognise them and assumed they must be day-trippers from the mainland.

By LATE MORNING, the shop was empty again. He had sold several books to the day-trippers and exchanged Matteo's copy of *The Remains of the Day* for *Klara and the Sun*. That had been awkward for a moment. He had looked inside the flyleaf and found a price written in pencil as with the books he had sold to the visitors, but when he had asked Matteo for the money he had shaken his head and passed his paperback across the desk instead. 'You want to exchange?'

Matteo nodded. His smile seemed relieved that Luke had grasped the concept and Luke decided to assume this was a long-standing agreement, rather than an islander taking advantage of the clueless newcomer.

The doorbell jangled and his chest squeezed when he realised it was Esme. She wasn't wearing her bulky coat today, but was swathed in a long woolly scarf and a thick navy cardigan with a knitted pattern of white trees around the hem and she was carrying her small rucksack. The only part of her body visible was the stretch of leg from above the knee to the top of her calf-length boots, sensibly clad in opaque (and probably thermal) tights. He dragged his gaze upwards, telling himself not to ogle the poor woman.

'You look good behind that desk,' Esme said.

He tried not to react to the compliment. She was just being friendly. Being nice. It didn't mean she thought he looked *good*. 'Not sure about that. I just let Matteo walk out of here without paying.'

Esme went still. 'What?'

'He swapped *The Remains of the Day* for *Klara and the Sun*.'

Esme relaxed. 'Well, that's payment. Islanders are allowed to swap books we've bought here before. Maybe mainlanders, too, I don't know. We don't get many return visitors.'

Luke felt his shoulders lower. He didn't realise how worried he had been until that moment.

Esme had wandered closer to the nearest shelves and was scanning the spines with the head tilt he was already finding familiar. The seasoned bookshelf-browser stance. She reached out a finger and touched a book before seeming to remember that he was there. 'I brought lunch. I wondered if you would like to eat. Together. It's okay if you're too busy, I can leave yours. I wasn't sure if you would have had time to get yourself sorted.'

He interrupted the flow of words. 'That would be great. Thank you.'

Esme slipped her rucksack from her shoulders and placed it on the counter. Instead of unzipping the bag, she looked around. 'In here? Or do you have a, I don't know, a break room? Or do you eat in the accommodation?'

'There's an office. With a fridge. It's not very big, though.' Luke was trying not to imagine being forced into close proximity with Esme. Having a crush was no excuse for acting like a letch.

'Through here?' Her voice floated through from deep in the shop.

He followed it and found her stood in front of a door he hadn't seen before. He looked back along the warren of bookshelves and located the door to the office/breakroom. Through a narrow gap, he could see the back room of the shop, lined with yet more shelving, and the sign that he had seen before. The one that said 'Shoplifters will be eaten.' But here was a door that most definitely hadn't been there before. 'Are you fucking kidding me?' He said out loud.

'Sorry?' Esme looked startled.

'Not you,' he smiled in what he hoped was a reassuring manner. 'I'm talking to the bookshop.'

THE DOOR OPENED EASILY ENOUGH, revealing a narrow winding staircase made of wrought iron. Manners told him he should let Esme go first, but since he didn't know what was up there, he decided prudence took precedence. 'I'll just nip up and... check.'

'Okay.' Esme sounded mystified, which was entirely fair.

The stairs opened directly into what must have been a converted attic. Skylight windows made the room bright, and a wide window, which must have been on the back of the building, showed a view that was like one of Esme's seascapes. There was a low double bed against the far wall, an oak chest of drawers, and a small pine table with two basic dining chairs. The walls were painted white and the bedding was blue. A patchwork quilt was folded at the end of the bed. Everything was worn, but looked comfortable. Cosy.

'Is this for me?' He asked out loud, feeling foolish. It occurred to him with utter certainty that if the bookshop didn't want him up here, he wouldn't be up here. He had a sudden vision of losing his footing on the stairs and falling awkwardly, his neck broken. 'I only asked,' he muttered, ignoring the realisation that he was talking to a building. And it was answering.

'Come on up,' he called down to Esme.

Her eyes were wide as she took in the view from the window.

He stood awkwardly, suddenly very aware of the bed. He had been thinking they would be able to sit to eat, but now he was worried it might have seemed presumptuous in some other way. It was too intimate.

'I don't see anything of Alvis's,' Esme said, when she dragged her gaze from the window and looked around the room.

She was right. There were no personal knick-knacks, no clothes left lying across the bed. Not even a half-read book. He wondered what he would find if he opened the top drawer of the chest.

'Did someone come and clear out her things?'

Esme was frowning again.

'I don't know,' he answered. 'I didn't get the impression that anyone had been here, but I might be wrong.'

'Maybe Bee?' Esme said. 'The Three Sisters have a way of sorting things out on the island.' She glanced over, as if for permission, and slid open the middle drawer in the oak chest. 'Belay that. Alvis's clothes are here.' She opened the others, quickly riffling through the items inside.

'I suppose I will need to bag that up,' he said, joining her. 'Charity shop, do you think? Or is there some sort of island thing...'

Esme didn't reply. Unless he was losing his mind, he had the distinct impression that she was attempting to look under the bed. Subtly.

He was about to ask what she was looking for, when he got his answer.

'Where is your stuff?' Esme looked at him directly.

Luke decided to be honest. 'I haven't been up here before. I've been sleeping in the front of the shop with my camping equipment.'

She looked around at the pleasant room and then back at him, eyes questioning. 'You felt weird about it?'

'I hadn't found it. This place is...' He stopped, unsure how to describe the bookshop while the bookshop could be listening. Which was crazy. But on the island seemed, somehow, not-crazy. Reasonable. The bookshop had feelings. Whatever.

'Alvis told me that there was a section devoted to witchcraft but she couldn't always find it. I'm still looking. Will you tell me if you see it?'

Esme's easy acceptance of the sentient building inched the whole situation another notch toward 'fine'. Luke felt his shoulders relax and he took one of the chairs at the small table.

'I'll help you move in,' she said. 'Let's get your stuff.'

'We don't have to do that, now...'

'Yes. Tidy home. Tidy mind.'

'But it's lunchtime.'

'You should unpack first.'

Luke was mystified by this abrupt change in conversation and Esme's insistence. But she was showing an active interest in getting him settled, which suggested she might not hate the thought of him sticking around. That was good enough.

He went back down the stairs, hoping he would be able to find them again, Esme close on his heels. He had packed his backpack in the morning out of habit, so he just needed to pick it up from the corner of the front room of the shop.

Upstairs, Esme watched him unbuckle the straps. 'I've been camping for a while so this stuff might be a bit...' He winced internally as the smell of unwashed clothes wafted into the air.

'I assume there's a washing machine tucked somewhere, but if not, one of the islanders will lend you theirs. For a fee or a favour.' Esme reached past him and upended the rucksack, spilling his possessions onto the floor. His high beam torch thumped as it landed on the carpet, and a forgotten orange rolled away.

As quickly as she had become enthusiastic about him unpacking, she seemed to lose interest. 'You're right.' She stood up, dusting off her knees. 'We should eat.'

Esme hefted the tower of Tupperware onto the table. 'It's just leftovers,' she said as she began to unpack.

There was a Greek salad with chunks of feta, half a quiche, a slice of lasagne, and a foil platter of sliced ham.

'Why do you do that?'

'What?'

'Minimise. This looks amazing. And not just because I've been existing on takeaway and motorway service station sandwiches.'

Esme's cheeks had flushed pink. He wanted to wrap his arms around her. He didn't move, though. He had never prided himself on being a genius at reading women, but he had picked up enough signals to tell him that she was not open to unsolicited physical affection. The way she went very still whenever he got closer than a couple of feet was a big clue. 'Thank you,' he said instead, trying to sound as warm and sincere as he felt.

Once they were sat opposite each other and began to divide up the food, the tension evaporated. Luke asked about her morning's work painting and then told her about the bookshop experience so far. He wondered if he ought to mention the lights. He hesitated to voice some of the oddities he had noticed, though, not wanting to sound unhinged. She had seemed to be alluding to the way the bookshop changed configuration when you weren't looking, but he was worried it would all sound that bit madder voiced out loud.

'Alvis was very attached to this place,' Esme said, gesturing with her fork. 'I found it hard to imagine you here in her place. No offence.'

'None taken.'

'And you never intended to settle on the island, did you?'

'Did you?' He countered. 'When you first arrived?'

Esme looked down at her food and Luke wanted to slap himself. For all her forthright speech and capability, there was something vulnerable about Esme. Something that he kept seeming to trample over, even though it was the last thing he wanted to do.

'The bookshop lights,' he began. He wanted to rebuild the fragile sense of intimacy that had been there until a moment ago. Until he had burst it like an elephant with a soap bubble. 'I haven't seen any bulbs. And they seem to go on and off automatically.' He wasn't going to mention them going out when he said he was going to sleep. That had to have been a coincidence. 'Are they on a timer?'

'I wouldn't know,' Esme said. Her tone wasn't unfriendly, but it was no longer warm either. She was packing away the tubs, too.

'I didn't mean to pry,' he said. 'You don't have to leave.'

She gave him a curious look. 'I have to get on. And you need to open up downstairs.'

'Right. Okay. Thank you for the food.'

'Don't get used to it,' she said. 'I just felt sorry for you being thrown in at the deep end. But you asked for it by staying, so I don't know why I did.' She finished on a rush, looking surprised.

'I've upset you.'

She shook her head, her expression closed and her whole body radiating tension. Then it seemed to drain away and she closed her eyes briefly. 'I'm sorry. It's not you. Well. That's not true, really. But it's not your fault.'

Luke stayed quiet, not wanting to fuck up again.

Those hazel eyes were on his and he could see she was thinking. She bit her lip. 'I've been here seven years and I still feel like an incomer. I'm the Ward Witch. I protect our borders and I still feel like I don't quite belong, like I might have to leave. And that scares me.'

He nodded to show he was listening, but didn't risk saying anything. He was pretty sure she had just said she was a witch, and he found he believed her. Next to everything else on the island, it seemed reasonable somehow.

'When you asked about the lights,' Esme looked around the room nervously, 'I'm not sure if I'm supposed to be honest. And that made me remember that I don't feel like I am part of this place yet. It's...'

'Annoying?'

She laughed. 'Yeah. A bit. I'm tired of feeling out of place. I want this to be my home.' She straightened her shoulders. 'It is my home. I'm being stupid. Ignore me. And now you really do have to open up downstairs. I've taken too much time...'

Without thinking, he reached out and took her hand. 'Stop apologising.'

She had gone very still and he carefully removed his hand, cursing himself for his stupidity. Still. He had started now, and couldn't seem to stop himself. 'You're not stupid.'

She smiled at him, but her eyes were filled with

sadness and something else that he couldn't identify. 'You're sweet.'

Well, that wasn't a good sign. Sweet wasn't what sent women crazy for a man in Luke's experience. He followed Esme down the steep stairs with a heavy feeling in his chest.

CHAPTER TWENTY

Having fled the bookshop, Esme went straight to Tobias's house. She wasn't going to speak to him about Luke, that was her own private conundrum, but she did want to tell him about the glass. It hadn't been in Alvis's room or downstairs in the bookshop. Or in Luke's rucksack. She had patted the whole thing down after emptying it, and checked his coat pockets on her way out of the shop. He had handily left his coat on the back of the chair by the cash register, which in itself suggested his innocence. Plus, he had seemed bemused by her going through the room and his things, not alarmed.

All in all, Esme was feeling mightily relieved. Nothing contradicted her instinct that Luke had nothing to do with Alvis's death. And it looked like he was going to stay on the island. Her heart leaped at the thought and she suppressed a smile.

Tobias opened the door and ushered her inside. As always, there was a fire crackling in the grate. Winter struggled to his feet and padded over to nudge at Esme's hands. 'I don't have anything for you,' she said, stroking his head affectionately. 'Boss's orders.' Tobias had Winter on a strict diet. Something that she occasionally felt guilty about when she let Jetsam eat butter.

'Would you like tea?' Tobias had been reading. A book was on the side table by his favourite chair and his glasses sat on top. He had the air of a man surfacing from another realm.

'I'm fine, thank you. Sorry to interrupt you.'

He waved a hand and indicated that she should sit. Esme wanted to pace the room, to work off the nervous energy that was coursing through her body, but Tobias was an old-fashioned gent and would never take his chair unless she was seated first.

'Alvis had a piece of glass. It was like sea glass, but a really big piece. Black. Do you remember it?'

Tobias shook his head slowly. 'I don't.'

'I know she was carrying it with her. She showed it to me and then put it in her jacket pocket. The coat she was wearing when she died.'

'Okay...'

'It's not at the bookshop. Or her bedroom, so I think she had it with her.'

Tobias raised his eyebrows. 'Perhaps she gave it away?'

'Maybe.'

'Or dropped it somewhere on the island.'

Esme shook her head. 'She thought it was important. She showed it to me and seemed worried about it, but she didn't really explain why. I don't believe she would have just dropped it somewhere. Buried it, maybe, if she thought it was dangerous... But I feel like she would have asked me to help if that was the case. To ward the area against someone stumbling across it.'

'Did it seem dangerous to you?'

'No. It seemed like a lump of unusual glass. But you know I'm not very...'

Tobias held a hand up. 'You are our Ward Witch. You would have sensed it if it had been dangerous. I'm sure that's why Alvis showed it to you.'

Esme digested it for a moment. The thought that Alvis had been seeking her expertise had literally never occurred to her.

'If it was still in her pocket when she died, that means somebody took it.'

He nodded. 'But we don't know for certain she was carrying it.'

'It's a fair guess,' Esme argued. 'Especially given that it's disappeared. And Alvis was right about it being important.'

'What makes you say that?'

'I saw it.'

'A vision?'

Feeling like a fraud, Esme nodded. 'At least I think so.'

'We need to tell DS Robinson.'

Esme was surprised. She had supposed that Tobias wouldn't be keen to share information with the mainland.

He must have seen her surprise, because he continued. 'We police ourselves for the most part, but we cooperate fully when the mainland law steps across the water. It doesn't much matter in the long run, but it makes it easier in the short term.'

Well, that didn't make much sense. 'What can the police do, though? They don't really understand... All our ways.'

'But Alvis could have been killed for a mundane reason. Greed. Anger. Poor impulse control. The police have resources and outside perspective. They might be able to achieve what we cannot.'

Esme frowned. 'You don't really believe that, surely?'

Tobias spread his hands. 'Live long enough and you

realise that all things are possible. And I think this mystery needs to be solved as quickly as possible. Otherwise it will be like a rot setting in. The community could turn on its own. There has been discord already and that will only get worse if suspicions grow.'

Suddenly, Esme understood his reasoning. 'And if an outside agency points the finger, it's more likely to bring the islanders together against them?'

Tobias smiled sadly. 'Exactly.'

ESME DID NOT RELISH the thought of speaking to the police officer, but she was willing to do whatever Tobias thought necessary for the harmony of the island community. She wanted to be a good team player.

DS Robinson was perched on the edge of her sofa at Strand House. She had declined a cup of tea, but asked for a glass of water instead. 'I'm trying to cut down on caffeine,' she said in explanation.

'I've got peppermint, chamomile, gooseberry...' Esme began to list the contents of her tea cupboard, but the other woman shook her head.

'Water's great. Thank you.'

Esme sat in the chair facing the sofa and folded her hands in her lap.

'You had something to tell me. About Alvis.'

'Something was taken from her when she died. A glass ornament.' She had decided that was the best way to refer to the sea glass that wasn't just sea glass.

'And how do you know that?'

'I don't know it,' Esme amended. 'I just think it. Alvis showed me the ornament before and I know she was carrying it around with her. Not leaving it in the shop when she went out.'

'Okay,' Robinson made a note in her pad. 'Anything else?'

'That's it,' Esme said, feeling deflated. She had expected more of a reaction. To her, the information felt key. Someone had taken the glass, which meant they had been there when Esme had died. Whether they had killed her deliberately or not, it meant that somebody on the island knew more than they were saying.

'Can you describe the ornament?'

Esme did her best. She left out the part about the colours moving inside the glass, as she could tell DS Robinson already thought she was eccentric.

When the police officer left, promising to keep her informed of developments, even though she knew she couldn't and wouldn't, Esme leaned against the closed door and took a couple of deep breaths to slow her heart rate. She was proud of herself. She had spoken to a copper and hadn't had a panic attack. Maybe she was getting better?

Esme was just feeding Jetsam some ham when there was a knocking on the back door. Hammer in her kitchen was a strange sight. He was too big for the small room and too rough-looking for the cosy domesticity. Esme felt bad as soon as the thought crossed her mind. It wasn't Hammer's fault that he looked the way he did. She wondered if he had harboured any hope of a different life or whether he had become an enforcer the moment he hit his teens. Predestined because of his size and the cast of his features.

'I know you like him.'

'Who?' Esme was pretty sure she knew who Hammer was talking about, but she didn't want her interest to be obvious. Hammer had never shown anything other than brotherly affection, but it felt too private. Besides, she had only recently admitted to herself that she felt something for the man.

'Luke Taylor. He's bad news,' Hammer said. 'I did some digging.'

'Is that where you've been?'

'Yeah, down south. That's where he's from originally.' Hammer made it sound like a dirty secret.

'You investigated him?'

'Alvis is dead,' Hammer said. His forehead creased into a deep scowl. 'He's the new Book Keeper. Fine. I accept that, but it doesn't mean I'm not going to check on him. Tobias might be happy to trust the island spirit or whatever the fuck he thinks makes the decisions around here, but I need a bit more than that.'

'Did you check my background? When I arrived? Did you go poking around in my past?'

Hammer shook his head. 'I didn't need to.'

'Double standards,' Esme said, even as she was glad he hadn't. She didn't need him looking at her with pity.

'I won't apologise. I trusted you. I still trust you. I don't trust him.'

Esme wanted to hold on to her righteous anger, but she couldn't. Hammer was looking out for the island. He was doing something she had never experienced before in her life, he was working hard to keep her safe and he wasn't asking for a damn thing in return. She put her hand on his large forearm and forced herself to look directly into his eyes and to speak gently. 'I thought island code was that we got to leave our past behind?'

He met her gaze. 'There are always exceptions.'

After a short pause, Esme dropped her hand. 'Fine. So what do you need to tell me?'

Hammer blew out a breath. It was relief, as if he had

truly expected her not to listen to him. 'Okay. You already know he's looking for his brother?'

'Yes.'

'The stuff I found... Let's put it this way. It would be better if he doesn't succeed.'

'But that's not Luke's fault,' Esme protested. 'He's not responsible for his family. Just because you've found out some bad stuff about his brother...'

'They are twins.'

'That still doesn't mean they are the same. Or that they have done exactly the same or will do...' Esme stopped. She couldn't help wondering exactly what Hammer meant by 'bad news'. It was her turn to take a deep breath. 'I think you need to tell me what you found.'

THE BELL on the door of Matteo's shop rang and two customers walked into the small space. Matteo replaced his bookmark and closed the paperback he was reading. Focusing on the visitors, he felt his stomach plummet. These two weren't tourists. For starters, they didn't have backpacks or binoculars, but that wasn't the only clue. Both men were in their twenties and heavily tattooed. One looked like he had been a boxer, both from his physique and misshapen ears, while the other had the lean kind of body that suggested a high metabolism, high stress, a penchant for amphetamine, or all three.

Matteo shifted his weight so that he was balanced on both feet. Ready to move. He didn't expect he would be able to make it to either exit before the two men caught him, though. The front door would mean navigating around the shop counter and walking right past the men in the confined space between the packed shelves. Behind him there was an opening with a bead curtain. It led to the downstairs toilet, a small stockroom and the fire exit. If he ran, they would follow, and they would catch him. He could feel it and the fear rooted his feet to the worn tile floor.

Skinny picked up a chocolate bar and ripped it open, taking a big bite while staring at Matteo in a way that was clearly meant to be disturbing. It was pretty effective.

Boxer put a large hand on the counter next to Matteo's book. It had letters spelling 'pain' on his knuckles. 'We are looking for someone. Family emergency.'

Matteo lifted his chin to indicate that he had heard. He felt like he was letting a breath out after years of holding it. He had been expecting something and there it was. There was a kind of relief in that, although this wasn't the sort of danger he had expected from Alejandro. That would come with business suits and leather briefcases. With false smiles and dangerous words.

'Lewis Taylor. You know him?'

Matteo shook his head. He was relieved they weren't looking for him, but he had the distinct impression that 'no' wasn't a word these two liked hearing. His hand reached automatically for the pen he kept handy on the counter.

Boxer put his hand over his and squeezed. 'How about Luke Taylor? He's tall. Like his brother.'

Matteo felt the bones in his hand grinding together and pain radiated up his arm. With his other hand, he slid his notepad from under his paperback and tapped it.

Boxer stopped frowning menacingly and frowned in incomprehension instead.

Matteo looked at the hand that was enclosing his writing hand. Then he took the pen he had been reaching for and put it on the pad.

Skinny began laughing around a mouthful of chocolate. 'I think he's disabled.'

Boxer let go of Matteo's hand as if it was contagious.

Matteo stretched his fingers and tried very hard not to look relieved. His hand hurt, but he forced himself to pick up his pen and write. *Don't know them.*

Boxer's eyes narrowed. 'We heard they were here. One of them at least.'

Matteo shrugged. He knew these two weren't going to leave without hurting him. Whatever he did. Whatever he did or did not tell them.

Skinny sidled around the side of the counter. It was open, just a little bit of kitchen worktop that had been repurposed. On the island, you often made do with what was available rather than get things shipped in from the mainland. It was a necessity when the weather was bad and the island was cut off, but a point of pride the rest of the time. Another way in which they were different.

He could hear skinny breathing heavily. The man was excited. Matteo's stomach lurched. This was going to be bad.

Boxer leaned forward and grabbed the front of Matteo's shirt, pulling him across the counter. His face was too close and he could smell the man's skin and breath. Sweat mixed with something weirdly sweet. He forced himself to keep his eyes open.

'I'm going to give you one last chance. Where is he?'

Matteo didn't answer. He had no particular loyalty to Luke as a person, but now that he was the Book Keeper, he would not direct these men to him. Apart from anything else, they might damage the bookshop.

'You've met him, I think.' Skinny's voice came from his left. He felt something sharp pierce his side. 'So you know we're serious people.'

A knife changed things. A beating he could take. Bruises would heal, broken bones would knit, but a stab wound could leave him bleeding out on the floor of the shop. Dead like Alvis before anybody came in for their pint of milk.

'I don't think this dumbfuck wants to play,' Boxer said.

Before Skinny could push the knife into his side and pierce his liver, Matteo did something he had vowed never to do again. He opened his mouth and spoke.

CHAPTER TWENTY-ONE

'Y ou want to put your knife away. You want to leave this shop and leave Unholy Island immediately.'

Boxer let go of Matteo's shirt so abruptly that Matteo stumbled back. He was relieved that Skinny had moved the point of the blade from his side so there was no accidental knifing. They turned and walked out of the shop. The bell tinkling as the door opened. They didn't even pause to shut it, so Matteo followed them and closed it after them. He ought to follow, to check that they weren't going to bother anybody else, but his knees had gone to jelly and he slid down the door instead and sat on the floor, trying to get air back into his lungs.

IN HAMMER'S PAST LIFE, he had known a lot of bastards. There were dodgy people trying to get by, others trying to get rich, and the truly desperate cases - people who would do whatever they thought was necessary because they were caught in a trap and could see no other way out. And then, occasionally, there were the ones who were just wrong inside. They wanted money, of course, and power within their little circles, but more than that they needed to feed something dark and hungry. An endless desire for causing pain, a need for domination. In short, the sort who just *liked* it.

He didn't know which category Luke's twin brother fell into, but Lewis had definitely got mixed up with one of the worst. According to gossip, Dean Fisher had learned his trade working for the Crow Family in London back in the eighties. He had moved up north to start his own enterprise, dealing drugs and girls, and now ran a small empire in Leeds. Lewis had ended up working a couple of jobs for him after he stumbled into a poker game and lost more than he could pay. Poker was a side hustle for Fisher. Something he did for nostalgia and fun. But the only way he could enjoy himself involved somebody losing big. And this way, he either made more money or drafted more people into his machine.

Hammer still had contacts. People he could tap for information and who wouldn't dare lie or refuse. One of these was an old geezer called Rab. He was ostensibly out of the life and somewhat looked up to by the young ones. Getting old in the life was no easy feat and Rab had gained a certain measure of respect as a result. Hammer had bought him a couple of pints in the nasty pub he spent his afternoons and walked him back to his shithole of a flat, stopping for ciggies and milk, before he got the whole story.

Lewis had been on the hook for cash, and he probably thought that a couple of jobs would pay it off. Problem was, of course, that once you'd done a job for Dean Fisher, you were considered an employee. He called and you answered. 'Once you ken something about something you cannae just stroll off,' as Rab put it.

Hammer knew all about that. He'd managed to walk away but only through a combination of being a bigger bastard than any of them, and by disappearing. There were certain key members of low society who believed him to be dead and at least one who prayed for it.

Lewis had been installed in debt collection. But Rab had heard he had been skimming and that was why Dean Fisher was keen to interview him. Hammer took that with a grain of salt. People talked, didn't make any of it true.

SOME PEOPLE SLID into bad relationships, unknowing and unwilling, and some people ran into them headlong. Esme had always known she belonged to the latter category. It was yet another source of guilt and confusion. How could you have been so stupid? No. That was his voice. But on some days, it was hard to tell.

Whatever. Her instinct had told her right away that Ryan Parry was the devil and she had still crossed the bar when he had crooked his finger. Still tripped along by his side on the walk back to his flat. Still stayed that night and the night after and the night after that.

She knew that she had been vulnerable. Some part of her accepted that, accepted that there were reasons for her being susceptible to Ryan's brand of certainty. His combination of flattery and coldness, the heady brew of intermittent punishment. By the time it became intermittent reward, the bad times greatly outweighing the good, it was too late. She was ensnared and too tired and uncertain to leave.

Before Ryan, Esme had been running headlong into a series of bad decisions. Bad decisions that felt reasonable and almost saintly by comparison to the standards she had been set. The examples from the people who had surrounded her as she grew up in the system, and with foster placements coming too late to paper over the damage already done.

Her instincts had always been there, though. She knew when a party was going to turn violent, when to cross the road, when to change the subject. Hypervigilance, a counsellor had told her once. She had been given a course of six sessions, focusing on CBT and coping strategies, after a bloodied knife had been discovered in her room at the Home. That and a criss-cross of healing cuts on her left thigh. Compared with the others, Esme hadn't considered self-harm much of a problem. It was a solution to her feelings. And next to the violence, drug addiction, eating disorders and psychosis of the other kids, it had seemed positively healthy. Neat. Quiet. Hurting nobody but herself. Sitting in the counsellor's bleak office, she had half-expected a gold star. *Good job. Only a touch of cutting. That's very restrained.*

But her instincts had become something she had buried. Something she wilfully ignored so that she could keep on running into bad decisions and muting the screaming of her own mind with self-harm, alcohol and iron-clad denial.

In fact, if you had told her she was a witch, she would have laughed in your face. When she arrived at Unholy Island, running from Ryan and her old life, Tobias and Bee had said the words with such matter-of-fact certainty that it had opened the door to the possibility. However insane the notion.

Whatever. It was certainly true that the island invited acceptance of the unusual. And once Esme had been told that her new role also came with a house rent-free and hers to own for as long as she was living in it, it became easier to go with the flow. Especially after she was shown a very sound-looking legal document backing up this outlandish claim.

She might have started out with the sceptical attitude of 'I will say I'm a witch and go through the motions of strengthening wards, whatever they might be if you will let me stay here, in this place that I feel safest, and with a roof over my head,' but it hadn't been long before it had morphed into acceptance. More accurately, it hadn't been long before she could no longer deny that her intuition was more than the usual, that she felt something spark when she did the ward ritual and that the Three Sisters were definitely not human.

ON THE MORNING of Alvis's funeral, the glitter on the sea was blinding. Sparkles like shining constellations twinkled just under the surface of the waves, dancing and diving in an ever-moving choreography of light. Bright sunshine on a sad day often feels like an abomination, but the islanders felt it was appropriate to honour Alvis and they thanked the weather.

Esme walked along the beach and said a private goodbye to Alvis before joining the others at the old church. The graveyard next to the ruined church was not bound by a wall or fence, but the slope of the land limited the space. It was a small hill, chosen for the church so that the residents would look up and see God. Or, possibly, so that the holy men of the church could look down on the islanders.

Hammer and Oliver had dug Alvis's grave the night before. Tobias, Hammer, Seren, Matteo, Esme, Fiona, and Oliver gathered around and threw handfuls of dirt onto her shrouded body. Gulls landed on the ruined stones of the broken-down church and watched in unusual silence. The sun shone through the window of the remaining wall and lit the ruins of the chancel arch, giving it a golden hue.

Esme stared into the grave and blinked back tears. She was the Ward Witch and she hadn't protected Alvis. She had finally found safety and a home, and someone had stomped on that safety by murdering an elderly woman. A selfish thought, perhaps, but she couldn't help it. The old panic was simmering under the surface, humming under her skin and singing in her blood. She was so tired of being afraid and felt exhausted at the thought of the sleeplessness and hypervigilance to come.

JUST WHEN THE service was over, Tobias was very surprised to receive a call from DS Robinson. He walked away from the others and put his hand over one ear to help him hear.

'I don't seem to have the body in the morgue. I'm very sorry. The coroner's office were supposed to collect last week. It was on the system, but it seems to have been missed. I can't find the original record, either, but...' The DS trailed off and then seemed to get a hold of herself. Briskly, she added, 'Anyway, that's not your problem.'

Tobias wasn't sure how to tell the officer that the body was now interred. Laid to rest. Especially as Robinson ought to have forgotten everything about Alvis. 'She's not on the island now,' he said.

'Oh. God, I'm sorry. They did collect after all?'

'Yes.'

'There must be a mix-up this end. I'm sorry. It's not good enough. I haven't forgotten you. I will...' Robinson trailed off, as if her mind had suddenly gone blank.

'Alvis.'

'Yes. Alvis. I will investigate Alvis's death, I promise-'

'Don't promise,' Tobias said.

'No. Right. Unprofessional.'

Tobias finished the call and stared out at the headland, thinking.

'It's strange that Bee didn't show,' Esme said, catching up to him.

'The sisters mark death in their own way.'

Esme nodded thoughtfully. Tobias wondered how much information Bee was passing along during their yoga classes. After a moment, her face creased in concern. 'You look worried.'

'DS Robinson just called. I would have thought that she would have forgotten about Alvis by now.' He saw her expression. 'I know you did the wards.'

Esme went very still. 'Will we get in trouble for this?'

He knew she meant the burial. 'I don't think so. If she asks you about it, just be honest. The mainlanders are in the wrong for not collecting the body and I don't think it will be high up their list of priorities. It's not as if Alvis has family to make a fuss about it.' His mind was still whirling, trying to work out why DS Robinson would have remembered about Alvis. Was it the island? Angry at her death and the lack of justice? Was the island telling Tobias that if he wasn't going to solve Alvis's murder, then the island would make sure DS Robinson did?

'You think she will come here again? The DS?'

'I fear so.'

CHAPTER TWENTY-TWO

Esme was trying to summon the motivation to go into her studio and finish the painting she had been working on before all this disruption. There was the sharp pain of losing Alvis, of course, and the awful ache that somebody on this island, the place she had finally felt safe, had committed the act. But alongside all of that was the sense that there was more to come. In a closed community like the island, Alvis's death wasn't a pebble chucked into a pond, it was a boulder. The big splash had happened, but the waves were immense and wide-reaching.

Jet was sitting on the kitchen table, legs akimbo as he attended to his bathing. Esme looked away from Jet's nether regions just as somebody started rapping on the door. Esme wasn't especially close to Seren and couldn't remember the last time she had visited the house. She stepped back, letting the other woman in along with a rush of cool morning air.

Seren had a long red scarf, which she began to frantically unwind. Her eyes were pink rimmed, as if she had been crying. Her expression, however, was furious. 'Is he here?' she demanded.

'No. He's probably at the shop if you need him.'

'Oliver's not here?' Seren's expression intensified.

'No. Luke's at the bookshop. I thought you were talking about him...'

'Oh, thank God.' Seren seemed to sag a little.

'I haven't seen Oliver.' She was surprised that Seren would expect to find him at her house. 'Is everything all right?'

Seren threw herself into the nearest chair, scattering Jetsam from his place at the table. He meowed indignantly.

'He and Fiona had another fight. I was going to have it out with him. Tell him what I think. I'm sick of it. I don't know why she puts up with it, she's better than that.'

'Why did you think he would be here?' Esme settled on one of the many questions that sprang to mind. It seemed politer than 'why on earth would you get involved in their marriage?'. She was also trying not to be hurt by the implication that Seren thought Fiona was stupid for 'putting up with' arguments. What did that make Esme? She had put up with far worse.

'He shouted about leaving. I can hear every bloody word through our shared wall... I thought he might ask you for a room.'

'No. I haven't seen him.' It was one downside of having the most spare rooms on the island. Esme mentally crossed her fingers that Oliver wouldn't turn up later asking about staying.

'They were like this years ago, but it had been better. I don't know what has happened, but it's relentless. Every night. I can hear through the wall and it's keeping me awake.'

Esme didn't know that Fiona and Oliver were having trouble. She wasn't surprised, but she wasn't sure if it would be insulting to show that. 'Oh,' she managed instead. Non-committal. 'I'm sorry.'

'He said he was going to speak to you. I thought...' She stopped and shook her head. 'I don't know what I thought.'

Esme tried not to be nervous at the thought of Oliver storming into her house in a similar state of agitation.

'Can I stay here? I need to get a full night of sleep or I'm going to lose my shit. I'm too old for this.'

'What?'

'Just for tonight. Or maybe tomorrow, too. I really need a break.'

People didn't talk about their pre-island lives as a rule, and Esme had followed their cues and not asked. Over the past seven years, she had gleaned a few scraps of information, though. Seren was a widow. She had grown up in Wales, and had arrived on the island at least five years before Esme, maybe longer. She always brought a hip flask to the fire ceremony. It wasn't a thick dossier, but it still represented more than Esme knew about Tobias.

Esme opened her mouth to say the only thing she could. Seren was her neighbour. A fellow islander. 'Of course.'

THE NEXT MORNING, Esme cooked Seren breakfast.

'You don't have to,' the older woman said. 'I don't usually bother with it.'

'Part of the package,' Esme said. She didn't understand how anybody could miss breakfast. It was her favourite meal. One she often repeated at lunchtime. Having already laid out a dish of homemade granola and a plate of cut-up fruit and berries in front of Seren, Esme was now frying bacon, eggs and tattie scones.

'Thank you.' Seren was picking at the fruit platter.

'Did you get some sleep?'

'Some. Yes.'

Esme flipped the scones and bacon. 'You're welcome to stay as long as you like.' The words weren't entirely true, but they felt like the sort of thing she ought to say.

'I'll go home today,' Seren said. 'I just needed the break. Thank you.'

Esme plated up two cooked breakfasts and brought them to the table. Sitting opposite Seren to eat felt as strange as being the one to cook and serve her.

As if she had just been thinking the same, Seren commented how unusual it was to eat something she hadn't cooked herself.

'How is your hand now?'

'All better,' Seren waggled her fingers. 'I'm running up quite a bill with you.'

'We're friends,' Esme said promptly.

'Are we?' Seren cut a piece of bacon and speared it with her fork. 'We're neighbours, but I don't know if I have any friends.'

It was like a slap to the face. Esme blinked. She had been stupid. She had spoken without thinking. She had been trying to be nice. *But she was stupid of course Seren wasn't her friend didn't want her as a friend.*

Seren had a hand over her mouth. 'I'm sorry. That was rude.'

Esme didn't answer. She was still hearing Ryan's voice in her head, and she was struggling to ignore it. The voice that had quietened over the years on the island, time healing as everybody always promised it would, seemed to have woken up. With Luke's arrival reawakening parts of Esme that she had shut down, other doors had also been opened.

'I'm not a morning person,' Seren was saying. 'And I've clearly been living alone for too long.'

Esme tried to nod her understanding. She told herself to eat her breakfast but the thought of food was sickening and she knew it would stick in her throat.

Seren sighed audibly. 'This is why I'm better on my own. You've been nothing but kind. If I was going to have a friend, you would be top of the list. I'm just not friend material.'

Esme forced herself to hear Seren's words. Ryan's old track was still playing, but he wasn't here. She wouldn't let it drown out real people in the here and now. And as soon as she did that, she knew there was pain behind Seren's words. Looking closer, Seren's cheeks were pink and her eyes bright. She was embarrassed and a little frightened.

Esme picked up the salt and sprinkled some on her eggs. 'We'll see,' she said airily. 'People change.'

At the other end of the village, Luke was walking to the Three Sisters' house. The sky was a blameless blue with wispy white clouds and he felt the warmth of the sun on his back. It was hard to believe the black storm that had recently ripped through the island, but he wasn't complaining.

He was hoping to find Bee and not have to see Diana or Lucy. He wasn't about to forget the intense and confusing effect that Diana had had on him on their last meeting, and everybody seemed terrified of Lucy, so he was in no hurry to make the youngest sister's acquaintance.

His luck was in, as Bee was outside the front of the house, tending to the pots of flowers. She was wearing her usual denim dungarees and a floppy sunhat. She put down her watering can when he approached. 'Greetings, Book Keeper.'

'Morning,' he replied. 'How are you?'

'You aren't here to ask about my wellbeing.' Bee smiled, which softened her words.

Okay, then. The questions that had been building spilled out. 'How much is the rent on the bookshop? Do I get paid for running it or is it in lieu of rent? Can I be evicted? Where is my tenancy agreement? How many hours do I have to open the shop? What about closing up for a holiday?'

Bee raised an eyebrow. 'You want to go on holiday?'

'No. Not at the moment. But maybe I will one day.'

'I suggest we cross that bridge when we arrive at it.'

'This isn't normal,' Luke said. 'You know that, right? People don't just get given a job and a home.'

'You weren't just given it,' Bee said sharply. 'Our Book Keeper died.'

'Right. Yes. That's another thing. What should I do with her things? I mean, it can all stay, I don't need much space. I don't have much at the moment...'

'Keep what you want, box up the rest. We will help move it out. You should make yourself at home, make space for the new Book Keeper. There has to be one.'

Luke let that settle for a moment. Bee had spoken in the tones of making a pronouncement. After what felt like a respectful pause, he spoke, trying not to make it into another question. 'And it's me.'

'Apparently,' Bee said, looking uncertain for the first time. She waved a hand. 'Either you are or you aren't. These things usually work out in the end.'

Well, that was as clear as mud.

'Why do you keep saying Book Keeper?'

Bee suddenly smiled a full and genuine smile and it

was like looking at the sun. In that moment he would have laid money on her being the same age as Diana and he felt an embarrassing stirring below the belt. For fuck's sake, maybe the sisters used some sort of pheromone perfume or there was Viagra in the island's water supply. Get. A. Grip.

'Think about it, Luke,' she said. 'What mischief would the books get into if we didn't have a Book Keeper?'

So she was teasing him. That was fine. 'Does the Book Keeper pay rent?'

'Not with money.'

'So the job is the payment.' He really wanted to pin down the details.

She shook her head. 'The job is the privilege.'

LUKE WALKED BACK to the bookshop, not feeling a great deal wiser than when he had left. A home and a job. Was he ready to settle down? He thought that he had accepted that his brother was dead, gone, unfindable, but there was a difference between deciding to stop looking and accepting a job and a home. He imagined roots growing from his feet, through the earth of the island. Anchoring him. Most worrying, it didn't make him panic.

He unlocked the front door of the bookshop and flipped the sign to open. The smell of old paper and glue, mixed with wood from the shelves, greeted him. He made a mug of tea and took it to the stool by the cash register. He had a view of the street outside and there were as many mystery novels as he could want within easy reach. He caught sight of his reflection in the window and realised that he was smiling.

CHAPTER TWENTY-THREE

Matteo had switched the lights on and unlocked the front door to the shop, but had not had time to do anything else when the mayor walked in.

'We might have a problem.'

Matteo raised his eyebrows and reached for his notepad, but the mayor wasn't waiting.

'Two bodies washed up at Embleton Bay.' Tobias said, naming a popular sandy beach south of the island on the Northumberland coast. 'Two men. They have been identified as Darren Evans and Calum Reed.'

Matteo went cold inside. He grabbed his pad and pen and wrote a question. *You know them?*

'They came to the island a couple of days ago. Seren remembers them trying the door of the pub. She hadn't opened yet, but she watched them through the window. Said they looked dodgy, so she was glad she hadn't unlocked the door that morning. Did you meet them?'

Matteo looked at the grainy pictures in the newspaper. Tobias was old-fashioned and liked to get his news via print and paper. Boxer and Skinny stared up at him. He shook his head, meeting Tobias's gaze.

'There was an abandoned vehicle in the car park. I found it on Sunday, but it could have been there for days. I haven't been monitoring the car park, but Fiona remembers seeing it when she took Euan to the mainland for a shopping trip.'

Matteo felt stupid. He hadn't thought to check the car park. When the men hadn't come back, he had known that his powers were as strong as ever and they had simply left, as he had instructed. Now he realised that they hadn't left in their car. He looked down at the laminated map that he kept on the counter for visitors. It had his shop marked clearly in red and the other important landmarks in a variety of colours. Blue for the pub. Green for the car park. Yellow for the paths to the beaches. In a flash, he saw what had happened. He had told them to get off Unholy Island. His Silver power meant that they would be compelled to carry out his order in the most immediate way possible. The shortest route to leave the island from the shop wasn't via the car park to collect their vehicle and drive the causeway, the shortest route led directly to the shore. From there they must have waded into the sea, unable to stop themselves and to take the less-lethal longer route. This was why he didn't speak. His Silver blood made every word a command. And commands were dangerous.

Where is car now? Matteo wrote. He felt sick. It had been so long since this particular churning regret. Regret for actions he hadn't intended and the guilt that he had intended *something*. And maybe that was enough to damn him.

'Hammer drove it to North Berwick and I picked him up in the Land Rover.'

Matteo closed his eyes. With traffic cameras, automatic number plate recognition software, and car registration data, it wasn't so easy to make a car disappear. He wished

Hammer had pushed it into the sea instead. He wrote 'traffic cameras' on his notepad and looked up at Tobias.

'Still needs somebody to be looking for it,' the mayor said. 'Let's hope they're not particularly missed.'

Matteo nodded, trying not to think about the men walking into the freezing water, the water closing over their heads. He swallowed.

Tobias was watching him. 'They don't appear to be upstanding members of society. You sure you don't recognise them? They didn't come into your shop?'

Matteo shook his head. He couldn't meet Tobias's gaze this time.

They had been going to hurt him. Maybe worse. And they certainly spelled trouble for Luke and he was their Book Keeper and had to be protected. But still. His brother Alejandro had been right when he had told Matteo that he was dangerous. His grandmother had been right when she had said Silvers were all going to Hell, but that there would be a special corner of it for him. And he had been right when he had chosen to hide himself on Unholy Island to take a vow of silence.

CHAPTER TWENTY-FOUR

The next day was a big event in island life. The winter festival. Esme had borrowed a soup pot from Seren in the summer and she took it back. She would probably need to borrow it again in a week or so, but the festival tradition was that all borrowed items were returned, floors were swept clean, and seaweed hung in the house. It was always tempting to cheat on that last one, but not worth the risk in Esme's opinion. She had collected swathes of sea ribbon and bladderwrack in the summer and hung it to dry in her greenhouse and distributed bunches to all of the islanders.

Another key part of Esme's job was to bake the winter bread. It was a large circle with notches around the outside to indicate the rays of the sun. Esme made the bread, but she cooked it at the pub as Seren's oven was biggest.

The warm spices and brown sugar smelled fantastic and the whole wheel was studded with juicy dried fruit. Throughout the afternoon, islanders popped in for a hot drink and a slice of the fruit bread. Hammer and Oliver had built the fire on the beach ready for the night's festivities, so Esme made sure that the largest pieces were left for them.

IT WAS FULLY dark and the bonfire was lit by the time Luke arrived. Logs were cracking and splitting, sparks shooting up into the night sky. The whole community was present, standing in groups and chatting, some holding thermal mugs, some hip flasks. His gaze found Esme first, without his brain's consent. She was standing in the fire-light, her face illuminated by its warm glow. She was wearing a long skirt that swirled around her legs and a flowing white blouse with an open neck. Her dark hair was loose and, as he watched, she reached up to tuck the unruly waves behind her ears.

Winter padded over and nudged his hand. He stroked his head before reaching into his pocket for a dog treat. Winter accepted the gift and stuck to Luke's side as he made his way close to the fire. Smoke streamed away from the assembled crowd, taken by the ever-present breeze. Seren said hello to Luke, Matteo nodded a greeting and Tobias walked across the sand to welcome him. 'Did you bring it?'

Luke handed over the book. Feeling a tug of something as he did so. A strange concern, like he was worried about the book leaving his possession.

Bee was on the opposite side of the fire to the rest of the islanders. She raised her arms and the assembly fell silent. Tobias opened the book and began to read. The faces of the crowd were all turned toward him, and Luke looked at each. Rapt attention, blank stoicism, and, when it came to Euan, a dreamy expression, like he was thinking about something else entirely.

Luke looked away from the faces of the crowd and back

at Tobias, illuminated by the firelight and glowing as if lit from within. The shadows cast on his lined face, made it older and more craggy than usual. Almost demonic. If the mainlanders could see the islanders now, it would confirm all of their suspicions.

'This sanctuary endures,' Tobias intoned. 'These walls shall not crumble. This sea will conquer all.'

That seemed contradictory to Luke, but he wasn't about to argue out loud. He wondered how long the recitation would go on for, but Tobias was already finished. He closed the book and held it with both hands.

The group was chatting again. What had been a small murmur rose in volume until everybody was speaking in their normal voices. 'It's fucking freezing,' Hammer said. Luke looked across, startled to see the man.

Esme was next to him. 'It's your own fault for putting style over comfort. If you cared more about warmth than looking cool, you would have a decent coat on.'

Hammer grinned at her, and Luke felt a twist in his gut. 'You think I look cool?'

She put a hand out and touched the front of his leather jacket. 'I think you look like an idiot who isn't wearing enough clothes on a beach in December.'

'Does this happen every year?' Luke's feet had taken him closer to Esme and Hammer. Only one of them seemed to welcome his presence.

'It's the start of winter,' Hammer said, sneering a little. 'So, yeah.'

'We all have to be together for it,' Esme said in a much friendlier tone. 'It's an island tradition to welcome the winter. If we aren't all together, then the winter will be a bad one with storms and terrible weather. Well, worse storms and weather, anyway.'

He couldn't tell if she was teasing him or not. Preferring to look stupid than risk offending Esme, he asked: 'It's a ritual? Like the wards?'

Hammer's face was never exactly pleasant, but at this moment it was clouded with dark emotion and uglier than usual. Luke widened his stance and forced a slow breath. 'What?'

'He shouldn't know about the wards,' Hammer said. Presumably, he was addressing Esme, but he kept his scowl fixed on Luke.

'He lives here, now,' she replied and Luke tried to ignore the way warmth flooded through his chest.

'I told Tobias you were trouble.'

'What am I supposed to have done?'

Hammer's lips clamped into a thin line and he shook his head.

'It's the festival,' Esme said. 'Play nicely.'

'I don't know you and I don't trust you,' Hammer said.

'Hardly my fault.' Luke's heart rate kicked up, but he tried not to show it.

'Is that a fact?' Hammer's fists were clenched.

'So, what? You going to tell me to leave again? I'm the Book Keeper, now.'

Hammer's features twisted further. 'I know that. Doesn't make you immune. You cause trouble and you can still be evicted. I look after this place and I'm not going to let you put these people in danger.'

Fear and anger speared Luke at the same time. The unfairness burned, as he hadn't done anything. And the fear stabbed at his gut. What if, somehow, Hammer was right? That he *was* bad news?

'You've been warned,' Hammer said, taking a step closer as if planning to add weight to his words with a little violence. Thankfully, he seemed to get hold of the impulse. He turned abruptly and walked away.

'That guy really doesn't like me.' Luke stated the obvious, trying not to sound as spooked as he felt.

'He's a sweetheart,' Esme said, ignoring all the evidence to the contrary. 'He's just protective.'

'Of you, maybe,' Luke conceded.

Esme looked surprised. 'Of the island. Of all of us.'

LATER THAT NIGHT, Esme was standing in her kitchen with a cup of chamomile and honey tea, contemplating adding a shot of something to it to try to shut off her whirling mind. Images kept leaping up: Tobias's face that night, hollowed out and painted red by the firelight like a storybook devil. Alvis in her yellow raincoat, holding out her knotted hand with the piece of sea glass that wasn't glass at all. Luke digging in the garden with his sleeves rolled up, the muscles of his arms and shoulders flexing.

It was galling that her mind kept looping back to the newcomer who looked like a Viking God. Why, after all this time, had she decided to develop a crush? And why did it have to be on the new Book Keeper? It seemed as if he was staying and that meant it wasn't safe for her to have feelings for him. Especially not when he seemed to bring baggage. Baggage that could endanger the islanders.

Hammer had said that men had been looking for Luke. And that they had 'bothered' Matteo. That was a phrase that could contain multitudes. Esme knew that Matteo was a member of the Silver Family, but that he had moved from London and left his Family behind many years ago. According to the rumours, the Silver Family had a facility for persuasion, which made them formidable barristers. Tobias had hinted that Matteo was the strongest Silver and that his gift went beyond the 'gift of the gab'. It was clearly strong enough that Matteo avoided speaking.

Jet was out, probably terrorising the local wildlife. She sipped at her tea and stared out of the window, her own face reflected back in the black glass. Bee was always telling her to follow her breath, to let her mind calm. It doesn't have to be empty, you just need to feel your breath, your feet on the floor, the air on your skin. Just be. Don't worry about the thoughts in your mind, that's what minds do. You just have to focus on your physical presence, your place as an animal on this earth. That way, you can detach a little from your mind. Become an observer of those thoughts as they flow past, rather than drowning in the river.

Slipping into a meditative state seemed to be easy for Bee, but Esme was always holding herself back. It was as if she had to keep a strong grip on her thoughts. She knew why, didn't need a psychiatrist to tell her that she was frightened of the places her mind would go if left to its own devices. There were locked boxes and closed doors to rooms and she couldn't have her consciousness go wandering free and easy. That was terrifying.

The tea was finished and she felt no closer to sleep. Every fibre of her body was humming with tension and, suddenly, the urge to move was too great. She was wearing thermal pyjamas, thick socks, and a dressing gown and she added her bulky winter coat, a hat and her sturdy boots.

The sky was clear and the moon was riding high, lighting the path from Strand House to the beach. Esme followed her instincts and walked toward the water. The sea was a black mass and the remains of the bonfire still glowed orange and red. Esme's heart leaped into her throat as she realised she wasn't alone. A slight figure stood at the end of the beach, their back turned.

Esme could count the number of times she had been

alone with Euan on one hand. Fiona had always been a protective mother and the boy spent most of his time in his room either working on his online schoolwork or gaming. Fiona had joked that even she hardly saw him these days. She had also expressed frustration that Euan didn't like to be outdoors more.

Esme patted Euan's shoulder gently. He hadn't responded to her voice, but he jumped at her touch.

'Sorry,' she said. 'I didn't mean to startle you. Are you okay?'

Euan had looked briefly surprised, but already his face had moulded into its usual blank expression. 'Fine, thank you.' Very polite.

'It's late,' Esme said, feeling suddenly stupid. He was nearly sixteen and had grown up roaming the island. And she wasn't his mother.

He nodded, acknowledging the truth of her statement.

'Are you looking for something?'

He had turned and was gazing out to sea. The islet was just a shadowed shape against the dark waves.

She waited for a few minutes, giving Euan a chance to answer. Some people were shy. Some people processed interactions differently. More quickly or more slowly than others. Esme knew these things and waited, not jumping to the conclusion that Euan was intentionally ignoring her. When it became clear that he wasn't going to respond, she turned to leave. 'Good night, Euan.'

'I just like the sea at night,' he said, his voice almost swallowed by the sound of the waves on the shore.

'Me, too,' Esme said, absurdly relieved that he had replied. 'I like it all times, really.'

After a little longer, the cool night air blowing through her clothes and beginning to chill her bones, Esme realised he wasn't going to speak again. She wondered if Fiona knew that her son was enjoying the outdoors on his own terms, taking to the beach in the middle of the night when he had it to himself. And she wondered what else Euan was getting up to when nobody was looking.

CHAPTER TWENTY-FIVE

L uke didn't want to make a habit of doing what Hammer told him to, but he did need to speak to Matteo. He was disturbed by the news that strangers were coming to the island looking for him. He couldn't think of anybody in his life who wouldn't just call him.

'Hammer said two men were looking for me.'

Matteo picked up a newspaper from a shelf underneath his shop counter and placed it on top. It was folded to show a story. Two men found dead at Embleton Bay, their bodies washed up. Luke could barely take in the information as his mind was whirling.

The pictures were grainy newsprint and one looked like it had been taken from a distance, but he couldn't ignore the fact that he recognised both men.

He hadn't seen that much of Lewis in the years before his disappearance, their lives having taken decidedly different paths, but on the last occasion he had been up north for work and had arranged to meet Lewis in a pizza chain at lunchtime. His plan had been to have a quick and calm meal and then to go on his way, brotherly duty discharged. Instead, Lewis had declared the pizza place as unacceptable and moved them to a dodgy pub. After several pints, Lewis degenerated into a terrible mood and Luke had left before it got messy. Not before he saw Lewis talking cosily to the two men who were now laid out in the local coroner's office.

Matteo was writing on his pad. He showed Luke. *They were looking for Lewis, too.*

'You know about my brother?'

Matteo shrugged. Then he wrote *Hammer.*

'I don't know them,' Luke said. 'I'm not like my brother. I was looking for him, that's why I came here first, but I'm not like him. I swear. He's my twin, my blood, but I won't let him bring trouble here.'

Matteo frowned, but it seemed to be because he was thinking, rather than anger. After a moment, he wrote. *Family can be tricky.*

LUKE'S LIFE had a rift in it. A divide between one life and another. His first life had involved a loving mother and father, a house with regular mealtimes and a garden with a swing and Lego, and a twin brother who was his playmate and shadow. There had been trips to the seaside, magical Christmases with stockings and chocolate coins and gifts under the tree, and being tucked into bed at night with a kiss pressed to his forehead.

His second life began after his mother died. It was coldness and confusion. An angry, withdrawn father that the eleven-year-old Luke no longer recognised. And then the rest.

Luke didn't like to think about what came next. There was no point dwelling. Besides, he was an adult now and only the truly stunted continued to whine about their childhoods after the age of thirty.

Luke had retreated into books at home and sport at school. He wasn't particularly interested in the academic side of school, but didn't find it taxing either so coasted pretty easily with minimum attention and effort. During the day he blanketed his mind with football training and athletics, running laps and lifting weights so that his blood sang, and at night he escaped into the written word. His drugs of choice were stories and history. Fact and fiction seemed the same to him, the characters of the world from Henry VIII to Gandalf all equally real.

Lewis went a different way. He was as angry as their father and didn't stop fighting from the moment their mother slipped away. At twelve he got into trouble at school, by fourteen he had stopped attending and had a whole new group of friends. An older crew who secretly terrified Luke, although he would never have admitted as much.

He fought with everyone, except Luke. When it was just the two of them, Luke would see flashes of the person he thought of as the 'real Lewis' but over time those flashes became more infrequent until he was hard pushed to remember the last time he had felt their old connection. Standing with Lewis in a local pub, aged eighteen, and watching Lewis pick a fight with a skinny rat-faced twenty-year-old just because he was bored, Luke couldn't recognise the boy he had known. Lewis kept pushing the guy, spitting slurs in his face and laughing in a high-pitched crazed way, until the older man had taken a swing. Then Lewis had started hitting and hadn't stopped until Luke and three others had pulled him off. He didn't know if he would ever have stopped, in that moment he seemed as if he would kill the man. Over nothing. That was when Luke realised something had broken inside his twin.

At home they were still bonded though. Against a

common enemy. Their father had not dealt well with the loss of his wife. He had started drinking heavily at the funeral and not stopped. The aggression and anger that had taken over Lewis was mirrored in their father. But a grown man had grown fists and it was many years before Lewis and Luke were large enough to hold their own against him.

It was still a mystery to Luke how a man could turn against his own children. Weren't they the only things left of the woman he had loved? How could he mourn her at the same time as loathing the sight of them? And what could they do about it? The slope of their noses that echoed their mother's, the colour of their eyes, these were not things that they could change. In the end, he endured it, stayed out of the house as much as possible, and then escaped. By then, Lewis was long gone.

ESME DIDN'T LIKE to think about her life before the island. The 'don't ask' policy suited her just fine and it meant that, consciously at least, she had packed those years away in a remote corner of her mind. She hadn't had to talk about it with anyone, which made it like it hadn't happened.

Or so she had thought.

She was managing as the island's Ward Witch, she knew she was doing everything asked of her and competently, but she also had the gnawing sense that she could do more. *Be more.*

Which was a novel thought. By the time Esme had been ground down by Ryan, she had been utterly convinced that there was nothing of substance or worth about her at all. Certainly nothing unusual, except for a freakish stupidity and an ability to irritate Ryan beyond all measure.

By the time she had gathered the strength to leave Ryan and her toxic life, she was a husk of a human. She would never have thought it possible that she could hold a respected position in a community. She could barely hold a conversation. Thinking back to that time, seven years ago, she could hardly believe she had managed to leave the flat she shared with Ryan. She sent out love and gratitude to her younger self for finding the courage. She pictured that younger woman, the bone in her upper arm still knitting back together and her handbag slung over her good shoulder. She picked up the filled carrier bag and stuffed some empty tins and bottles into the top of it. Told him she was going to buy milk and take the recycling on her way. When she looked back to that woman, she knew she had been brave. Knew she had found a reserve of strength.

And strength meant facing difficult things head on. It meant speaking to people directly, not festering and worrying and allowing her imagination to run riot. There had been people looking for Luke and his brother. Hammer had told her that Luke's brother was dodgy, but that didn't automatically mean that Luke was the same. She ought to let him defend himself. Explain.

The bookshop was unlocked, the bell above the door tinkling as she opened it. Luke was sitting in Alvis's reading chair, a stack of books next to him on the floor. For a moment, Esme was shocked by the image. She realised that, until that moment, a tiny part of her had expected to walk into the shop and find Alvis behind the counter, pottering around the shop as if nothing had happened.

Luke got to his feet as soon as he saw her, closing his paperback and looking adorably concerned. 'Is everything okay?'

'I'm fine,' Esme said. 'Just wanted to chat.'

'You're not the only one. Seren was here earlier. She heard from Fiona who heard from Oliver that my missing brother is the devil and wanted to check my head for horns.' He stopped speaking, looking embarrassed and uncertain. 'Not really. And it's understandable. I get it.'

'Do you think it's over?'

'I think so. I hope so. But I don't know all the things Lewis was into. We had lost touch a bit before he disappeared.'

'And you don't know why he would want to disappear?'

Luke grimaced. 'I mean, he had been on a bad path for a long time. Maybe it finally got too dark even for him and it was the only way he could see to get out. He was working for a guy called Dean Fisher who doesn't sound like he's keen on his staff retiring.'

Or it got so dark that somebody made him disappear against his will. Esme didn't want to say it out loud, but Luke voiced the thought as if he had read it in her face.

'I know he's probably dead. It's the most likely.'

His voice had been flat, but she could see the spark of pain in his eyes. 'I'm sorry.'

'And now those men are dead, too. I know they were pals of Lewis's, or acquaintances at least, but hopefully that's the end of the line.'

'End of the line?'

'They probably heard the same rumour that I did and finally came looking. They won't be telling anybody else and I don't imagine there will be a host of other people looking for Lewis. I mean, it's been a year and a half. Why now? I've pretty much given up and I'm his twin.'

. . .

216

That evening in the pub, Tobias was seated next to Hammer during dinner. Still, he waited until Hammer had finished his haddock and chips before raising Matteo's concerns. Tobias knew that timing was very important with people and Hammer would be more amenable after he had a full stomach.

Hammer wiped his mouth with a paper napkin and crumpled it before answering. 'I left it in a lock-up in Scotland. Different country, different police. And the lock-up isn't in my name. And even if it does get found, I would be extremely surprised if the car could be traced to those men.'

Oliver was sitting opposite and he raised his head to look at them, his face questioning.

Tobias leaned closer to Hammer and lowered his voice. 'What do you mean?'

'It didn't belong to them.' He picked up his pint and took a sip.

'The car was stolen?' Tobias wanted to be sure he had it right.

'Or borrowed from a friend.' Hammer's lips twitched into one of his almost-smiles. 'But I would lay money that they nicked it. Full service record, travel sweets in the glovebox, and a bag of kid's stuff in the back. Looked like a car for a nice middle-class family.'

Tobias didn't approve of thievery, but in this case he would make an exception. 'Let's hope so,' he said with fervour.

'Are you talking about the newcomer?' Oliver leaned across the table. 'I told you I don't trust him.'

Tobias was glad that Luke had already left. 'He is our Book Keeper now. Bee has spoken, and the island clearly wants him here.'

'Don't know about that,' Oliver replied. 'I heard there's been trouble.'

'I told him,' Hammer said. 'He's a right to know. His kid lives here.'

'Step-kid,' Oliver said. 'But, yeah. I've got rights. And things have been wrong since he turned up. Or have you both forgotten about Alvis?'

Hammer was a very useful member of the community, but at that moment Tobias could have happily thrown him into the sea. 'Discretion,' he said, staring down Hammer. 'Let's keep this information to ourselves. We don't want a panic. Or unnecessary conflict.'

'I don't trust him,' Oliver said. 'I've said it and I stick by it. Something's not right there.'

Tobias knew it had taken Oliver a long time to adjust to the island and its unusual residents, and it seemed he was still a little jumpy. For a single unkind moment, he imagined showing the man his true nature. Instead, he leaned forward and locked eyes with him. 'All will be well, Oliver. Do not concern yourself.'

CHAPTER TWENTY-SIX

The next morning, Luke was dressed and downstairs in the bookshop. He had tea in one of Alvis's mugs. It was orange and said 'I prefer books to people' on the side in a seventies-style font. He had taken off his watch and put it on the oak chest of drawers in his bedroom before bed and he realised it was still there. He was just thinking about going upstairs to retrieve it when dark shapes moved past the cluttered window at the front of the shop. His instincts told him that trouble was coming and every hair on his body stood up. The shelves of the bookshop creaked, as if sensing that something was wrong.

He was standing very still, his mug still halfway to his mouth when he heard a low laugh, confirming his instinctual reaction. A second later, someone tried the handle of the locked door. The islanders wouldn't be attempting to open the door at this time in the morning. If they needed access out of hours, they would knock. Or someone would have phoned him. As if conjured by his thoughts, the landline began ringing.

And then whoever was outside the door knocked loudly.

The bookshop lights went out. 'It's okay,' Luke said. He knew it was mad to be talking to the building and the books, but it felt comfortable and right.

The knocking became hammering. 'Luke Taylor. We want a word.' More laughter, loud this time.

The weak morning light illuminated the inside of the shop, washing everything in grey tones and shadows. A face appeared at the window and he stepped back, knowing that he had probably already been seen. The hammering and shouting went up a notch and the telephone continued to ring.

He snatched up the chunky receiver. It was Tobias. 'Three individuals have arrived and they don't look like typical tourists. We all need to look-'

'They're here,' Luke said, raising his voice over the noise.

'I'll get Hammer. Sit tight.'

The door shook in its frame as the hammering continued. There was a pause and one of the three called his name in a creepy singsong voice. 'Come out, come out, wherever you are.'

The shelves to his right shuddered, as if there had been a tiny localised earthquake. 'I won't let them hurt you,' Luke said.

The banging was shaking the door in its frame. Luke could imagine the wood splintering and breaking and then what? What would they do to the books? It didn't even strike him as strange that he was more worried about the books than his own safety.

He imagined the gang throwing their shoulders against the door, crashing through it and splintering the wood. Heavy boots on the worn rugs, clumsy shoulders bashing into the bookshelves. And worse. He patted the counter.

'It's all right,' he said to the bookshop, to the books. 'I won't be gone long. This will all get sorted out and I'll be back before you know it. I'll go out to them.' The lights flickered as if answering him.

The racket at the front had changed in tone and violence and he realised that they were kicking the door now. He patted the shelves as he walked past, trying to reassure the shop. He wasn't going out the front, that was madness, and he picked up his car keys and jacket on the off-chance he made it to the car park before they caught him.

The backdoor was easy to find, the shop making his exit easy. And this gave him a sense that he was doing the right thing. 'Thank you,' he said, before taking a deep breath and opening the door. It was unlocked, even though he was sure he had locked it the night before. The side street was deserted but he could still hear the shouts and banging from the front of the shop. His instinct was to cut away before they saw him, but then they might trash the bookshop in their frustration. He had to let them see him and lead them away.

He allowed himself to go numb, to accept whatever happened to him. This was when his past came in handy and he knew from experience that if he accepted the possibilities and decided they were fine, he didn't get paralysed by fear. It didn't mean he relished the thought of being caught by the gang, but he could live with it.

As he rounded the corner and saw the group, his calm resolve cracked just a little. What if he couldn't live with it? What if they meant to kill him? Still. It was too late now, one guy at the back of the scrum had spotted him. He had a second to register that it wasn't a guy, but a strong-looking woman with a buzz-cut. He turned and ran.

. . .

LUKE STARTED OUT STRONG. He was in decent shape and ran five miles twice a week. This was different, though, the adrenaline and fear of the chase made him fast, but he could feel it was a short burst and that he would tire quickly. His heart was already pounding and his breath coming in harsh gasps.

The shouts had stopped quickly as the group set in to catch him. They were conserving their breath and this also ramped up Luke's fear. They were serious. Not just making noise. Not needing to whip each other up.

His feet pounded the pavement along the main street and as he ran past Esme's bed and breakfast he wondered if she would see him and raise the alarm. Tobias had said he would get Hammer, but would he come to his rescue? If not, would Tobias attempt to help? Without wanting to be insulting, he didn't know what an old man could do against three thugs. And he didn't want Tobias's getting hurt on his conscience. And definitely not Esme. He didn't want her in any danger.

He had had a good start and was running with determination and purpose, but his strong lead was waning and the gap between himself and his pursuers was closing rapidly. He used the fear to boost his speed, ignoring the pain in his lungs. He ran out of the village, leg muscles burning, and along the rough track to the car park.

If he hadn't been on the island, he would have slashed their tyres and made his escape, but he needed them to follow. His only thought was to get them off Unholy Island and away from Esme and the bookshop. His breath was coming in harsh rasps, but he was at his rust bucket Ford Fiesta, wrenching the door open and flinging himself into the front seat.

The car started just as the fastest of the group appeared

at the entrance. It was the woman and she stood in the exit for a moment, as if planning to block it with her body. Luke sped up to indicate that he was more than willing to run a woman over and she reconsidered, moving to the side just as Luke swung through the gap, small stones spraying.

The causeway was ahead, the black tarmac covered with sand and water in places, but definitely still passable. He glimpsed the men in his rear-view mirror as he accelerated away. They had arrived at the car park and were heading to join their speedy friend.

It was close to the end of the safe time to cross the causeway, and the sea was up to the boundary markers on either side of the road. It pooled amongst seaweed and muddy sand, blurring the margins. Shallow water stretched away from the road, mirroring the sky and the poles that marked the footpath. The water was already over the footpath and he knew that the road wouldn't be far behind. It was dangerous to cross on a rising tide, but Luke didn't have a choice.

He was driving too fast, water spraying up on either side of the car. He knew he had to slow down to pass the point in the middle of the causeway where the tide covered the road first and it would already be deep. If he had Tobias's Land Rover it would be no problem, but his Fiesta was significantly closer to the ground. He slowed down as little as he dared and splashed through the water, praying silently that he didn't stall.

While he worried about the drive, another part of his brain wondered at the gang and their intentions. He assumed they had planned a quick beating or to grab him and leave. Or, equally likely, they hadn't allowed for the causeway opening times. These were the kind of knuckle-draggers who didn't read signs or tide maps. If they were the crew from Newcastle, they probably didn't leave the city often, probably couldn't imagine a place in which shops closed on a Sunday, let alone a road twice a day.

It meant that if he got them across to the mainland, they wouldn't be able to return until the next low tide. And by then then he hoped he would have come up with a genius plan.

In his rear-view mirror he saw the Subaru coming through the low-lying water. From this perspective, he could see just how high the water was coming up the tyres of the car and he wondered if it would get stuck. Seconds later, the water lowered and the car was free.

The spurt of adrenaline ran through his body, making all his muscles jittery. He gripped the steering wheel more tightly and tried to focus on the road ahead, not the vehicle that was gaining on him from behind.

The sea and sand gave way to grassy wetlands and then, after a circle of tarmac which allowed people to turn their cars around before they hit the causeway proper, the road widened into a two-lane highway. Soon he was at a T-junction for the main coastal route. Luke turned right, heading north on instinct more than anything else, and not wanting to waste precious seconds dithering.

He was keyed up, every nerve jangling as he drove just above the speed limit. The black Subaru was only a couple of cars behind him now, but he wasn't going to risk reckless driving. Besides the risk to the rest of the road-users, being pulled over by the police would not solve his problems. While the presence of a traffic cop might deter his pursuers, it might not. Luke didn't know how dangerous – or unhinged – the gang was. And if a police stop did deter them, it would only delay them for a while. They could wait, watching, until the cop moved on and then he would be caught on the side of the A1. He drove on, his mind spooling through possibilities and outcomes, searching for a solution, a way out.

CHAPTER TWENTY-SEVEN

Esme had made a pot of gunpowder tea, but it was cooling on the kitchen table, abandoned. The feeling that she was missing something important was gnawing at her insides. Why had her intuition sent her to the beach the night before? Was there something she was meant to ask Euan? He was just a child, though. It was inconceivable that he was somehow connected to Alvis's death. She knew that his quietness might make some people uncomfortable, but she assumed he was neurodivergent or shy. But what if she was falling to the same prejudice? Reacting to his lack of social skills, rather than getting a genuine message from whatever witchy ability she had.

One thing was definitely true, however - Euan had seemed sad last night. His demeanour didn't give much away, but there had been a melancholy hanging around that seemed more than the standard teenage angst. Not that she was an expert, her teenage years had been spent around kids who had more reason than most to be depressed.

Knocking on the Three Sisters' door, Esme wasn't sure

if she was doing the right thing. This feeling intensified when the door opened seemingly of its own accord.

Esme waited a moment before stepping inside. The open-plan living room was empty. The curtains were shut against the daylight and every surface in the living room was cluttered with lit candles.

'I was hoping to see Bee,' Esme called out, trying to keep her voice loud enough to carry, while also a respectful volume. Not easy. 'Is she in?'

A girl peered out from behind the enormous monstera plant in the corner of the room, making Esme's heart stutter. Her long black hair was glossy in the candlelight and Esme caught the impression of pale skin and red lips. A strange singing rang around the room which, however unlikely, had to be coming from the girl. She stepped out into the room and Esme realised that she wasn't a girl. Not really. She had curved hips and round breasts, with a narrow waist and slender neck.

Esme couldn't stop staring. The woman was enchanting. Her skin was so pale and so perfect. She wondered if it felt like marble. Her own skin was prickling with the desire to touch the girl's skin, to feel it smooth against the pads of her fingers. There were speckles at the edges of her vision and Esme realised that she wasn't breathing.

The sound of footsteps on stairs and then Bee's voice cut through the air. 'Breathe, Esme.'

As if a spell had been broken, Esme found herself gasping in oxygen. Her fingers tingled.

'Go back to sleep,' Bee said to the young woman. 'It's still early.'

The woman smiled those disturbingly dark-red lips, flashing bright-white teeth that looked almost feline. She danced toward Esme, lightness in every step, and reached out a hand as if to touch her face.

'Lucy!' Bee said sharply. 'She's our Ward Witch.'

The lips turned into a pout. And the smooth skin of her face wrinkled in momentary displeasure. She was, as if it was possible, even more magnetically beautiful when frowning. Esme had the urge to take the girl in her arms and comfort her, to hold her head against her chest and to stroke that shining hair, feel the silk of it. She also had enough of a self-preservation instinct to know that it would be the last thing she ever did.

'Go on back to bed,' Bee said.

With a final sly look at Esme, the youngest of the Three Sisters spun around and danced out of the room.

'Right,' Bee said, clapping her hands together. 'Tea?'

Once she was sitting cross-legged on a floor cushion, a pottery mug of smoky tea in her hands, Esme felt her heart rate finally return to normal. Bee kept shooting glances toward the stairs as if expecting a return appearance from her youngest sister. 'She liked Alvis,' Bee said, 'and she's very attuned to the island. She'll settle down again in a while.'

'Things have definitely been feeling 'off',' Esme said without thinking. She felt herself blush at her own audacity. Who was she to presume to claim any sort of intuition or knowledge? To one of the Three Sisters, no less. She paused, waiting for Ryan's voice to start heckling her, but he remained silent.

'What did you want to talk about?' Bee said, focusing on Esme. 'Or is this just a social visit?'

'Something was taken from Alvis when she died. A chunk of black glass.'

'That's good. If you find the glass, you will know who

killed her.' She shot another look toward the stairs. 'And everyone can calm down.'

Esme wasn't so sure it would calm things down. Not if an islander was responsible. How did a community recover from something like that? And what would they do with the culprit? She tried to imagine DS Robinson leading Euan away in handcuffs, but the image wouldn't form. It was wrong.

'You know who has the glass. You know who killed Alvis.'

They weren't questions and Esme didn't answer. Instead, she said something she hadn't intended. 'I'm ready to stop being frightened. It's not serving me any more.'

'That's good.' Bee smiled in a comforting way. 'That will help the island to heal once all this is over.'

Esme squashed the urge to scowl. Bee had a fondness for speaking in riddles and, in times of stress, it made her want to roll her eyes. She would never do something so dangerous, of course, but still.

'You doubt me?' Bee clicked her tongue against her teeth. 'Why do you think you need the blood for the ward ritual?'

Because it's always blood, Esme thought. Anything that matters hurts and nothing hurts more than blood. Losing your own or the people who share it. A piercing pain, remembered, throbs in her side. Ryan had kicked her there once. The bleeding had been internal that time.

Bee took her hands, the sudden contact sending an electric feeling through Esme's body. 'The ritual needs your blood because you are the Ward Witch.'

'I know that,' Esme said. 'That doesn't...'

Bee shook her head, impatient. 'It works because you are part of the island. You belong to it. The island recognises your blood as its own.'

· · ·

LUKE HAD BEEN DRIVING for almost half an hour and the tension had made his back and shoulders lock painfully. The petrol gauge was showing less than a quarter of a tank and he knew he needed a plan.

Looking at the signs, the turning for Berwick-Upon-Tweed was close. He didn't think he had ever been to the place, but he imagined it was a small town. Probably not big enough to lose his pursuers. Approaching the turn-off, he saw that there was a modest retail park on the outskirts. He realised that unless he planned to drive forever, he ought to stop where there were plenty of people around. Otherwise it would be a test of who ran out of petrol first and he didn't like the idea of that being him on some remote country lane. Another thing he had learned in his early life. If you couldn't be sure of getting away from a problem, you had better face it.

Taking the turning and making his way to the retail park, Luke tried not to focus on the car that was driving too close to his bumper. They weren't risking losing him or getting bored of the chase, that was for sure. He parked close to the shops and watched as the black Subaru pulled up in a bay opposite. He killed the engine and pushed his head back against the seat, his extremities tingling with adrenaline and tension. Suddenly, the situation seemed utterly surreal. A family walked in front of his windscreen, the small children hanging on their parents' hands and dragging their feet. The normal people were out with shopping bags and takeaway lattes, living normal lives in which they spent their weekend looking at sofas or bedding plants and had arguments about whether to let the kids have McDonalds afterwards. It was a life that Lewis had turned away from and, in so doing, seemed determined to take away from Luke, too.

He heard the sound of car doors opening and closing and knew that he couldn't stay in the relative safety of his car any longer. He got out before his pursuers reached him and forced himself to face them, his back against the car door. He hoped the public place would inhibit the scale of the confrontation, but looking at the little gang he wasn't confident. 'I don't know you,' he said. 'What's this about?'

The leader spoke. He had a tattoo of a spider on his neck and a nasty expression. Not helped by the fact that his eyes were too small and close together for his face. 'You just made a big mistake, running.'

'I did you a favour,' Luke said. 'Cardio is very good for your health.'

Tattoo neck hesitated, his tiny eyes narrowing still further. He clearly wasn't used to people not being impressed by his scariness. 'Your brother owes us.'

'And you think that's my problem because?'

The smallest and slightest of the group took a step forward. 'Because we say it is.'

It wasn't fair, but Luke knew it was pointless to argue. 'How much?'

The man seemed surprised by this sensible question. His companions looked disappointed as the potential for immediate violence receded.

'Five grand.' A smirk.

'Well, you're stupider than you look.'

'What?' Tattoo neck bunched his hands into fists and Luke took note. They were definitely low-rent muscle or higher-end professionals with some kind of personal problem with Lewis. His twin had a talent for making enemies, so the latter was very possible.

'Lending Lewis that kind of cash.'

'It was for a deal,' the woman with the shaved head said. She laughed softly. 'A big one.'

'And how did that work out for you?'

The man with the spider tattoo went red and Luke wondered what was wrong with him. Why was he baiting the pissed-off gang member when he was standing there with his pals? And they were probably armed.

His head snapped back and pain shot through his nose and eyes. He hadn't seen the punch coming, had been watching the leader of the group. Stupid mistake. He reached up and felt his face. His nose wasn't in the right position and his eyes were streaming. Burning pain radiated from the centre of face, but he put his nose back quickly, ignoring the crunching sound. It was always better if you did these things straight away while the adrenaline was running and dampening the pain. 'Fuck.'

He wiped his eyes to clear his vision. The leader was glaring at one of the others, presumably the slugger.

'Give me a couple of days and I will cover Lewis's debt.' Luke's voice was muffled, like he had a terrible cold, and he was ignoring the small issue that he didn't have five thousand pounds handy. 'I will get you the cash and then we'll be square.'

The leader visibly relaxed and Luke realised he probably had his own boss. His own problems. 'It's just business,' he said. 'We've got no need to drag this out. But we've got to get paid.'

'I'll get it. I want this over with. I'll be back here on Friday at three to hand it over.'

'If you don't, we'll come to you. And no funny stuff. Come alone, yeah?'

'I can leave it at a drop, if that's better,' Luke said, keen to wrap up the details and get away before the rest of the gang decided that punching looked fun and they wanted to work off some of their energy.

'Nah, mate. I want to watch Lewis's brother hand over the cash like a good little lamb. And it's not over until I say it is.'

HAMMER HAD FOLLOWED the gang who were following Luke. He told himself that he was just checking that they left. Seeing them off the property like any decent guard dog. But he kept following even as they took the main road toward Scotland.

Hammer couldn't always see Luke's car and had to assume that the black Subaru was still following him. When they took the turning for Berwick-Upon-Tweed, he conceded that Luke wasn't a complete fool. He led them to a busy retail park on the outskirts of the town. He parked in front of a pet supplies store, presumably relying on the CCTV and public witnesses for protection.

The location also meant that Hammer could park unobtrusively a few rows away and observe proceedings.

It wasn't a long chat or a friendly-looking one. Hammer watched one man get steadily closer to Luke while he was distracted by his conversation with the leader. The man was bouncing on the balls of his feet and twitching. Clearly ready for action and not enjoying all the polite chit-chat. Hammer wasn't in the slightest bit surprised when he sucker-punched Luke in the face. He had his hand on the door handle, ready to intervene if the group looked ready to bundle Luke into their shitty car, but the punch seemed to hasten things along. A few passers-by were staring and the group of not-so merry men appeared to have registered that they were in a very public place.

They let Luke get into his crappy Fiesta and drive away. Hammer stayed until the gang were stowed in their own car and when they peeled out of the car park, he followed.

CHAPTER TWENTY-EIGHT

Getting a cushion, Esme sat cross-legged on the floor of the living room. Sylvie was glowing contentedly and Jetsam was curled up in front of her warmth. He appeared asleep, but Esme knew he would probably come over and start bothering her now that she was at floor level. Whenever she tried to do yoga in the house, he got underneath her and meowed in her face.

Still, as Bee kept telling her, practice was the only way she was going to get better at it. And she needed to be a better witch. Not just because it would make her feel secure in her position on the island, but because she wanted to help. Somebody had hurt Alvis and the islanders needed to know who and why. Bee had told her that the island recognised her blood, that it meant she belonged here. She would protect her home and the people inside it. She closed her eyes and slowed her breath.

Almost immediately, an image of the black sea glass popped into her mind. It wasn't in Alvis's hand. It was sitting on a flat surface that was domestically familiar. Fabric. A blue and grey patchwork quilt. Esme felt her stomach rolling but she stayed in the vision, trying to look around the glass and see more. She got a flash of blue walls and posters before she had to open her eyes and lurch upwards, hands held over her mouth. She made it to the kitchen and threw up into the sink, running the water to wash the vomit away.

ESME KNOCKED on Fiona's door. There was no answer, but she tried again. After an agonising minute, the door opened. Instead of Fiona, it was Euan. Esme ignored her stomach flipping over and asked if she could come in for a quick chat.

Euan shrugged and turned away. Perhaps he meant for her to wait for Fiona in the living room, but she followed him to his bedroom and stepped inside before he could object. She had to keep moving before she lost her nerve, and she was on high alert looking for signs that she was right.

And found exactly the thing she hadn't wanted to find.

Esme didn't want to believe that one of their own could have killed Alvis, let alone a child, but there was no getting around the evidence of her own eyes. The lump of glass looked blacker than Esme remembered. She would have sworn it had been dark blue with swirls of aqua and ultramarine when she had seen it last, but she still knew it was the same object. Alvis was dead and the piece of glass that had been missing, that must have been in Alvis's possession, was now sitting on the neatly smoothed cover of Euan's bed.

'That's not mine,' Euan said flatly. He looked at Esme with an eerily calm expression.

'It's all right,' Esme said, which she knew was daft the moment the words were out. It wasn't all right. Not at all.

He cocked his head, as if listening. The movement was

jerky and unnatural, and Esme felt a shiver of fear run up her spine.

'I had to move it. I couldn't sleep with it under my pillow.'

Esme didn't know what to say. Did Euan see the glass as a trophy? Or had he been hiding it, frightened of it being discovered? If so, why had he led her into his bedroom when it was sitting on his bed in plain sight?

'My parents will be home soon,' Euan said, his voice still flat. His arms hung loosely at his sides and his face betrayed nothing. 'If you're going to do it. Do it.'

'Do what?'

'Kill me.'

Esme took a step back, horrified. 'I'm not going to hurt you.'

A look of confusion crossed Euan's face and, in that moment, he looked like the boy he was. 'Mum said...'

'Whatever happened with Alvis,' Esme said quickly, 'and I'm sure that was an accident... we don't kill people. I'm not here to hurt you.'

Euan sat on the bed, his expression smooth and blank once more. 'She said you would. I heard her.'

Esme couldn't work out his tone. Was he upset? In shock? Disappointed? 'She said I would...' Esme couldn't say 'kill', that was too much. '...hurt you?' Why would Fiona say such a thing? Her mind was whirling.

He shrugged.

'What happened, Euan?' Esme's eyes were drawn to the black glass. It was darker than before, a truer black that seemed to be absorbing light.

'I wish you would,' he said. 'Just get it over with.'

'I know it's scary,' Esme said, thinking of the police. A trial. Jail. Or would it be a place for minors? Same thing, really, of course. Or was Euan right...Would Tobias and

Hammer take matters into their own hands? What would island justice look like? They wouldn't kill him, she was sure of that. But what would they do? What could they do? Pushing aside the unhelpful thoughts, Esme focused on the frightened teenager. 'But you can start by talking to me. Tell me what happened. I'm sure you didn't mean to hurt Alvis. People will understand.'

He shook his head.

Esme willed him to say it had been an accident. And that he had taken the shiny glass in a moment of bad judgement. That he hadn't phoned for the air ambulance or called an adult for help because he had panicked. All of which was understandable. And, in a young-for-his-age fifteen-year-old lad, completely excusable. Instead, Euan just stared blankly ahead, looking like he was waiting for a bus.

Esme wanted to be closer to the door, to escape, but she forced herself to move in the opposite direction. Euan had killed Alvis but he didn't seem out of control now. He had a strange, disaffected manner and it made her skin prickle, but she found that she couldn't really believe that he had hurt Alvis in cold blood or that he was going to hurt her now. Either her instincts were working and she was safe, or they were failing her at a catastrophic time.

She pushed away that second thought and focused on Euan. He was a teenager, which was much the same thing as a frightened child. She felt her protective instincts override everything else and she took another careful step toward the bed, as if approaching a wounded animal. 'Did you have an argument with Alvis? Did she say something you didn't like?'

He shook his head again, more forcefully this time. 'I hardly spoke to her. I never... I didn't really know her.'

The door to the bedroom flew open and Euan's father

appeared, his face twisted in fury. 'You shouldn't be here.' Oliver's voice was harsh and he was breathing heavily.

'Where's Mum?' Euan asked, sounding unhappy for the first time.

Oliver ignored his son, focusing on Esme. 'You shouldn't be talking to my son without my permission. And certainly not on his own.'

'I didn't say anything,' Euan said quickly. He had gone pale and there were two spots of colour on his cheeks, making him look even younger.

Oliver didn't look away from Esme. 'This is my house. You can't just waltz in here and start throwing around accusations.'

Esme was paralysed. The man was shouting. He was so close and the room was suddenly too small. She felt the walls shrink and her head spin as the anxiety took hold. The instincts that had told her she was safe a moment ago were now screaming the opposite. Here was danger. Here was violence. Her chest was tight and she couldn't take a breath. Oliver's face was red with fury and Esme couldn't see anything else. He was shouting, his mouth moving, but Esme couldn't understand what he was saying. There was no room for anything else in her brain, just terror, and the realisation that she couldn't breathe.

Oliver's hands were on her arms, squeezing, and his red face was too close.

She was dimly aware that Euan had moved from the bed into the corner and was staring at the wall, his back turned as if he couldn't bear to see what was going to happen next. It made her stomach drop even lower. It was like Ryan's friends in the pub, turning their attention to their drinks when he got nasty. Pretending they didn't notice that he was pinching her arm hard enough to bruise.

Esme knew she should struggle, try to twist out of Oliver's grip. Or say 'stop it', something to remind Oliver this wasn't acceptable behaviour. The man was unrecognisable from the person she knew as Fiona's husband and Euan's father, and the fear had grown to fill every corner of her mind. She was in Euan's bedroom on Unholy Island, and she knew that, but part of her was back in her old flat with Ryan. His face blood-red with fury.

Just as little speckles were clouding Esme's vision and she realised that she was going to pass out, she thought she heard a voice. For a second she thought it was Alvis's, but then she realised it was somebody even more familiar. *You are Esme Gray. You are the Ward Witch.*

'Let go!' Esme brought her hands up and shoved Oliver as hard as she could. He stumbled back, letting go of her arms.

The voice inside her head had been her own. And she had listened.

The brief moment of triumph was followed by relief as a figure appeared behind Oliver. For a second she wondered if she was hallucinating, but then she recognised the figure. She saw Seren push past Oliver and into the room in a series of staccato images, her brain still having difficulty processing as the panic ran through her nerves and muscles, making everything sharp and jangly.

'What the hell is going on?' Seren planted herself between Oliver and Esme. She was wearing jeans and a checked shirt and the familiarity and normality of those details, and the knowledge that she was no longer alone with Euan and Oliver, helped to turn down the deafening alarm call that was sounding in her head. Seren was speaking, Esme realised. It was a steady sound, but she still couldn't make sense of it. No words. Just a roaring in her ears.

'You need to calm down,' Seren was saying. She didn't

sound frightened. She sounded angry but in a way that was controlled. She was outraged but masking it for the sake of de-escalating the situation. It was sane behaviour. Grown up. And it helped Esme's brain to come back online. She dimly expected the violence and fear to bring back Ryan's voice, for his litany of bile and hate to start playing again. But it didn't. She realised something – it had gone for good.

Seren turned back to her briefly, concern in her eyes. 'Sit in the desk chair. Put your head down.'

The clear instructions unlocked her paralysis and she made it to the swivel chair. With her head between her knees she could think more clearly and the black edges of her vision disappeared, but she also felt vulnerable with the top of her head exposed to the room and not being able to see.

She straightened up so that she could see the dangers. Euan was still in the corner, his back to the room and staring blankly at the wall. Seren's back was still facing her, a block between her and Oliver. Then Oliver moved and she caught sight of him. His fists were clenched and she felt her heart rate kick back up.

Seren was still talking in a calm and steady voice, and nobody was shouting. It was better.

'Leave him out of this,' Oliver was saying. Yelling, really. He still sounded terrifyingly out of control.

Tobias appeared in the doorway with Fiona. The room was very full now, but Esme could breathe again.

'Take your son out of here,' Tobias said.

'He's not going anywhere,' Oliver said, his voice cracking.

Fiona walked over to Euan, not looking at her husband as she passed him.

'What did you say to him, you bitch?' Oliver spat at Fiona and she flinched.

'Come on, love,' she said, putting her hand onto Euan's shoulder. He turned, moving in a mechanical way, his face still perfectly blank. They moved around Oliver in as wide a circle as was possible in the bedroom and Fiona pushed Euan out of the door ahead of her.

With the departure of his son, Oliver seemed to lose energy and he sagged onto the bed. Sitting on the edge with his hands dangling loosely between his knees and his shoulders rounded, he looked defeated and small.

Seren moved and Esme stood up. Oliver might no longer look like an immediate threat, but Esme's nervous system was a long way from believing that. She needed to stand with Seren, to provide a united front against the threat.

'All right,' Tobias said. 'It's okay, Oliver. Let's just talk about this.'

When Oliver raised his eyes to meet the mayor's gaze, Esme felt a twist in her stomach. She had expected him to look relieved, but there was something else behind his eyes. Calculation. A tinge of disappointment. He was danger-ous. That much she knew, as every instinct in her body screamed it. She reached for Seren's hand and squeezed it in warning, knowing that speech was out of the question.

'He's not been himself,' Oliver said slowly. 'But he's just a teenager. He can't be blamed.'

'We know it wasn't Euan,' Tobias said, more firmly this time.

Esme jerked in surprise.

Something slid behind Oliver's eyes. Esme could see him making a calculation and she wondered how she had ever thought of him as just Fiona's slightly boring husband.

'Thank God. I've been so worried.' Oliver ladled on fake emotion with his voice, but his eyes stayed cold, watching the faces of the assembled islanders to see if they were buying it. 'But of course it makes sense... He's just a kid. It's obvious who is responsible. Who must have planted this evidence.' He glanced at the chunk of glass on the bed and then at Esme.

'What are you talking about?' Esme felt light-headed again.

'You brought it with you, didn't you? Trying to protect the mainlander. You've probably got a crush on him. Don't want us to realise what he really is, but we know. He killed Alvis and took this thing. Then she,' he jabbed a finger at Esme, 'brought it here to try to frame my son.'

'I didn't bring it. Euan will back me up on that.' She hoped. Then something occurred to her. 'And how do you know it's connected with Alvis? The only way you would know it was evidence of her murder would be if you took it from her yourself.'

Oliver ignored her, directing his words at Tobias. 'Come on, Mayor. You know it makes sense. We didn't have any problems until Luke Taylor showed up. He brought those bad people here, looking to make trouble. And if he's mixed up with that sort, who knows what he's done in the past? Who knows how many other people he's hurt? He chose the wrong place to hide out, though. We won't stand for it, will we?' His voice had been rising as he pontificated, gaining in confidence and volume.

Tobias shook his head and when he spoke, his voice was flat. 'It wasn't Luke.'

'If he's so innocent, why did he run off?'

'Just stop.' Tobias's tone had more authority and finality than Esme had ever heard and the hairs on her skin raised.

He looked at Oliver with something approaching pity. 'Fiona told me you're not happy. You sensed that Euan was changing, taking after his mother. You didn't like that. I'm guessing you decided Alvis had some kind of cure.'

'She wouldn't give it to me,' Oliver blurted. Then he looked shocked, as if he couldn't quite believe the words had escaped.

'What?' Seren said, at the same time as Tobias asked, 'So you pushed her?'

Oliver smiled and it was as if a mask had fallen away. 'I had to,' he said. 'She wouldn't even show it to me and I need it.'

'What do you think it does?' Tobias asked.

Oliver's smile widened. 'You think I don't know. You think I'm stupid. Failing at my job, can't look after my wife and kid. I know you all talk about me. I know what you say. Whispering behind my back. I know.'

Having hardly even thought about the man, let alone talked about him in the seven years she had lived on the island, Esme was confused. 'Why do you need the glass?'

When Oliver spoke, his voice was so violent again that Esme's stomach flipped. 'For Euan. To cure that little freak.'

CHAPTER TWENTY-NINE

Luke arrived back on the island, still vibrating with the leftover adrenaline of his encounter. His face hurt and he felt shakily relieved to be otherwise in one piece. He didn't know if Esme had heard about the gang from Tobias and didn't want her to be worried, so he went to see her at Strand House. Finding nobody home, he was walking towards the bookshop when he saw Esme walking in the opposite direction. For a moment, he remembered seeing her walking away from him on the beach, carrying a bin bag and collecting rubbish. It seemed like years ago, not weeks. She had been a stranger to him, then, and the island a quirky stop on his quest. Now the island felt like home and Esme felt like... He stopped his brain before it could fill that part in.

'Your face,' Esme said, as she reached him, her eyes wide with concern.

'Are you okay?' He asked at the same time. She looked pale and unhappy and it made him want to hit something.

'Come down here,' she said briskly. 'So I can take a look.'

He obediently bent his legs so that they were at eye-level. She examined the black eye carefully, tilting his head to get a better look.

'It's nothing,' he said, aiming for strong and stoic. 'What's happened? You look shaken up.'

'It's Oliver... He just flipped. He grabbed... It's fine. I'm fine. Tobias and Seren turned up, but Fiona took Euan away. Your nose was broken.'

'I put it back,' Luke said. 'What did Oliver do? Did he hurt you?'

'Tilt.' Esme said, ignoring his question.

She pulled a slim penlight from her jeans pocket and examined his nose. He tried very hard not to wince.

'It's swollen, of course, but it looks like it'll heal all right. You really shouldn't set your own bones, you know?'

He straightened up. The pain in his face had been steadily increasing and he was really looking forward to taking some painkillers and lying down. But something wasn't right with Esme and he needed her to tell him. He had been holding onto his patience by a thread, but it was about to snap. 'Please tell me what's going on. You look...'

'Do you want me to pack it for you?' She was still staring at his face with a mix of professional curiosity and a kind of dazed horror.

'Nah, it's fine.' He said quickly. The thought of anybody touching his nose right now was not pleasant. 'It'll heal as it is and the bleeding's stopped.'

'Are you in a lot of pain?'

'No,' he lied. 'But you need to tell me what's happened. I can see you're upset. Please. Tell me.'

'Oliver killed Alvis.' Esme shook her head lightly as if clearing it. 'He just confessed. I don't think I've quite... It was... Actually. Shit.' Her eyes widened as if she had just realised something. 'Could you go into Fiona's? Tobias has

248

him contained in Euan's room but I think he would appreciate the back-up.'

'Fuck. Of course.'

He was already moving around her when she said, 'Oh, good' in a relieved tone.

He turned and saw Hammer striding along the street. Marvellous.

'You can go and lie down. Hammer will help Tobias.'

'I'll go,' Luke said stubbornly. Esme still seemed worryingly calm. She had to be in shock and he didn't want to leave her. On the other hand, if Hammer was going to go and be all manly and help to restrain Oliver, then he was bloody going to go, too.

'Be careful,' Esme said, and he felt warmth flow through his body.

WITH HAMMER AND LUKE HELPING, Oliver meekly allowed himself to be led to the spare boat shed next to Hammer's home. They locked him inside and as soon as they were a few paces away, Luke and Hammer turned to Tobias for a recap.

He filled them in on Oliver's confession, including the disturbing revelation of his dislike of Euan.

'What are you going to do?' Luke asked Tobias.

'What are we going to do,' the mayor corrected. 'This is a community decision.'

'We can't execute a man in cold blood,' Luke shot an uncertain look toward the boat shed prison.

'Technically,' Hammer said, 'we can.'

'Make him leave? Could Esme strengthen the wards so that he couldn't get back? But then nobody could visit, I guess...' He thought of food deliveries. 'Or is there a way to make a specific ward? Just for one person?'

Tobias shrugged. 'I have asked Fiona and Euan what they want. Naturally, they are the closest to Oliver and I think they should have the loudest voices.'

It made sense. But it was a terrible burden for a kid. Luke opened his mouth to say as much, but Tobias carried on.

'Euan won't know that his opinion carries any weight. We have made it clear that it is an adult decision. That way we can hear his thoughts and desires and, hopefully, keep his personal sense of guilt to a minimum.'

'Right. That's good.'

'Nothing about this is good,' Tobias corrected. 'And it's going to be hard to know what he truly thinks. He might perform protectiveness toward his father because he feels he ought to, out of a sense of duty. Or fear.'

Luke thought about what Tobias has told him. Oliver spitting out that he wanted Alvis's glass to cure the 'freak'. Putting aside the questionable grasp on reality, he knew that would stay with Euan. Chase him into adulthood. 'Why did Oliver call him that? His own father.'

'Oliver is Euan's stepfather. And he has been uncomfortable with his wife's nature for quite some time. I suppose now that Euan is growing up, beginning to change, that discomfort became hatred. Humans usually hate what they fear.'

Luke wondered if Tobias knew that he sounded as if he was speaking about a different species. It wasn't until much later that Tobias's words about Fiona struck him as strange. At this moment, all he could really think about was going home, taking some painkillers and going to sleep.

THEY WERE ALMOST at Tobias's house and Luke realised that he wanted to go home. He wanted to be in the quiet of the shop, surrounded by the books. But he also wanted to check in on Esme.

Tobias was watching him, a small smile on his lips. 'Go on home. Esme will be asleep by now. You can visit her tomorrow when you've both rested.'

'I don't know what you're talking about,' Luke lied. 'And don't we need to have a meeting or something? This isn't over.'

'I think we should all sleep on it. Oliver isn't going anywhere.'

Luke had the urge to yawn, but he managed to stifle it, mindful of his painful nose. Instead, he stretched so that his spine cracked. 'Yeah. You're probably right. And we shouldn't rush into something while we're upset.' He thought of Esme's pale face earlier, how shaken she had seemed, and he felt a wave of anger. Judges and juries weren't supposed to be angry.

'Besides,' Tobias said, unlatching the gate to his front garden. 'We need to give Fiona a chance.'

Luke wasn't really sure what Tobias meant by that, but the tiredness was back. It enveloped the residual anger and blanketed his mind in a thick fog. He needed to go to the bookshop and climb the spiral stairs and get into bed. Sleep for a week.

THE NEXT DAY, Esme sent a message to Luke to ask about his broken face. She had slept a deep and dreamless sleep and had followed the impulse to check on Luke before she could talk herself out of it. The reply came back quickly.

Still pretty.

She hesitated for a moment before texting to offer to bring him breakfast and painkillers. He replied with a 'yes, please' and to let her know that the bookshop front door would be unlocked for her.

Walking along the main street of the village and into the bookshop, Esme felt a sense of peace. Something had shifted and the island was no longer in turmoil. She didn't question the feeling, just accepted it.

Climbing the stairs to the studio above the shop, she found Luke sitting up in bed, the blankets around his waist. His upper body was bare and she was struck by his muscular frame and the tattoos that inscribed his upper arms, shoulders and chest. His face, however, was still a swollen mess with both eyes and his nose blackened.

'Those bruises are going to be spectacular,' Esme said, trying to cover her physical reaction. She knew she had gone bright red, like a schoolgirl with a crush. It's just a body, she told herself. Nothing to get in a flap about. You are both adults. Don't be ridiculous.

He shifted and Esme tried very hard not to think about the rest of his body, hidden by the blankets and what that might look like. 'You are a lifesaver.'

Despite trying not to look, Esme had automatically read the writing. It was Latin and she didn't know what it meant. But asking would reveal that she had been looking. Too late, Luke dipped his chin. 'It looks pretentious, I know.'

'No. I just...' She just hadn't expected Latin. Which would sound rude to say out loud, as if she thought him uneducated.

'It's the family motto,' Luke said, glancing at his chest where the black script curled along his clavicle. 'It means "learn to suffer".'

'Cheery.'

He grinned. 'I'm guessing my great-great-grandfather wasn't a fan of school.' Then his face fell. 'I'm really sorry.'

'About what?'

'Not being here yesterday. Tobias told me what happened with Oliver. I wish I'd been here.'

'It's all right. I was right.'

'About Euan?' Luke frowned. 'But he didn't do it.'

'I know that. And I wasn't scared of him when I went to his room. Not really. I wasn't scared until Oliver came in.'

Luke winced, his eyes filled with concern. 'I'm so sorry. Did he hurt you?'

'No.' Esme struggled to find the words. She wanted to explain her happiness and relief. Her instincts had been right and she was alive and well. If she got it right once, she could do it again. She wasn't broken. 'I saw the glass in Euan's room. In my mind. That's how I knew it was there and that he was connected to Alvis somehow. But I wasn't scared of him and that was right.'

She didn't feel frightened of Luke and now she could, maybe, believe that meant she was truly safe to be his friend. That it wasn't her old death wish pushing her head-long into another catastrophic decision.

There was something tugging at her mind. A vision of Luke that was accompanied by, not fear exactly, but a discomfort that she didn't usually feel around him. Now that she was beginning to believe that she could trust her feelings, she wondered what it meant. A second later, the truth clicked into place.

Luke was searching for his twin brother. His identical twin brother. 'Do you and Lewis still look very alike?'

He frowned at the conversational swerve. 'As far as I know.'

'I saw him in a vision.'

'A vision like a prophecy?'

She appreciated the effort it must have taken him to sound so neutral and accepting.

'Don't know. Bee thinks I'm more likely to see what is happening or has already happened, but not stuff I would usually see. Like I'm tuning into another channel that's broadcasting live.'

'Or showing a re-run? That sounds more like you're jumping into somebody else's mind.'

'I don't hear thoughts or opinions or feelings. Not so far, anyway. Just visions. I'm working on controlling them.'

Luke looked intrigued despite himself. 'Will you start seeing the future?'

'Apparently, prophecy is extremely rare. Bee said I don't have the right sunny disposition for it. Hurt my feelings a bit. I'm always upbeat. Around other people, anyway.'

'I must have missed that,' Luke said, ducking when Esme raised her arm as if to throw the box of painkillers.

'It's okay,' she said, placing them on the duvet. 'I'll make you pay for that once you're not an invalid. It's time for coffee.'

LUKE THOUGHT about putting on a T-shirt while Esme was out of the room, but the thought of pulling it over his head wasn't appealing. Instead, he got up and found a shirt that he could button up the front. He pulled on a pair of joggers, too, before getting back into bed. He had been too groggy to think properly when Esme had taken him by surprise by texting him. Having her in his room while he was half-naked was definitely not okay. She seemed less jittery around him and he wanted it to stay that way.

He heard her feet on the stairs and then she appeared with two mugs. The smell of coffee wafted through the air, waking him up a bit more. His stomach rumbled loudly and he realised he hadn't eaten since lunch the day before.

She passed him one of the mugs and perched at the very end of his bed.

'I wish you hadn't gone to confront Euan on your own.' He knew it wasn't his business to police her behaviour, but he also didn't care. There was a fierce feeling of protectiveness that wasn't shifting. She had to be more careful or he was going to have heart failure.

'Who were those guys?'

Luke let his head fall back onto the pillow. 'My brother owes them money. They got sick of waiting for him to pay up, so they passed the debt onto me.'

'That's not fair.'

He smiled weakly. Her face was the picture of wholesome outrage. 'I don't think they care about fair.'

'You could go to the police. I mean, they are trying to steal from you. And this,' she indicated his face, 'that's assault. Doesn't matter what your brother has done, they can't do this to you.'

It felt nice to have her angry on his behalf. She might not have other feelings for him, but it was clear she cared. 'I don't think the island wants attention from the police. Especially not after Alvis.'

'Well, that's true.' Esme looked unhappy. 'But I would support you. And I'm sure Tobias would understand.'

'I can handle it.'

'Clearly.' Her tone was dry, but the soft concern was still apparent in her eyes.

'I will make it go away. No police. No more trouble. I promise.'

'You really are an islander, aren't you?'

'I hope so,' he said, surprised and pleased.

'So Bee was right.'

255

'What do you mean?'

'As usual,' Esme said to herself. She smiled brightly at him. 'I'm going to make you breakfast. Anything you want.'

You, he thought. A fresh throb of pain in his face reminded him that even if Esme was willing, he was probably better off with a fist full of painkillers and a plate of eggs. 'Surprise me,' he said.

'You do love to live dangerously,' Esme said, her smile even wider.

CHAPTER THIRTY

Matteo had sworn not to use his Silver ability ever again and now he was about to break that promise for the second time in a week. He suspected what Fiona was and, if he was right, she was more than capable of dealing with her errant husband. She could swim out to deep water and drop him near a tidal stream and let the strong currents take whatever was left far away from the Northumberland coast. But to have to do that would take a toll. Fiona couldn't help her nature, any more than he could help being born part of the Silver Family, but he could save her from crossing a line that you didn't come back from. There was a cost to taking a human life. He ought to know.

The waves rolled onto the shore, the swell and the crash making a continuous roaring soundscape that was both soothing and slightly alarming. A thin line of silver shone at the horizon below the place where the sun was hiding behind clouds.

Matteo walked across the harbour bay to the boat sheds. A curl of wood smoke lifted from the chimney in Hammer's.

He unlocked the padlock on the boat shed next to it, and began speaking even as he opened the door. He wasn't going to give Oliver a chance to rush him. Having told Oliver to stand still, the man was stuck fast to the floor. His eyes bulged with the effort of trying to move his limbs. He couldn't speak or breathe, either, because still meant his lips and diaphragm couldn't move. Matteo hadn't intended that, and he felt the weight of his terrible power.

'You brought this on yourself,' he said out loud. Then he stepped up to Oliver and whispered into his ear.

Matteo turned away as the man crumpled to the floor, dead before he hit the dusty wooden boards.

CHAPTER THIRTY-ONE

E sme placed the piece of black glass onto her kitchen table and made a cup of spiced tea. With the smell of cloves and cinnamon in the air and Jetsam winding around her legs, she felt a sense of calm blanketed over her jangling nerves. The fear had receded but she still felt on edge. Exhausted and keyed up at the same time. Her mind managing to be both blank and somehow racing, the thoughts fragmented and blurry so that they were impossible to follow.

She ought to visit the Three Sisters. Bee might be able to tell her more about the black glass. Maybe tell her what Fiona and Euan were going to do about Oliver. Although she had the sense that she would find out soon enough. And, the thought surprised her as it fell into place. Alvis had asked her about the glass, not Bee. She could look into it herself, maybe do some research at the bookshop. Oliver had thought that the glass would stop Euan from becoming like Fiona. However wrong he had been to want that, there was a chance he had been right about the glass itself.

She sipped the hot tea and inhaled the spiced steam and thought about Oliver. How had she missed his nature so completely? Her instincts had warned her to be careful around him, but she had put it down to her mistrust of all men. The fear that she had carried with her since her disastrous marriage. Bee's voice sounded in her mind. *When are you going to start trusting yourself?* When indeed. If she hadn't dismissed her intuition around Oliver as her own particular paranoia, maybe Alvis would be alive.

Something seemed to move in the surface of the glass. She had been staring at the shining black surface as she berated herself and now her thoughts stopped in surprise. She looked more closely, examining every millimetre for what she thought she had just seen.

There. A wisp of dark blue curling like smoke and then disappearing. A lighter greenish blue rippled near the bottom edge and then faded. Jet jumped onto the table and butted his head against her chin.

'Did you see that?' She asked the cat.

Seeming to understand her, he looked at her and then at the glass. He sat and stared at it for a few minutes and Esme did the same. The surface remained black and she began to think she had imagined the colours. Then, a waving line of ultramarine swirled in the middle of the glass for a few seconds before fading away. Jet turned his head to lock eyes with Esme, unblinking.

'I know. Weird.'

Jet let out a loud meow. The kind that said, very clearly, that he required some food. Something tasty. Esme realised she was hungry and made herself a plate of cheese and crackers. She fed Jet a small piece of cheese as a treat and some morsels of ham.

She knew Fiona's nature. She didn't expect Oliver to still be breathing in the morning. And when she remembered him spitting the word 'freak' at his son, she couldn't find it in herself to feel particularly sorry. As a kindly doctor had told her once, when she had been in A&E with a broken wrist, claiming to have clumsily fallen over: when somebody shows you who they are, believe them.

Esme thought about phoning, but this was a conversation to have face to face. She didn't want to go anywhere near the house, let alone go back inside, but she knew she had to. Euan might have been uncanny, but he hadn't hurt Alvis. And he was a child. She was the grown up and she had to do the right thing by him.

Fiona opened the door with dark circles under her eyes. 'I'm not really up to visitors...'

'This won't take a moment,' Esme said, stepping into the house with a confidence she didn't feel. 'Where is Euan?'

'Walking on the shore. I thought the view would do him good.'

'I'm sure you're right.'

'Can I come in for just a moment?'

Once they were in the living room of the cottage, Esme got straight to the point. She had to get it out before she lost her nerve. 'I need to tell you something. About Euan.'

Fiona's face went even paler, the dark shadows under her eyes standing out in stark contrast.

Esme ploughed on. 'It's something he said, just before...' She stopped. Before Oliver had stormed in and attacked her. She couldn't think about that now. Had to breathe and stay on point. 'I thought you should know.'

'What did he say?' Fiona crossed her arms and hugged her sides, as if holding herself together.

'He said he overheard something and I thought I should tell you. I'm sure he misheard, but it sounded really bad. Sorry.'

'What?'

Fiona's expression was closed, clearly preparing herself for the blow. Esme took another deep breath and launched in. 'He heard you say that he would be killed. By the island.'

Fiona's brow creased in confusion. Whatever she had expected, it wasn't that. 'I don't... I don't understand. I would never say...' She trailed off and Esme could see that something had clicked.

'He thought I was going to kill him,' Esme said. 'Like it had been ordered and I had drawn the short straw.'

Fiona nodded. 'I think I know what he overheard. Oliver was saying that it wasn't safe for him to grow up as... Well, like me. That people would hunt him, kill him. He was talking about Euan needing to resist his nature.' She shook her head. 'As if it was that easy.'

'He should never have said that,' Esme said. She didn't know exactly what Fiona was talking about, but she knew one thing. Unconditional love and support did not sound like telling a person to change something essential to their nature.

'I can't believe it took me so long to realise what he was like. How bad it had got.'

'I'm sorry,' Esme said, trying to put all of her understanding into her words. 'There's more, I'm afraid.' She took a deep breath. 'Euan told me to do it. When he thought I was going to hurt him... That doesn't mean he's suicidal or anything like that, I'm not trying to frighten you.'

Fiona let out a bark of laughter. 'Sorry.' She put a hand up to her face. 'It's not funny. It's just... I don't think I could be frightened right now. I was with that man for all those years. He has been living with my son. *My child.* And he's a murderer. How could I have been so...' She trailed off, her eyes staring past Esme and into the distance, filled with a bleak horror.

Esme knew that expression. 'It's not your fault,' she said, trying to put every bit of conviction she had won over the years into her voice. Trying to gift it to Fiona so that she would feel it in her soul. She knew it wasn't something you could be given, though. Fiona would have to forgive herself first.

'I'll talk to Euan,' Fiona said. 'But I know my son. I know he's in a tricky phase. I remember it myself and I know he'll feel better once he has... Finished developing. It's a confusing time in the best of circumstances.'

Esme didn't want to pry, but it didn't sound as if Fiona was just talking about puberty. The break in tension ought to be good but she felt unaccountably sad. Like a gulf had opened between her and Fi.

And then Fiona threw her arms around Esme and hugged her tightly. She wasn't the touchy-feely type so it was a shock. After a moment, Esme squeezed her back.

When she drew back, Fi's eyes were damp. 'You're a good friend and a good person. I know you find Euan a bit odd, I know that everyone does, even here. But you still care about what happens to him. You still came to tell me this even though it was awkward and sad and I might have bitten your head off.'

Well, that was an image.

'I'm not frightened,' Fiona said. 'But I do appreciate you letting me know what he overheard. I'll need to explain.'

Esme waited for a moment before realising that Fi didn't mean explain to her. She was still reeling a little from Fi calling her a good friend. She felt a little glow inside that extinguished some of the darkness. The island recognised her blood and she had a friend.

263

CHAPTER THIRTY-TWO

In Victorian times, Unholy Island had been rumoured to house some of the worst cases of nervous collapse in the Northumberland and Southern Scotland regions. Those poor unfortunates who were resistant to the new treatments for mental weakness, women with persistent hysteria or promiscuousness, men who had unnatural urges, and most especially those who had been found to have an unhealthy interest in the occult and the devil, were sent to the island as a kind of free-range institution.

It wasn't true, of course. The island had been resisting newcomers for centuries. It chose who it sheltered, not the woeful mental health system of the eighteen hundreds.

And once the wards were strengthened in the early nineteen hundreds, the rumours died away as people forgot about the island all together.

What was true, however, was that the island had been providing sanctuary to the more unusual members of society for centuries. The causeway kept the island remote and secure from the casually curious or malicious, and the ever-changing sea provided a meditative backdrop that was soothing to the troubled soul. Tobias had been mayor of the small community since before the ruined church had been built by some optimistic residents. A spell of Christianity brought by a devout villager that had taken root for a couple of hundred years. The island was, by nature, tolerant of differing beliefs and the residents of the time had mucked in to help the pious individual build his church and had then happily attended on Sunday mornings and holidays. There was, after all, very little entertainment to be had at that period. Now they had high-speed internet and streaming television. Tobias wasn't particularly interested in either of these advances, but then he hadn't particularly enjoyed the church sermons either and he had heard so many things over the years that it was difficult for modern stories to seem anything other than an echo of something he had heard many times before. He wasn't the kind to need complex distraction. He could watch the frost patterns forming on his living room window or the flames leaping in the grate for hours and feel perfectly content. And he had lived enough stories to review his memories for entertainment.

The fire was built up nicely now, and crackling in a comforting way. Winter was lying on the rug in his favourite spot and Tobias was sitting in his preferred chair. It was warm and quiet and comfortable.

When the doorbell chimed, Tobias was expecting Hammer. Instead, it was Fiona.

He ushered her inside and offered refreshments.

She shook her head. Her hair was still wet and the smell of sea salt and ozone wafted with the movement. Fiona had been drawn to the island when Euan was a toddler. She had recently got together with Oliver, and he was providing emotional, practical and financial support while she navigated the tricky early years of motherhood.

Thirteen years had passed in the blink of an eye and

Tobias felt he could reach out and touch the moment Fiona had stood in this same room, a sleepy Euan in her arms, and asked him if the cottage next to the pub was available to rent. He hadn't known that she was a shifter, not at that moment, but he had sensed that she wasn't human. And that she had needed sanctuary.

'I am taking Euan for a trip,' Fiona said now. 'A holiday.'

'Is that a good idea?'

Her shoulders sagged. 'I have honestly no idea. But a change of scenery might do us both good. His first change is coming, but it won't be for another few months. This could be his last chance to experience the mainland while he is completely...' She trailed off instead of saying 'human' or 'normal'.

Tobias prided himself on retaining tact, despite his long years in this world, so he didn't ask about Oliver. Matteo had told him that the man was in the boat shed, but no longer breathing. When Tobias had gone to see for himself, he found a broken lock and an empty shed. He assumed that Fiona had taken to her seal form and towed the body out to sea.

'We'll be back in a few days,' Fiona said. 'If that's okay? With you?'

'Of course. This is your home.'

The tension drained away from Fiona's stance and her face softened. 'Thank you.'

LUKE SPENT the next couple of days taking regular painkillers and trying not to move his head too much. By the time Friday rolled around, he was feeling more robust and the swelling in his face had gone down. He was almost at the car park when he heard his name. The last person he expected to see had appeared from the path that led to harbour bay.

Hammer was close in a few long strides and Luke widened his stance, ready for whatever extra shit today had brewing.

'I know where you're going.' Hammer was scowling, as if Luke had demanded he follow him.

'Okay.' Luke didn't think Hammer was about to deck him, but he wasn't completely sure. There was a strange energy coming from the man mountain.

Hammer glanced away and then met Luke's eyes. 'Meeting's off.'

Luke squashed his automatic impulse to say 'what meeting?'. He needed to curb his instinct to match Hammer's dickishness with some of his own, and try to get along with the man. He wanted to stay on the island, and that meant being a good team player. Instead, he asked, 'How do you know about it?'

Hammer, who apparently didn't give a flying fuck about being a team player, ignored the question. 'I had a word. They decided they don't need your brother's debt paid after all. Agreed to write it off.'

'That doesn't sound likely.' Understatement of the century.

'I'm very persuasive.'

'I don't know what to say.' Luke wanted to ask whether Hammer was absolutely certain there wasn't going to be further repercussions. Some other, higher-level gang member who would come looking for the missing cash. But that might seem churlish. Ungrateful. 'Thank you,' he managed instead.

'Five hundred.'

'Sorry?'

'My fee.'

Luke counted out the cash and handed it over. 'Very reasonable,' he said, trying to sound properly grateful. He couldn't shake the feeling that it couldn't be this easy. Hammer might be persuasive, but five grand was a lot of debt to forgive.

'It would have been a grand, but I'm giving you a discount.'

'I can pay the full amount.'

Hammer shook his head. 'I would rather you owed me.'

Well, that was ominous. 'I would rather pay you a grand.'

'I don't really care what you want, mate.'

Luke was battling the high provided by the profound sense of relief that the situation with his brothers' associates was sorted. He also recognised that he was up four and a half thousand pounds, which meant he could put the money back onto his credit card before it crippled him in fees and interest. 'Fine. I owe you.' He tried to sound gracious but knew he had missed the mark.

'So don't run away.'

Hammer was staring at him in an unnerving way. Trying to lighten the atmosphere, Luke said. 'I thought you wanted rid of me.'

Hammer didn't smile. 'It's no longer my call. You're the Book Keeper. So just stay out of my way. And then come when I call.'

Definitely ominous.

CHAPTER THIRTY-THREE

That evening at The Rising Moon, the main table was full and conversation flowed easily. Bee talked to Esme about house plants, Tobias and Matteo played a game of hangman on Matteo's notepad, and Seren took a break from serving to join them for a post-meal coffee. Matteo had just asked Luke whether he had seen the latest episode of the murder mystery they both enjoyed, when Hammer moved from his position at the other end of the table and stood behind his chair.

Luke felt his shoulders tense up, but Hammer didn't seem to be in an antagonistic mood. Wonders would never cease.

'Just wanted to say sorry.' Hammer's eyes flicked to Esme who had stopped talking.

Luke tilted his head to look up at the gigantic man. His first impulse was to be unhelpful, to say 'what for?' in a sneering voice. But this was his home now. And having a home meant getting along with your neighbours. It was a very adult and rational thought and he was proud of himself.

'I shouldn't have jumped to conclusions. There wasn't

evidence on you so I shouldn't have pursued...' Another glance at Esme. He cleared his throat. 'It wasn't you. And I should have realised that sooner.'

Luke stood up and was gratified when Hammer took a step back, making room for him. 'That's okay. I was the new variable. If I was you, I would have suspected me.' He held out his hand. 'No hard feelings.'

Hammer looked faintly surprised. He looked at Luke's outstretched hand for a moment before grasping it. Luke was not a small man but Hammer's hand enclosed his completely. They shook briefly with, mercifully, none of the macho squeezing as hard as possible that both men had used at different times in their lives.

'Very nice,' Seren said, rising from her seat. 'Now are you lot buggering off so that I can finish for the night?'

Tension well and truly broken, the group began to make moves to leave. Chairs were pushed back, scarves retrieved and coats pulled on. 'Any news from Fiona?' Luke heard Seren ask Tobias in a low voice. He didn't catch the mayor's reply but knew it would be negative. Fiona and Euan would return when they were ready.

Esme was chatting to Hammer by the door, but then she hung back and waved him on ahead. Luke realised with a rush of pleasure that she was waiting for him.

Outside, the cool air felt freezing after the warmth of the pub, but in a refreshing way. Luke said as much and Esme laughed. 'You're definitely an islander now.'

They walked in companionable silence for a few minutes, Luke taking the route to Esme's house even though it was the opposite direction to the bookshop.

'Did you want a glass of wine?'

The offer was unexpected and he shot her a questioning look.

Esme's cheeks were pink in the glow of one of the few streetlights in the village.

'Yes. Please.'

'I mean, it's the least I can do after you've walked me home. Very gentlemanly.'

He couldn't tell if she was teasing him.

'Who knows what might happen to me on this godless island?'

Definitely teasing, then. He nudged her gently. 'I was new. It's not kind to tease the clueless.'

Inside the cottage, Esme added wood to the banked burner and coaxed it back to life. There was a bottle of red wine warming on the hearth, so Luke fetched glasses from the kitchen.

Once they both had a drink in hand and were sitting opposite each other, Luke on the sofa and Esme in the armchair closest to the fire, they raised their glasses in silent toast and drank.

'I'm glad you're staying,' Esme said.

'Me, too.' Luke took another sip of the wine. He wanted to tell Esme that he liked her in a way that wasn't just friendly, but he still didn't know whether that would be welcome news. She sometimes looked at him in a way that seemed promising. Sometimes held eye contact for longer than was casual and these days she sometimes touched his arm when they spoke. He didn't think she realised she did it and that felt precious. An unconscious sign that she had decided to trust him.

And then there was the time she had brought him lunch at the bookshop, and, more recently, the time she had invited him in for a post-dinner glass of wine. On the other hand, she had taken the armchair rather than sitting next to him on the sofa.

The conversation flowed well enough and Luke gradually stopped worrying about whether she liked him in the way he liked her and just enjoyed her company. There was something very comforting about Esme. That wasn't something he would use if he ever got up the nerve to ask her out. 'You're very comforting' probably wasn't what a woman wanted to hear, but nonetheless it was true. And after so many years of feeling on edge and the last twenty months of hellish searching, he felt that calm comfort was a highly underrated quality. Plus, he felt a lot of other things about Esme that were X-rated and also not the sort of thing to blurt out. Not unless you were already together and were pretty damn certain the other person wanted to hear them.

They talked about the bookshop and Luke found himself waxing lyrical on the unusual books and first editions he kept finding.

A strange smile played on Esme's lips. 'There's going to be a lot more to discover. Once the place trusts you.'

'The shop?'

'And the island.' She pulled a wry face. 'I know how it sounds. Like I'm trying to be all witchy and mysterious. I know it sounds mad...'

'Not mad,' Luke broke in. 'This place.' He stopped, trying to formulate the right words. He had no desire to go back to their early days together when he had continually said the wrong thing, constantly offending Esme. He might not know much, but he had come to realise that Esme loved Unholy Island and was deeply protective of it. She spoke as if it was a sentient being, not a rock in the North Sea. 'I feel at home here. And in the bookshop. I know I want to stay and I've never wanted to stay anywhere in my life.' A memory of being a small child flashed into his mind. 'Not since I was a little kid, anyway.'

Esme was smiling at him, now. She looked genuinely happy and her cheeks had gone pink. 'I hope you do stay.'

CLOSING THE DOOR BEHIND LUKE, Esme wanted to punch herself in the face. When was she going to get the nerve to tell him that she was ready for something more than friendship? She wasn't an idiot, she could tell that he liked her. Or, at least, she had thought she could tell. The fact that he had accepted a glass of wine ought to confirm things, but then he hadn't made a move. She felt a rush of energy through her body and wasn't at all sure how she would have reacted if he had done. The uncertainty that had been momentarily chased away in a rush of pheromones and attraction came flooding back. She liked Luke. In a looping-stomach nerves-fizzing kind of way. She could admit that. But was she ready for anything to happen? She wanted to be ready, but that wasn't the same thing at all.

Frustrated, Esme left the wine-stained glasses by the sink and went upstairs to bed. Jetsam was curled up in the middle of the bed and she squeezed in under the covers, curving her body to accommodate his sleeping form. 'I don't need a man do I, Jetsam?'

The cat opened one eye and glared at her for disturbing his sleep.

'I love you, too,' Esme said.

LUKE HAD WALKED AWAY from the cottage before doubling back and standing in the street and looking up at the first floor where Esme's bedroom was. The light in the living room had been switched off and he wondered if she had gone straight up to bed. Then he felt the chill of the cold night air and imagined how it would look to an onlooker. He was standing outside Esme's house like a creep. Hammer would kill him.

He turned toward home and walked the short distance through the village. The moonlight glinted on the glass fishing floats and there was the cosy glow of light behind shut curtains in some of the windows. The Rising Moon was shut and the downstairs dark. There were no lights visible and he assumed that Seren had retired for the night to the living quarters at the back of the building. He turned down the narrow lane to the bookshop and stopped outside, tilting his head to look at the scattered stars. It was a good view, but he knew that with a few more steps onto the beach and away from the few lights on the island the display would be breath-taking. He felt a wave of pure contentment as he contemplated his options. Beach for stargazing or straight into the paper-scented haven of the bookshop to carry on with the book he was currently reading.

LUKE'S PHONE dinged a couple of times as he walked into a service spot. He had got used to the patchy reception on the island and it felt normal to get messages and emails sporadically.

Glancing at the screen, his whole world went still. It was a WhatsApp notification on his home screen and the name of the sender stopped his breath. Lewis.

Stop looking for me.

THE END

THANK YOU FOR READING!

I am busy working on my next book. If you would like to be notified when it's published (as well as take part in give-aways and receive exclusive free content), you can sign up for my FREE readers' club:

geni.us/Thanks

If you could spare the time, I would really appreciate a review on the retailer of your choice.

Reviews make a huge difference to the visibility of the book, which make it more likely that I will reach more readers and be able to keep on writing. Thank you!

ACKNOWLEDGMENTS

I wrote this book while suffering from a frozen shoulder so I would like to start by thanking ibuprofen, hot baths, ice packs and, most of all, my extremely patient husband who has had to drive me around, help me to dress, and do the lion's share of the cooking and cleaning. I offer no thanks whatsoever to adhesive capsulitis which can, to be frank, jog on.

To my writing coven, Hannah Ellis and Clodagh Murphy, heartfelt thanks for the support, advice and laughter. Writing and publishing is so much more enjoyable with good friends who understand the madness. Thanks also to Nadine, Sally, Keris, LK, and Julia.

Huge thanks to my wonderful readers. I was very nervous about writing something new and I am so grateful for the messages of support and enthusiasm. In particular, thank you to my brilliant ARC team for their early feedback: Jenni Gudgeon, Karen Heenan, Melanie Leavey, Caroline Nicklin, Paula Searle, David Wood and Beth Farrar.

Thank you to everyone involved in the publication of this book, especially David Painter, Kerry Barrett and Stuart Bache.

I'm extremely lucky to have fabulous friends (who are very understanding when I disappear into the writing cave and/or steal their names for characters). Thank you Emma Ward, Lucy Golden, Mike Taylor, Isla Duncan, Catherine Shellard, and Rachel Bodey.

I also want to give a shout-out to my brilliant family for all their support and encouragement. Special thanks to Matthew, Bea, Alex, Chris and Christine, and my lovely dad, Michael.

As always, my deepest love to my children, Holly and James, and my husband, Dave. I am the luckiest woman to know and be loved by three such outstanding people. Thank you for everything.

ABOUT THE AUTHOR

Sarah is a bestselling author of contemporary fantasy and magical realism. She writes the Crow Investigations series, a London-set urban fantasy featuring private investigator Lydia Crow.

Having always been a reader and a daydreamer, she now puts those skills to good use with a strict daily schedule of faffing, thinking, reading, napping and writing – as well as thanking her lucky stars for her good fortune.

Sarah lives in rural Scotland with her husband and extensive notebook collection.

Head to the website below to sign-up to the Sarah Painter readers' club. It's absolutely free and you'll get book release news, giveaways and exclusive FREE stuff!

www.sarah-painter.com

facebook.com/SarahPainterBooks
twitter.com/SarahRPainter
instagram.com/SarahPainterBooks

THE CROW INVESTIGATIONS SERIES

Find out more about the magical families of London - the Crows, Silvers, Pearls and Foxes

The Night Raven is the first book in the Crow Investigations series

The Crows used to rule the roost and rumours claim they are still the strongest.

The Silvers have a facility for lying and they run the finest law firm in London.

The Pearl family were costermongers and everybody knows that a Pearlie can sell feathers to a bird.

The Fox family... Well. The less said about the Fox family the better.

For seventy-five years, a truce between the four families has held strong, but could the disappearance of Maddie Crow be the thing to break it?

Made in the USA
Las Vegas, NV
30 January 2024